Here Cometh the Son

The Gospel
According to
Jesus H. W. Christ

Courtney Jensen

Plagiarism upsets Jesus

Introduction

Here Cometh the Son was written by Jesus Christ nearly two millennia ago. It has been missing since the second century.

In June of 2000, it was discovered in the Ionia region of Turkey.

The following pages are a faithful translation of the original codex, in print for the first time.

Chapter One

[1] Notes on what this isn't:

This isn't "good news".

Nor is it a "further", "last", or "really, really, really new" testament.

And don't call it a "revelation". It's no more a revelation than when, with great fanfare, your two-year-old declares an impending poop.

Although I have no testament, revelation, or covenant in mind, I've spent the past two thousand years listening to the crap that many of you spew in my name. I'm tired of it and I have a few observations I'd like to share. Beginning with this:

[2] "In Jesus name" is never an acceptable thing to say. You need to come up with something else to precede your "amens".[1]

I have two problems with "in Jesus name".

The problem that irritates me less is that people are laundering their words through my doctrine. Every time they pray, they affix the entire prayer to my name, implying that I'm the billable party. So I end up being held responsible for every stupid thing they say.

While this annoys me, the *real* crime here is the grammar.

Let me explain why "in Jesus name" is so annoying with a story about an American male named Courtney:

In A.D. 2008, Courtney coaches high school baseball. He does it for one season and then he is fired by a me-worshiping man whose smile always exposes a set of bloody gums.

Pre-firing, Courtney coaches a Chris and a Jake.

---

[1] And "amen to that!" in the place of "yes" or "sure" or "oh, good!" is also inexcusable.

One day, Jake forgets to bring his bat to practice. So Courtney tells him to "use Chris's bat."

Notice Courtney doesn't tell Jake to "use Chris bat." If he did, I would have bloodied up my smile and fired him myself. Because cavemen don't understand the nature of high school athletics. So having one in charge would be a bad idea.

But apparently having a caveman at the pulpit – "in Jesus name" – is perceived as okay.

It's not though. It's not okay.

I, like Chris, require an apostrophe to indicate the possessive. And I demand an extra syllable when spoken. When you deny me that syllable *while* laundering your words through mine, I get annoyed.

³ And I'm sick of anyone over the age of six still thinking that "A.D." means "after death" (as in "Courtney coached baseball 2008 years after Jesus died").

Not only does it not mean that, but the A.D. comes before the year, not after. It stands for *anno Domini*, which means "in the year of our Lord". And I am that lord. So when you refer to me, at least have the reverence to do so correctly.

One would never say: "in 325 in the year of our Lord, Constantine assembled the First Council of Nicaea."

Rather: "in the year of our Lord 325, Constantine whatevered."

If you don't stop messing this up, my dad is going to send you straight to Hell.

⁴ And don't think that you can save yourself by wearing a crucifix. I'm not a vampire.[2]

---

[2] Or a werewolf or whatever it is you're trying to ward off with your little apotropaic tricks.

A huge cross dangling in your cleavage will have as little effect on your salvation as would a big garlic bulb.[3]

But at least the garlic wouldn't be incredibly cruel – to me, that is.

Think about it: that thing between your hairy man-boobs is the thing that killed me. It hurt up there. A lot.

Do you honestly think I want to be reminded of this every time I look at you? Especially when you're constantly badgering me:

"Jesus, hear my prayer! And look, here's a really graphic representation of you being tortured!"

What the fuck is the matter with you people?

If your daughter was killed by a drunk driver, would I come to your house wearing a necklace with a tiny, crumpled Toyota hanging from it? And a little girl inside with a snapped neck?

Would I show you my new tattoo of a steering wheel smashing her face in?

Or maybe I could just give you an engraved flask with the date of her death. Or some chocolate eggs to commemorate the event. Isn't that what you do with my death?

The eggs are weird, but the crosses are thoughtless and insensitive. You're better than that. Seriously. Take them off.

[5] And while we're at it, stop saying "everything happens for a reason", as if anticipating the emergence of a greater good in every terrible situation.

---

[3] Or, to put it in more carnal terms, your crucifix will not ward off damnation any better than it will insemination, when inserted into the vagina like an IUD. It is not a ticket to Heaven any more than it is a contraceptive.

"My daughter died needlessly, but everything happens for a reason."

This is always declared in an accusatory tone. The speaker seems to think *I'm* that reason, as if I'm somehow responsible.

Yes, everything happens for a reason.

Take earthquakes for example. Those are caused by tectonic shifts. That's the reason.

Sometimes the reason is physics.[4] Other times it's chemistry.[5]

It could be the effects of prior psychological trauma: a bad childhood, bad parenting, or a bad experience with mushrooms.[6]

Or maybe it's genetic. Whatever the reason, it ain't me. I'm not sitting up here, perched on a little throne in the sky, "testing you".

So I would appreciate it if you would stop pointing a finger in my direction and accusing me of such. Stop trying to pin all of your problems on my celestial scheming.[7]

[6] And don't try to honor me with rock music either. I don't feel complimented by your bad riffs and corny lyrics.[8]

Those "lyrics" are usually just a bunch of clichés lifted from one of the testaments (e.g., "my cup runneth over" or "though I walk through the..." or something about "breaking bread").

---

[4] Given the vehicle's mass and speed, and the coefficient of friction when the brakes were applied, it was unable to stop in time.

[5] Or otherwise biological. Maybe my Petri dish wasn't exposed to the right environmental conditions.

[6] All plausible explanations for why your son killed himself on the day you married his stepdad.

[7] Or referring to them as "blessings in disguise".

[8] We won't get into the dancing because even you must realize how embarrassing that is.

Not only are these not lyrics, they're not even yours. So if you try to pass them off as lyrics (let alone *your* lyrics), I'll make sure you (and all of your fellow "Christian rockers") spend a fiery eternity surrounded by the Mormon Tabernacle Choir.

[7] And I hate people who think the Immaculate Conception had something to do with *my* conception. It didn't. It was about my mom and *her* conception.

If you're going to wear crucifixes and sing embarrassing songs about me, this really is something you should know.

[8] And something else you should know: I didn't become a person so that I could issue salvation (strictly to those who live after me).

That's what everyone seems to think. "Jesus became a man to atone for our sins", or some such.

This is an awfully peculiar thing to believe.

Keep something in mind: I'm Jesus. My dad is God. We're not idiots. If the two of Us were all that concerned with forgiving everybody, don't you think We might just have, oh, forgiven everybody?

Do you remember that passage in the bible where God, with nothing better to do one day, sends his only begotten son to Earth, who then says "I forgive you all" and goes home? No? Then maybe there's more to the story.

Why would I have volunteered to be beaten, whipped, and crucified[9] if all I wanted to do was accept your apology?

Is that how you forgive little Tommy when he steals all the raisins out of the Raisin Bran?

"Of course I forgive you; now nail these stakes into my ankle."

---

[9] To say nothing of using those first-century toilets.

The reason I had my dad impregnate a sassy Jewish virgin was so that I could have a better understanding of the human experience. It was just a study. I was curious.

So in mid-December, 5 B.C., Dad had me conceived.

The following September, I burst through Mommy Mary's intact hymen and into the world. Jesus the Grey, they called me.

In my thirty-third year, I was tortured, crucified, and buried. Darkness took me. And my spirit strayed back to Heaven.

But I hadn't completed my study. There was still so much more I needed to learn about mankind. So I returned, entering the world as a new man.

Again and again I returned, body after body. For two thousand years, while the stars wheeled overhead, I popped in and out of earthly life. Until A.D. 2013. That's when I completed my study. But I hadn't yet completed my task. So my father unwound the clock and sent me back.

I returned as Jesus the White, a spooky ghost who startled some women carrying spices.

After emerging from my tomb and startling those women, I began work on my task: writing the gospel before you.[10]

When I'm done, I will have created an account of all the ways in which human beings annoy me. Every single behavior that people need to change if they want to keep their afterlife asses out of Hell.

So in my name, listen up.

---

[10] A codex which Ephesians will soon hide, Germans will coin "Q", and Americans will ultimately discover.

Chapter Two

[1] People have this idea that I'm constantly watching them.

They're never alone because I've always got my eye on them, spying down from my eternal post in Heaven.

While that isn't true (and would be awfully strenuous if it were), I *have* spent a lot of time looking at people.

Sometimes I look at a kid – he might be ten years old – and he hasn't done anything wrong, but I can tell he's going to grow up to be the kind of person who hits his children at a Walmart.

So I hate him.

[2] I also hate people who talk about "tough love". It's usually just an excuse to be an asshole.[11]

[3] I hate adults who still shake Christmas presents. Once you become a teenager, this is no longer acceptable.

You're supposed to be celebrating me, not chopping down trees, dressing them in tinsel, and then guessing the contents of the boxes sitting beneath them.[12]

[4] Also, I hate adults who enthusiastically celebrate their own birthdays.

If you're nine years old and think you're a fairy princess, that's one thing. I blame your parents. But if you're thirty-three? Enough. Seriously.

---

[11] There's no such thing as "tough love". It's just the name that pathologically violent parents have given to punishments that don't scale with their behaviors.
[12] Though December twenty-fifth isn't *really* my birthday. This should be obvious enough; you don't see a lot of people herding sheep in the winter.

At thirty-three I was getting rusty nails hammered into my palms. So it's time for you to examine your priorities. You should be home alone boiling meat.

[5] I hate people who think that singing the Happy Birthday song is somehow festive.[13] It's sad and unoriginal. It no more makes you "fun" than does wearing a Santa hat and a funny tie.

Worse, however, are people who sing variations of the Happy Birthday song (e.g., "happy, happy birthday from all of us to you!").[14] These are usually waiters.

[6] If you want to get into Heaven, there are only two roads to the Kingdom (two that I've thought of so far anyway). And accepting me as your "personal lord and savior" travels neither.[15] I thought that would be cool when I was a first-century Palestinian Jew. I was like thirty at the time. I'm two thousand years old now; I'm not that guy anymore. I've done a lot of growing up since then. And today, one of only two paths into Heaven involves being a waiter or waitress (or, for twenty-first century American readers, a "server").

Here's that path (I'll explain the other one later):

A server approaches a table of diners. One of those diners makes an announcement about another: "it's his birthday today!"

The server now has two possible responses, each guaranteeing his celestial invitation:

1) He can stare blankly at the speaker.

2) He can say "okay" and offer a pained smile.

---

[13] A five-year-old's birthday is no excuse to sing something this stupid.

[14] The only sing-along worse than this is "For He's a Jolly Good Fellow".

[15] "I believe Jesus was tortured so that I could be forgiven" is not a pearly gate passport. Peter is totally unmoved by your "faith".

If he does either of these, then he may murder and pillage with impunity.[16]

But if he so much as says "happy birthday", or in any other way dignifies this sorry exchange, then Heaven has no vacancy.

[7] I hate people who noticed the gender non-neutrality of the previous verse.

I could have chosen to make the server an "it"[17], a "he or she"[18], a "she"[19], a "s/he"[20], or a "they".[21]

But I didn't.

And if you're going to be bothered by something as picayune as this, then I'm not letting you into Heaven. Ever.

No matter how much repenting you do.

[8] Similarly, I hate people who describe themselves as "feminists".

---

[16] Long-suffering and apathetic waiters, welcome to the Kingdom of Heaven.

[17] Creepy.

[18] Clunky.

[19] Self-consciously progressive. After bearing witness to thousands of years of civilization, I still find this incredibly obnoxious.

[20] Not a word.

[21] Doesn't make sense how one server could become multiple people. And I'm unwilling to accept "they" as a gender-neutral singular pronoun. In the King James days (what one might call my glory days), English had a more precise pronoun system. For example, "ye" was the subjective second-person plural pronoun and "you" was its objective case. Consider John chapter eight, verse thirty-two: "And ye" (subject) "shall know the truth, and the truth shall make you" (object) "free." There's a lot of precision in that sentence. At least in its grammar. But when it's translated to "Good News" prose, it's just you and you. Because languages evolve. And in the evolution of English, most of the second-person pronouns (ye, thee, and thou) go extinct. "You" replaces all of them. Likewise, there will soon be a day in which "they" can be used with the same sweeping imprecision as "you". But this won't happen until the twenty-second century. Until then, when referring to an anonymous "server" of either gender, it's a "he".

Not people who believe in things like respectful treatment of human beings and rightful distribution of resources regardless of gender. That's just not being an asshole. Using the *word* "feminist" though; all that tells me is that you're a bore.[22]

[9] Like self-described "feminists", I've grown to hate all flag bearers. Because they make it impossible to be black, gay, or female and contribute to the world quietly.

Want to be a writer? You're the one who is a gay, black man; let it be known! You're the voice of a generation!

Want to be a physicist? You're the one who is a single mother; let it be known! You're the voice of a generation!

The best perk of being born straight, white, and male is that life insists on the waving of no flag.

All things are permitted in peace.

[10] I hate people who use drinking fountains.

---

[22] Plus, use of the word "feminism" reveals far more about what you're *not* than what you *are*. To declare yourself a feminist is to assert your belief in fairness as it applies to women, but *not* as it applies to senior citizens; otherwise you'd be just as vocal about "elderism". And you don't believe in fairness or the ethical treatment of newborns; otherwise you would have identified yourself as an "infantist". And I haven't heard anything about adolescentism, so you must not care for the wellbeing of people in their most awkward years. And you clearly have no qualms about the mistreatment of animals, as I haven't heard you mention *anything* about being a baboonist, a lobsterist, a barn owlist, an arctic foxist, etc. If you need to specify a very narrow direction in which you're not an asshole, the implication is that you're an asshole in pretty much every other direction. If that weren't true, all you would have to say is "I'm not an asshole." This is why I, Almighty Jesus, consider it a good rule to distrust every self-identified "feminist". Personally, despite all of the Eden stuff, I believe that snakes deserve ethical treatment. When discovered in the garden, they deserve to be left alone (instead of being chopped up with gardening tools). Referring to myself thusly as a "serpantist" is exactly as stupid as calling myself a "feminist" owing to my pro-fairness vote when it comes to women. Just say you're not an asshole and I'll get what you mean. "Ists" and "isms" need never be applied.

I realize there are a *few* people who use them innocently. Not enough to make any exceptions though. Sometimes the fire and the brimstone need to be scattered indiscriminately. Just ask the corpses of Sodom and Gomorrah.

What people need to understand about drinking fountains is that the water is actually *ejected* from the nozzle. It shoots out in a parabola. It goes up and then it comes down. You don't need to create your own little vacuum. A drinking fountain is not a giant, metal nipple. Stop sucking on it.[23]

[11] I hate people who think they can sing well. These are usually sixteen-year-old girls about to become infested with transmittable diseases. Or impregnated with future reality show aspirants. The VD and the babies just keep coming.

[12] Girls with musical names like Melody or Harmony don't even have to think of themselves as good singers in order to expel a lot of avocado-colored discharge and nicotine-stained babies.

Despite popular insistence that Jesus loves "Little Children", I do not find these babies even remotely appealing. So don't bother baptizing them. Unless it's their only way of getting a bath.[24]

[13] Sometimes, just before becoming bad moms, teenage girls decide to pursue singing careers. In an attempt to display their skills, they do things like change notes really fast in no particular order or key (i.e., melisma).

Unless you're a Hasidic Jew chanting the Torah, you need to fucking stop it.

---

[23] I hate people who think "suckling" is what babies do. Babies suck on nipples. The mother whose nipple is being sucked is the one doing the suckling.

[24] Besides, when I said to go baptize all nations, I didn't mean every last infant (see Matthew, chapter twenty-eight, verse nineteen). No child anywhere in the bible is baptized. Tiny babies aren't capable of understanding and believing My Word or repenting any sin, original or otherwise. So why are you trying to dunk them in holy water pails? It's the Roman Catholics who become the creepiest about this.

[14] When the teenage girls abandon their singing careers (because of failure, never self-awareness)[25], that's when they begin to have terrible-smelling babies. This, unlike singing, is something for which they have considerable talent (which they share among many partners).

[15] I also hate the partners.

[16] It's usually because these mullet-headed boys have last names like Handcock.[26] Or sometimes their names have the word penny in it, such as Pennybaker or Pennypacker. Or other people might be named things like Kenny Swedish.

Once upon a time, people made up their names. That's the only reason they exist; they're not natural accompaniments of human birth. Surnames just get passed down through the same semen that transfers ancestral sin. Thus, every person with a ridiculous one shares a genetic constitution with the person who thought it was a clever idea to call himself that.[27] This is also why I hate people with first names like Brenner or Chip or Archibald or Topher (unless they were named by foster parents).

[17] And obviously I hate people who insist that I know how their names are spelled. "Hi, I'm Kathy with a K." Or "hi, I'm Cathy with a C."[28]

Who cares? You just introduced yourself to me at a house party; I'm not arranging people in alphabetical order.

---

[25] Sometimes the moms believe they stopped *because* of the baby. Or other times they don't stop *despite* the baby. In either case, each of these mothers is sure that her child will be the next "next-gen" pop diva.

[26] Or maybe a Plankbuster. Don't see as many Turban-Sterbas as I used to.

[27] This makes every Pennypockets-Cubclaw guilty by means of inheritance.

[28] Especially people whose names are pretentiously misspelled as an effort to make them "unique" or "interesting". Kaytlynn, Caitlin, and Kate Lynn all feel deeply wounded whenever their names are misspelled correctly as Katelyn. Because that means someone has failed to appreciate how special they are. "You said your name is Mary? How do you spell that?", I have to ask. Otherwise I risk having a "Maerie" become very upset with me.

[18] I have even more hatred for people who name their kid one thing but then insist everyone call him something else. "This is Jasper, but we call him Noodles."

[19] Or people who demand that their child be addressed either by middle or multiple names.

Mary Jo Anne Lavender Davenport Brunswick's name is Mary. It's not Mary Jo, Jo Anne, J.A.L, Lav-Dav, or any other waste of my time. She's going to Hell anyway; why would anyone care what to call her in the meantime?

[20] The worst parents are those who insist that they started a trend when they find out other kids are named Leo as well (or whatever other common name their child was given).

[21] I also hate people whose rectums prolapse suddenly in public and spray fecal matter all over my shoes and shins.

Though, granted, this happens infrequently.

[22] Something people do much more frequently: refer to their cars as "rigs". I don't like this one bit.

Sometimes it's just construction employees referring to their company trucks though. That's okay.

Unless it's an Archibald or a Goldcock or a singing girl.

[23] I hate people who perform feats of strength as an "art form". This usually involves ripping medium-sized phonebooks in half or bending things that appear to be difficult to bend.

During the performance[29], people in the audience may be inclined to experience thoughts like: "this person is physically fit!"

---

[29] Which usually happens in a public school gymnasium as part of a mandatory "assembly".

That's never been one of my thoughts. What I usually think is "just because you use mechanical advantages to tear lots of paper all at once doesn't mean you're not going to die of cardiovascular disease. So go blow up a canteen or whatever your next trick is while I mock your atherosclerosis."

[24] After the performance, the people sitting next to me leave the gymnasium (having called it an auditorium) impressed. And I decide that my hatred for the performers themselves is somewhat shallow. Much deeper is my hatred for the people who were *impressed* by them (or at least more impressed by the performers than by my jokes *about* them).

After realizing this includes all of my bleacher neighbors, I spend the rest of the "assemþly" looking for people who will share my perspective on the event. People who will find my jokes funny. And once we're dismissed, I seek out each one of them and repeat my punchlines about the men and their canteens.

Some of these people try to respond, attempting observations of their own. Others just laugh.

If all someone does is laugh (and they do so at the appropriate times), I decide that person is funny. And I go home and tell my wife as much. And these polite laughers *might* be admitted to Heaven. They at least have a chance.

[25] Despite this, lots of people still try to respond to my jokes. They try to contribute; they want to have a voice of their own. And when they can't think of anything to say that might be interesting, they say this instead: "what's your favorite color?"

These people will not be ascending to Heaven.

[26] I was just kidding about having a wife.

I killed her in a haystack.

Literally.

[27] Everyone already knows this, but when people say "literally", what they *technically* mean is figuratively.[30]

For example: "Bethany Hembolt's response literally threw me for a loop." Or: "when Darryl saw his car, he literally went ape shit." Or maybe he "literally shit a brick." And now all of this stress is "literally eating me alive." And I stay up all night "crying my eyes out… literally."

[28] And "technically" is almost never technical.

But technically, I did kill my wife in a haystack. Literally.

---

[30] And I hate people who pronounce literally as "litrully". I'm looking at you, British people and Rob Lowe.

Chapter Three

[1] Presently, I will sacrifice some korbanot at the Second Temple. Because it's not going to be around for all that much longer. And while it's here, this is where we do our worshipping.

[2] "Presently" does not mean "in the present". It means the present will be arriving shortly. As in: I can't see the Second Temple being destroyed right this second, but perhaps presently.

[3] The people who most frequently misuse the word "presently" also say things like "I'm a bad test taker."

I'm not sure I understand what that means.

It's like saying "I have a really skinny waistline, but if it's being measured, it messes up and gets huge."

[4] When a bad test taker decides to make a sandwich, he will reach into the bread bag, maneuver the heel piece out of the way, take some pieces from the middle, and then put the heel back.

When I ask this person (whom I hate) a question like "why did you do that?", he always responds with "the bread molds faster if you eat the heel."

No it does not. I'm Jesus. I would know. You just don't want to eat something that has less white, fluffy stuff.

But even if that weren't true (it is), why do these assholes feel compelled to run grain experiments in their kitchens?

Just eat your food. Put it in your mouth and chew it.

And be grateful. You should see the first-century shit I had to eat.

[5] And by the way, the "greatest thing since sliced bread" happened about thirty seconds after the first slicing.

[6] I hate people who say "that's a good question" as an immediate response to every question anyone asks about anything.

Very few questions are good.

"Is a pumpkin more orange than an orange?"

"What does sadness smell like?"

These are good questions, sort of.

But "what's the best route to Hillsdale?" is not "a good question"; it's just *a question.*

And if you need to stall with "that's a good question", don't expect me to say "that's a good answer" when you finally provide one.

[7] I hate people who nod their heads while I'm speaking.

No matter what I'm saying, their heads are constantly bobbing in the direction of "yes".

Once again, I feel the need to remind everyone that I'm Jesus. And as Jesus, I'm secure enough to finish my thought without constant affirmation that you agree with me. Just let me talk and then you take your turn. That's how conversations work.

[8] I hate people who begin a conversation with "guess what?!", and then they pause as if expecting a guess.

So I guess: "you're pregnant?"

"Nope, guess again!"

"You discovered a fungus in your belly button?"

"Nope, guess again!"

"You got 3.5% financing on your home loan with no out of pocket costs?"

"Nope, guess again."

"Wow, I give up."

Those ten seconds needn't have occurred. You will never get them back. Even I, who have eternal life, regret their wastage. And I'm adding them to your time in Purgatory.

[9] When people say "you wouldn't believe what happened!", the story that follows is always totally believable.

"You wouldn't believe what happened in the Sox game last night!"

"No, I probably would."

My response has, in over two thousand years of hearing rather mundane stories introduced this way, never once been "you know what? I *don't* believe it! That seems completely contrary to the laws of physics."

Instead, it's usually "huh… how 'bout that."

[10] Among the "you'll never believe it" crowd, if the story that follows is autobiographical, it generally begins with "oh my god, the x-est thing just happened to me!" The craziest, the funniest, the most outrageous, whatever.

I've encountered the "x-est" person enough now that I can confidently respond with this: no it didn't (as evidenced by every story that has ever followed such an introduction).

[11] I hate people who think what they do for a living makes a difference in the world (e.g., computer programmers, lawyers, nurses, train conductors, animal whisperers, etc.).

On a case-by-case basis, none of these people makes a difference.

If they stopped showing up to work one day, someone else would step in. And that person would perform the duties exactly as well. So if you think you're contributing to the world in a meaningful way, please know that you aren't.

The only difference you're making is that you get to cash the checks and someone else doesn't.[31]

[12] I hate people who are "waiting for my big break".

These people can usually be found blaming their failures on a recession. Or referring to their latest project as "groundbreaking" or "breaking a glass ceiling" or "pushing the envelope" or "cutting edge". None of these is okay. Or true.

[13] "It's so thick you can cut it with a knife", people sometimes say about the tension in the room.

Okay, you can cut almost anything with a knife. Given the right utensils, you can cut knives with knives. If it were something you could cut with a napkin, that'd be saying something.

[14] I hate people who, when serving themselves from a fruit salad, put too much discrimination into the course of the serving spoon. Every time it's my turn to have any, all that's left is cantaloupe.[32]

You know who you are.

[15] I hate people who use "vanilla" as a metaphoric adjective.

---

[31] Perhaps Shel Silverstein made a difference because no one else would have written *The Giving Tree*. Likewise, Lady Gaga may have made a difference in that nobody else would have written "Poker Face" (however little that means). But your personal trainer or financial advisor (or even your orthopedic surgeon) is not making a difference. He's just cashing checks in exchange for a service that someone else would happily do in his place.
[32] And it's always underripe to the point of being squeaky.

It does not mean "ordinary" or "normal" or "plain" or "regular".

It *can* describe an ice cream, a yogurt, a non-dairy creamer, or a flavor of protein powder. But it *can't* be used as a description of one's sexual proclivities.

[16] Similarly, the only thing that can be likened to an onion is a scallion. The layers of your best friend's personality cannot be described as "like an onion".

[17] And "Greek" needs to take a sabbatical from describing anything.[33]

[18] The same goes for "bittersweet". Even if you're talking about a stinky cheese with syrup on it.[34]

[19] And "transparency" when not describing an individual sheet of transparent plastic used on an overhead projector in an elementary school classroom in the 1990s.

Using "transparency" to describe government agencies or business practices is not acceptable and never accurate.

[20] "Complementary". How many syllables can you add to "free"?

[21] "Guilty pleasures". Eating cupcakes or reading vampire novels or playing Magic: The Gathering is not a guilty pleasure.

Rape is a guilty pleasure (providing you feel horrible about what you've done following your orgasm). But I've never heard the words "guilty pleasure" spoken in the same sentence as "roofies".

[22] I hate people who say "when the shit hits the fan."

Worse: "when the you-know-what hits the fan."

---

[33] May the words *Greek yogurt* nevermore be uttered together in my Kingdom.
[34] Describing life circumstances as "bittersweet" is totally out of the question.

Neither of these, but especially the second (but also especially the first) should be an expression.[35]

[23] And shits (rather than kicks) needs to stop introducing giggles. "For giggles" is a bad expression to begin with and it's only made worse by the addition of a second noun.

[24] "You must be smoking crack!", in response to anything done or spoken that was a little bit unusual. Unacceptable.

Comparing anything to crack is a bad comparison.

"This kettle corn is like crack!" or the latest Netflix series is "like crack!" or whatever.

You're not allowed to refer to anything but crack cocaine as crack. I'm officially decommissioning it as a metaphor.

[25] I hate people who use the word "vicious" to describe a cycle. It's never a vindictive or malicious cycle. Or: "that's one nasty cycle you've got there." It's always vicious. This needs to stop.

[26] And I hate people who begin a description of anything with "against a backdrop of…"

[27] Or describe something fast as "breakneck speed".

Is this a phenomenon of biomechanics? Is there truly a speed at which spinal severance occurs? If so, Jesus remains unaware.

[28] I like people who describe unpleasant things as "the pits", but I know I shouldn't. Even Jesus isn't perfect.[36]

---

[35] Say anything else. "When the ship hits the sand" or something. Something that actually makes sense. If you're going to use a stupid expression, at least adapt it a tiny bit (e.g., "when the poop deck hits the khamsin").

[36] I haven't decided if I hate or don't mind this: "can I be a son of a bitch and ask for a refill on my cola?"

[29] I hate people who whisper during television commercials.

Not the people *watching* the commercial, who are trying to keep their voices down so that they don't disturb the other viewers, but the people *on* television, *doing* the whispering. Whispering about some sort of product.

[30] I also hate the people who respond to commercial whispering with a greater interest in the product being whispered about.

Whenever something is being discussed in this way (with more lung than larynx), the sentences are usually directed at women. Maybe guilt-free chocolates or a feminine hygiene product.[37]

This strikes Jesus as unrealistic.

[31] I hate tabloid journalism. Not for any high-minded reason but just because it doesn't interest me. But, then again, I also dislike professional hockey.

I'm aware that both industries doubtless contain many fine human beings putting a great deal of effort into their jobs. I can appreciate the skill involved and recognize the work it takes. But none of this makes it interesting.

Whether the puck goes in the goal or Oprah is impregnated by an alien[38], this particular messiah just can't get a boner going.

---

[37] But only certain kinds of hygiene products. Like a French cream that firms or revitalizes. In my (albeit limited) experience, people rarely whisper sensually about urinary incontinence devices or extra-heavy-flow tampons.

[38] I also hate people who think of aliens as galactic monsters that look nothing like bacterial colonies. They're upright, bipedal creatures that mirror the human form but for their green, quasi-scaly skin, really narrow necks, and big bulbs for heads (as though such a tiny, twiggish neck could somehow support all of that cranial mass). The people who imagine in this way are those who are capable of believing that aliens have visited earth, made appearances to stupefied American hicks near the Mexican border, abducted them, and tried to extract important information about human civilization from their anuses.

[32] Along vaguely similar lines, I hate people who weren't parents or children or siblings or spouses or mistresses of Charlie Sheen who somehow managed to find his drug use compelling.[39]

[33] I hate people who flush their pot or alcohol or cigarettes down the toilet every time they "quit".

You and I both know (although I would, wouldn't I?) that they're going buy it again in a week. And that they don't have sufficient income to afford twice the drugs they consume. So they need a Courtney to pay for lunch.

Once such a Courtney agrees to cover the cost of this person's weak will, the weak-willed individual decides it's a great opportunity to overeat.

[34] I hate people who throw away a bowl of milk because the cereal that used to be in it is all gone.

[35] And people who throw away apple cores that are larger than a stem.

[36] Far deeper than my disdain for the wasteful is my hatred for people who say "no pun intended."[40]

Those who say this either intended the pun or, more likely, are really pleased with themselves for backing into it. If they weren't, they would just let the awkwardness die. Like they did with me on the cross.

[37] I hate adults who are involved in Boy Scouts.

[38] And people who use words like "tangentially".

"I'm tangentially involved in Boy Scouts."

---

[39] And people who know anything about the Kardashians. Anything at all.
[40] It would be more respectable if they just said "*did you catch that?*" after uttering their puns.

The tangential hatred also applies to "pontificate". And "bolus". And "minutiae". And "abscond". And "consternation".[41]

I find the use of such words to be an "opprobrious" act.

Partly because the *actual* definitions of the words have to be stretched – applying serious semantic gymnastics – for them to make any sense at all in the context in which they appear (see "opprobrious").[42] Or there is just a better, shorter word that has the same meaning.[43]

But a much larger portion of my hatred results from the *reason* people use these words. The person who says "nugatory" instead of "unimportant" or "bolus" instead of "bunch"[44] is someone who thinks of himself as a "writer".

Use of the word "refulgent" or "inveigle" or "opprobrious" disqualifies you from a literary career *and* from salvation.

Consider the unfortunately common: "he asked in consternation." Here, the "writer" has shoehorned a fancy word into his sentence solely for the purpose of impressing himself. If he thinks anyone else is impressed by this giant, pointless word, he's an imbecile. We already know he's an asshole.

[39] Jesus harbors an awful lot of disdain for self-styled "writers". Especially those who indulge their craft publicly.

They head to a trendy café, purchase the single coffee which they feel entitles them to occupancy of a table for six hours, and ostentatiously reveal their new Apple product. Then they check their email, make a few cringe-worthy Facebook posts,

---

[41] "Inveigle", "sequelae", "milieu", "refulgent", "nugatory", the list goes on.
[42] In the very applicable words of Inigo Montoya, "you keep using that word. I do not think it means what you think it means."
[43] "Bolus" is never okay. You're just trying to sound scientific. And failing.
[44] Pulling them from an online thesaurus, assuming all synonyms to be interchangeable.

and eventually communicate (by means of their deeply contemplative pose) that they are "working" on a "novel".

Jesus guarantees both that it is not a novel and that it is terrible.

There is a bottomless supply of these would-be artistes and none of them is capable of producing something Jesus wants to read. I would say "very few of them", but it's so close to none that I'm just going to round down.[45]

To every one of them, I redirect Truman Capote's criticism of Jack Kerouac.

[40] I hate people who thought I was going to quote the line I just referenced. It's famous. Had I felt constrained to repeat it, that would be an insult to Capote.

[41] It would be the equivalent of introducing someone with "a man who needs no introduction!", and then following that line with an introduction.

"Ladies and gentlemen, it is my distinct pleasure to introduce to you a man who needs no introduction! I first met Benny Carlisle when he was re-fitting his penile prosthesis..."

Every time someone's introduction is described as unnecessary, that person's entire résumé will be read aloud. Immediately.

No one ever says "a man who needs no introduction!", puts down the microphone, and just points at the person taking the stage.

But if someone did do that, Jesus would love them longtime.

---

[45] Among this group of "writers", it's those with the highest regard for their own skill who have the least. They've never sat down and worked on the craft, practicing the drills as a musician plays his scales. Instead, they're under the delusional impression that they can just play. And that's why their talent in writing is comparable to my talent in knife throwing.

Chapter Four

[1] "I'll give you something to cry about!" is not a very helpful or observant thing to say. To threaten in this way is to declare your lack of situational appreciation.

I'm crying *now*. You've clearly noticed. I must therefore have something to cry about. That's how it works.

If my eyes were dry, I would understand the offer being made; there may be some utility to it. If I had abnormally parched eyeballs, it could potentially be a non-medicinal substitute for eye drops.

But that's never the case. I've only ever heard it addressed to people with a case of the moist-alreadies. And at that point, somebody aggressive (or at least someone paternal) offers the weeper even *more* tears (another helping of what he already has in spades).

Tears seem to be among the few commodities proffered when clearly not in demand.

Nobody comes up to me after dinner, when I'm moaning, belt undone, grease dripping down my chin and says (angrily):

"Now I'll *give* you a jumbo enchilada!"

Never happens.

[2] And on the subject of tears, I hate people who lived west of Irvington, north of Fort Lee, south of Tappen Park, east of Elmhurst, or don't know where all of those places are, who wept over 9-11.[46]

---

[46] Today, they can be heard issuing sentences like "I remember exactly where I was – what I was doing – the moment the first plane hit the tower."

You're trying too hard to own the pain here. It doesn't belong to you. You're just sobbing to impress. It's theatrical grieving, so that even people in the back row can know how deep and caring and sensitive you are.[47]

3 I hate people who take high school dramatic productions seriously. The ones who stay in character in the lunch line. Then in the actual performance, they deliver their lines with too much enunciation and way too much volume, sometimes attempting an English accent.

4 I hate people who write "you need to annunciate more" and think I'll understand what they mean.

Or people who have "up most" respect for me, for all intensive porpoises. (These are all mute points.)

5 I hate people who pronounce "you" as "chew". "Without you there" becomes "without chew there". "Don't chew know?"

6 Much deeper is my hatred for people who write me back the instant I write them.

I send a three-paragraph email, into which I've put a lot of thought, and within one second, I have a response that says this:

hi :)

These people clearly didn't read my opus. They just see my name in their inbox, become aware that I'm currently online, and then take advantage of that awareness so that we can "chat".

I don't care who you are; I do not want to "chat" with you.

---

[47] Do any of these 9-11 weepers grieve when hail kills a thousand people in some fourth world country they've never heard of? Of course not. But if they legitimately cared about the loss of human life, then they absolutely would. This seems obvious. So what is it that they *actually* care about? Being perceived as a person who cares. This is as gross as it is pathetic (a lot of both).

Not even a little bit. About anything.

I would much rather you read my paragraphs and then didn't click the reply button. For a while. A pretty long one.

Just read my words and ponder. When that pondering starts to coagulate into thoughts of your own, don't send them to me. Wait. Let them let them mature; let them ferment. I don't want to receive anything from you until the vintage is auctionable.

If you have a four-digit IQ, then maybe I'll take your five-minute vintage. But otherwise don't insult me; I'm not into Welch's wine. So hang onto your thoughts. I'll talk to you in a month.

[7] The worst among the immediate responders are those who get irritated when I don't reciprocate the "hi" with a hello of my own. They know I'm online – that I must have seen the greeting – and they feel snubbed.

"Helloooooo!?", they write after a five-minute silence. And I respond to that email with a lifetime of estrangement.[48]

[8] I hate people who never write me unless they need help doing something really inconvenient.

Will I help you get your washer and dryer out of your ex-boyfriend's storage shed? Sorry, I'm kind of busy.

"Oh come on, where's your sense of adventure?!"

[9] I hate people who refer to women as "broads" (e.g., "a couple a' broads I grew up with").

[10] I hate childless "broads" who are just passed reproductive age and are obsessed with their nieces.

---

[48] These people will be getting to know Jim Carrey very well in the afterlife.

They aren't yours. Nobody wants to hear you talk about them. And your siblings would appreciate it if you would stop trying to usurp their role as biological parents.

[11] I hate anyone who owns a single decorative pillow.

[12] I hate people who wear watches that don't tell time. Some of them just need batteries; others are "modern", which means ugly garbage. Just wear a bracelet.

[13] I hate men who buy jewelry for women.

[14] I hate women who want men to buy them jewelry. And those who buy jewelry for themselves. And those who don't think that jewelry is stupid.

[15] I hate people who spend money on any fashion line that begins with "the", has a word in the middle, and ends with "collection".

[16] I hate people whose fashion is currently fashionable. And I can already tell it will be unfashionable by this time next year.

Hairstyle, belt thickness, pant tightness, sock height, etc.

There are much better ways to keep the economy moving than the perpetual updating of one's "look".

[17] These are the same people who get a new phone more than once every five years.

"Is that a new phone?"

"Yeah."

"Didn't you just get a new one like six months ago?"

"Yeah, but I had an upgrade."

"Do you think maybe you're paying too much for your monthly service if that service periodically issues you a $500 phone?"

"Well I also have an unlimited data plan."

"Isn't that what every internet service provider gives you on every device that isn't a phone?"

"Yeah, but this phone has features that the last model didn't."

"And it's necessary that you own those features? Every time a household appliance boasts new technology, do you upgrade it too? Every year you update your vacuum cleaner, dishwasher, iron, toaster, and stove?

"A phone is different."

"No it isn't."

[18] I hate people who purchase their clothes at trendy, mid-mall destinations. The kind of shops that struggle to look like dirty garages (exposed beams, unpainted particle board, shirts hung on iron pipes, etc.). Inside this store, music will be playing at a deafening volume. This eliminates the awkward pressure of *having* to talk.

[19] I hate people who look at new cars parked inside malls.

"Enter to Win!", the sign says. And people do. (They enter; they don't win, of course.)[49]

[20] I hate people who admire Abercrombie skills.

These aren't just casual shoppers, but teenagers who hang posters in their bedrooms. Teenagers who get a special feeling when they see twenty-year-olds casting longing gazes at nothing, or sensually frolicking in black and white.

---

[49] I hate anyone who registers for a chance to win a "sweepstakes".

²¹ I hate people who *have* Abercrombie skills.

Sometimes these skills are exhibited by lying down and kissing someone while shirtless, the top person's hair draping into the bottom person's face. Other times the two young lovers are standing, kissing each other ridiculously slowly. Usually with exaggerated lip gestures.

If these young adults aren't on grass or bed sheets (or sometimes a boat), they're on a beach. While on that beach, they're always wet. If it's a guy, he might be waxing his boat (shirtless). If it's a girl or an especially androgynous guy, her (and/or his) hair is messy. But just a little bit. It's more luscious than messy. And sometimes the wind is blowing through it.

If something is happening that isn't slowly kissing or boat waxing, it's probably a girl setting a volleyball or a guy catching a football (shirtless, arms outstretched, camera focused on his abs). Or that same shirtless guy is giving the almost-shirtless volleyball setter a piggyback ride. And they're ankle deep in the ocean, laughing at whatever is supposed to be funny about this.

²² I hate the people in black and white ads who laugh at nothing.

These people are not funny. They're not ever funny about anything. To each of them, I quote Luke, chapter six, verse twenty-five:

"Woe unto you that laugh now! for ye shall mourn and weep."[50]

---

[50] That was from the King James Version. Excepting Wycliffe's translation, this is the only version of the Bible that will ever be written in the English language. It is not okay to quote passages from a translation that says "Good News" on the cover. Or has words like "Contemporary" in its title. Or "Easy Reading" or "Clear Word" or "Modern Language" or "New Century" or "New American" or "New English" or "Living English" or "Common English" or "Revised English" or "English Standard" or "International Standard" or "New International" or any other "revised" (e.g., "Revised Version" or "Revised Standard Version") or "new" or "standard" anything (worst: "New Revised Standard").

23 Before the age of digital entertainment, people had to actually *be* funny. This is no longer necessary. After the invention of things like YouTube, they just have to be able to *recognize* what's funny.[51]

24 I hate people who are too eager to recognize what's funny. People who have already been sold on "this is so funny!" before anything funny has happened.

I realize you paid money to see a comedian, and you're expecting him to make you laugh, but at least make him work for it. Make him earn it. All he's doing is walking on stage and you're already giggling.

He approaches the microphone and shouts: "what's up New Jersey?!"

"Hahahaha!" goes the audience.

"I gotta tell 'ya: those goddamn toll booths are everywhere!"

"Hahahaha!" goes the audience.

Are you just worried you won't get your money's worth? You better start laughing now lest you regret the cost of the ticket? If so, that's really pathetic.

25 These are the same people who buy tickets to *The Exorcist*, get a bag of popcorn, take their seats during the previews, and begin screaming and spilling that popcorn during the opening credits.

I'm confused here. What specifically about "directed by William Friedkin" induces that degree of terror?[52]

---

[51] "Did you see the one where the girl poops the hot tub?" Or something about a British child's thumb or a homeless woman's rhubarb or a sneaky cat. At some point in life, people's standards are reduced to such a depth that quoting a movie or a YouTube video is considered a worthy contribution to a conversation.

[52] The kind of terror that has you making noises. Loud, pointless outbursts that liken the theater to a special needs classroom full of kids with Tourette's.

If he were directing *Airplane 6* or *Scary Movie 15*, would those noises be restrained giggles?

[26] When I hear someone say "weird funny or haha funny?", I don't hate *that* person, but I do hate the person who caused this question to be asked.

Just describe things with meaningful words the first time and you won't have to follow up with an explanation of what you meant.

[27] Anyone who calls anything a "practical joke" deserves a good amount of hatred. There's nothing at all *practical* about practical jokes. Nor is there anything funny about them. Like this:

"What's that on your shirt?"

Victim looks down.

"Whoop!", as the perpetrator pokes the victim in the face – mostly in the lips and nose – and then says "hahaha!"

That's not funny at all.

There's nothing even a tiny bit funny about it.

If someone asks "what's that on your shirt?", why should I not look down? There's no reason why I shouldn't look to the spot where you're pointing and asking me to look.

And when I do, why should you then poke me in the face?

What about this is *practical*?

[28] People who find humor in poking other people's faces in this way are unlikely to be compulsive hand-washers. So when their fingernails enter my mouth and scrape against my gums, and then I can feel how wet they are as they poke me in the pupil, I'm not going to say "haha, you got me! You *totally* got me!"

29 I hate people who think The Three Stooges are funny.[53]

The Three Stooges, like the people laughing in an Abercrombie commercial, were never once funny. They never did a single funny thing.

It is an unbreakable law, established by my dad at the birth of the universe, that physical humor is not humor.

Jim Carrey? Jerry Lewis? They will spend eternity having Mo, Larry and Curley poking their eyes in and bashing their faces with frying pans. And if you have ever laughed at the Three Stooges (even once) so will you.

"Nyuck, nyuck, nyuck!!!"

---

[53] Young boys who grow up thinking The Three Stooges are funny become teenage boys who fake-punch each other and say "dude!" a lot.

Chapter Five

[1] I hate people who talk "in tongues". I can't understand a single syllable of what you're saying. So you're clearly doing it for you, not for me. Nor at me, to me, because of me, and certainly not *through* me. I'm not involved here.

[2] But I am, unfortunately, involved in your prayers. These are almost always at me (or otherwise to me). And I find them offensive.

My dad came up with this world design – His master plan – and gave it life. He put it into motion. So when you pray to either Him or Me, asking that one of Us change that plan (e.g., "please make it so my wife *doesn't* die of cancer"), what you're really saying is that you don't like what We're doing. Or what We've done. You don't like the plan. And if it were up to you, you'd be doing things differently.

To me, your prayers sound like this:

"Look, Christ, I see what you're doing here. I see where you're going with this, but you're getting it all wrong. You're clearly missing the boat. You *have* a plan; I get that. It's just not a particularly good one. Either that or you don't have a very good handle on it. So let me give you some pointers on what a better plan would look like." You then request the revisions: cure this person, fix this situation, etc. "…Amen."

When someone prays in this way, it means he thinks he knows more about my dad's design than I do.

That's *really* conceited.

The reason your wife is dying is because I anticipated your conceit. And I was irritated by it. So irritated that I've decided to take her away from you. I'm just using cancer as my vehicle. And I'm starting with her breasts, which you loved the most about her.

Don't ask me to do anything differently or I'll kill you too.

I've already got my crosshairs on your prostate; I'm just waiting to pull the trigger.

3 Worse than people who privately pray for change are people who publically pray for anything. See Matthew, chapter six, verse five. 'Nuff said.

4 Worse still are those who ask the Courtneys of the world to pray for them.

"I'm going through some hard times right now; it'd really mean a lot if you prayed for me."

There's a reason you're going through hard times: you're the kind of self-centered asshole who asks heathens to pray for you.

5 And the worst of all are those who ask other people to pray for yet other people. Consider the Facebook post: "here's a picture of a sick kid I found; everybody pray for him!"

6 I don't even like it when people pray *thanks* at me. No decision I've ever made is about you. Your sanctimonious rectum-kissing isn't going to persuade me to alter any part of the grand plan to your benefit.

7 I hate people who talk about "feeling blessed", even outside of the spiritual realm. Things like "thanks for the b-day wishes!" Or: "I feel so blessed to have such great friends in my life."[54]

One should never announce specific things one is grateful for to other people. Especially those who make a ritual out of it.

This isn't even worth doing at Thanksgiving.

---

[54] Hashtag blessed!

[8] I hate people who call Thanksgiving "turkey day" (or any other such attempt to be cute or creative by saying the same un-cute, uncreative thing everyone else says).

[9] And people who play or watch football on Thanksgiving.[55]

[10] I also hate people who run toward (and then burst through) huge, decorated sheets of butcher paper at the start of a sporting event.

Sometimes people (i.e., "fans") are expected to watch this happen from cold, metal bleachers.

The people doing the butcher-paper-bursting are usually rapists.

[11] Before they raped women, back when they were just little kids, they rebelled against their parents by not washing their hands. Sometimes they would even turn on the faucet, but not touch the water, and then turn it off. This *really* fooled their parents.

[12] Later in life, their hand washing is even worse. They will turn the faucet on, rub their hands together under the water for a single second, and then turn the faucet off.

With hands that are still dirty, but are also now wet, they pump out a ten-foot band from the paper towel dispenser, crumple it in and around their dirty, wet hands, and then throw the sort-of-wadded-up hunk of 90% dry paper pulp into the wastebasket.

I (along with everyone else who has ever thought about it) would rather these people just didn't wash at all.

---

[55] These are the people who go shopping on "Black Friday". Sometimes they're just accompanying their wives; other times they're trying to upgrade their televisions. If you can get over the bragging (euphemized as gratefulness) enabled by Thanksgiving, it's one of the only holidays worth celebrating. It's a good excuse to overeat good food while in good company. But when Black Friday enters the celebratory equation, Thanksgiving dinner becomes nothing more than a pregame meal, an effort to carb load for tomorrow's performance.

[13] After the age of dry fake-hand-washing, but before the age of wet fake-hand-washing (just before their first birth through the butcher paper cervix), most of these men went through a phase in which they took karate classes. And took those classes seriously.

Their seriousness came from the belief that what they were practicing was real. The belief that the moves they were learning would enable them to fly through the air, defeating villains. Life is not that exciting though.

[14] And these future rapists had already earned their purple belts in taekwondo before they realized that it could be lumped together with hacky sack (and phonebook ripping) under the group of activities known as "performance art".

[15] Eventually these boys give up their "martial" performance arts, outgrow the AstroTurf (and the butcher-paper-filled hula hoops on the sidelines), and become sad adults. Sad adults who tell stories. Stories that include expressions such as "suppose to" and "use to". For example: "I use to have a Camaro."[56]

[16] And they begin their life of "billiards".

I hate people who play billiards and say things like "putting English on it".

A lot of them grew up at the Boys and Girls Club. This by itself is not damning, but upon reaching adulthood, the need to display one's skills in air hockey, foosball, and cue sports should be relinquished. And it never is.

[17] People also need to stop using the expression "up the wazzou".

[18] This is as bad as "any which way but loose".

---

[56] Sometimes it's the slightly more grammatical "remember that one time when I…" Every sentence that begins in this way will end with something boring. And the implication is always "weren't those just the glory days!?"

Or confusing loose with lose. I don't understand what it means when somebody looses a game any more than I understand what wazzous are and what's hidden up inside of them.

[19] Worse: people who say "I'm going to switch gears now" as a lead-in to talking about something else.

This is not what gears do. Gears change the velocity of a downstream motion. They don't switch subjects. That's what changing a TV channel does. And TV channels have nothing to do with gears.

So whenever anyone says "I'm going to switch gears", that person should be killed before he has the chance to change the subject.

Now you could say, "Jesus, you don't know how that person was going to finish his sentence."[57]

Yes, I do. I know perfectly well. Not just because I'm a Christ, but because no human mouth has ever said "I'm going to switch gears here", and then started talking about the exact same subject way faster.

[20] Just as bad: "I've been running around like a chicken with its head cut off."

No, you haven't.

Ignoring that your behavior does not resemble a dying chicken's in any way, you're not even "running around".

You're making phone calls and sending emails and occasionally driving somewhere. And then you sit cross-legged on your closet floor and organize your shoes and blouses for three hours. What part of these activities is relatable to those of mutilated junglefowl?

---

[57] Or *her* sentence, since it was usually Courtney Jensen's female ex-boss who used that expression. Every single time she changed subjects.

[21] I hate people who have really organized closets. Especially when it comes to shoes and blouses.

[22] If you exit this person's closet and head to the kitchen, you'll find signs that say "Live Laugh Love" or something about "Hope".

Hopeful people need no reminders to remain hopeful. And if you must be told to laugh, you have a painfully unfunny life. The same can be said about living and loving, but it would be a bore to say it. So instead, I'll say this: if you're in the "Live Laugh Love" class, you probably keep dead plants in pots.

[23] I don't mind male cheerleaders. Mostly because that degree of oblivion takes real work. I can almost admire it. The girls though, these are just the pre-moms who don't yet have thick, deep, purple veins running down their legs.

[24] I hate the coaches and athletes who gather themselves into a really tight circle, each reach their dominant hand into the center of that circle, and then raise and lower that mass of hands while grunt-shouting their team name in unison.

[25] And I hate people whose cheering involves hollering some sort of chant that rhymes.

"We want a pitcher, not a belly-itcher!"

That doesn't make sense. We should not pretend that it does.

[26] I hate people who, while standing at the finish line of a child's running event (e.g., middle school cross-country), issue the exact same cheer to every passing child, even if it does make sense.

"Woo-hoo, go Eastbrook!", with exactly four claps.

[27] I hate people who cheer at sports events that don't involve their children.

[28] And people who pretend to love minor sports (this includes soccer if you're an American) to exhibit "culture".

Expressing too much appreciation for a particular minor sport is equivalent to being a groupie of an "indie" band. If that band were actually good, they would be selling out stadiums, like the talented bands do. And like the major sports do.

[29] I hate people who think I care about the outcomes of any sport (regardless of how many fans it has).

My hatred is not limited to the coach who organizes a team prayer before his newly-blessed athletes take the field. Or the devoted fan who offers a prayer at the start of every inning.

[30] I hate the actual players just as much.

The baseball player who, upon stepping up to the plate, with one foot in the box, uses a batting-gloved hand to mark the points of a crucifix across his chest (assuming such a gesture will help guide the ball to the "sweet spot" of his bat).

Or the football player who, after scoring a touchdown, makes a big display about me. He gets down onto one knee, bows his empty head, and points a crooked finger up at the sky.

These idiots behave as though I had something to do with the events that enabled an arbitrary thing to happen to adult men who are playing a child's game for millions of dollars.

Chapter Six

[1] "Who's taller: me or you?"

Sometimes I'll hear a teenager ask that question as he presses his back against another person's and makes his posture as erect as possible.

    A) I hate anyone who has ever asked that.

    B) The answer to the question is always the person who didn't ask it. The one who doesn't care. Because it's pathetic if you're taller and desperate for someone to notice.

[2] I hate people who are too enthusiastic about barefoot running. If they're unable to go barefoot, they'll wear those shoes with the individual toe slots ("to simulate the barefoot experience", they'll explain to me, though I didn't ask).

And then they'll explain that the shoes I've chosen to wear are terrible for my posture and joints and bone health and are not conducive to athleticism. "Nature gave us the perfect anatomy for running and we're covering it up with a bunch of supportive rubber", they'll say.

Perfect anatomy? Are you sure?

"Perfect."

Huh. Have you ever watched a nudist run?

"No."

Well let me tell you, it's something to see. Jockstraps and sports bras were clearly invented for a reason.

"No other animal wears shoes though."

Okay. So what? If our anatomy resembled theirs a bit more, we wouldn't need shoes either. I've never seen *National Geographic* footage of a cheetah in slow motion, sprinting after a gazelle, with giant, pendulous tits flapping uncontrollably, obstructing its gait.

Damn, the gazelle got away. If only the cheetah had a sports bra.

Why are we treating human feet as though they're different from breasts and scrotums?

[3] The people who commit themselves to the barefoot experience are the same ones who feel the most compelled to tell me about their "all natural" diets.

"My diet is 100% natural", they inform me as they eat another handful of "raw nuts".

Okay, everyone's diet is 100% natural. Everything everyone has ever eaten is derived from nature. The alternative is that your diet is supernatural. Like you eat ghosts. So unless you were the inspiration for the Pac-Man character, your diet is totally natural.

If the barefoot naturalists have anything else to say (anything other than repeated descriptions of their raw nuts and shapely arches), you can expect an effort to sound philosophical.

[4] I hate people who study philosophy and are sincere about it. They never contribute anything to the conversation. All they ever do is comment about how the conversation is being held.

[5] And sometimes those comments include the word "persons".

As long as the word "people" continues to be a word, I hate people who say "persons".

If "persons" can be a word, so can "mans" and "womans", as in: "how many mans does it take to screw in a light bulb?" Or: "how many womans are in line for the bathroom?"

^{$6} I also hate every man (no woman does this) who rubs his index and middle fingers together with his thumb in a semi-circular fashion[58] to indicate money or some type of financial thing.

"Moo-lah", he might say if he's especially retarded.

[7] Even worse than this are the people who point at themselves with their thumbs.

I hate the people who use both thumbs simultaneously twice as much as I hate the people who just use one hand's thumb at a time.

[8] I hate people who use erasers. Just get it right the first time. If you're not good enough to do that, then start over a lot. The sound of you scraping a dry eraser against a sheet of computer paper can't be allowed to continue.

[9] And I hate people who think that good weather exists in Florida or Arizona. If scalding heat were pleasant, why would my dad have spent so much time and energy trying to get African men and women onto slave ships where they could be transported to cooler climates?[59]

It wasn't just so that the hypo-pigmented people who preached the hardest about me could own hyper-pigmented people (who would go on to preach about me pretty hard as well).

My dad and I have both grown to hate all of those people (the hard preachers). Whenever someone *really* commits himself to the two of Us, it always turns out that he's done something bad. And his "born again" fanaticism is merely an attempt to absolve his guilt.

---

[58] If using the left hand, the thumb goes counter-clockwise.

[59] I hate people who tell me about dry heat. "Do you want to come help me in the yard for a bit?" "Not right now; it's way too hot out." "Yeah, but it's a dry heat." "Okay, but wetness doesn't change the temperature." "Yeah, but it's a different heat." "Okay, but it's not a different temperature and the temperature is the problem". "Fine." "I'll help you this evening if you want." "No, don't worry, I'll do it myself." "Okay, have fun."

Either that or he's just an alcoholic. But lucky for him, I, Jesus Christ, lend my hallowed hand more to the chemically diseased than any other demographic of persons.

[10] But an alcoholic who has not yet introduced himself as such to a group of likeminded failures is not yet a Christian.

Just like his Christian counterpart, every one of his conversations is about drinking. However, instead of framing it as a problem, he thinks of himself as "wild" and his stories are told under the false impression that they're interesting.

100% of his stories go like this: "so I'm drinking last night, right?"

"Okay?"

"And I'm fucking *hammered*. Like I'm fucking *wasted*. It was *awesome!*"

And then?

(There's never an "and then". That's the end of the story.)

The Sumerians were brewing beer before Adam ever set foot in Eden. Wine and mead were being made around that time too. Alcohol isn't new. It's been around for a while. And this story has been around for exactly as long. And never once, in those thousands of years, has it ever entertained a single person.[60]

For this reason, my response is always: "that wasn't a story. Those were just a bunch of words. All you did just now was demonstrate, inefficiently, that you're a boring asshole."

---

[60] Relatedly, any story that begins with "I was at my bible study last night…" is not told for the edification, entertainment, or enlightenment of one's listener. It's an indulgence. Nothing more. It would be far more respectful to your audience if you just said "I'm better than you", and left it at that. Same overall summary, but you would not have wasted as much of their time.

This person then leaves and immediately tells someone else the same story.

[11] Even worse are the people who say things like "I don't remember last night. I totally blacked out."

Girls say this more than boys.

A) You didn't black out, but you did fall asleep at some point.

B) Of course you remember last night. You remember it perfectly. You're just embarrassed by it.[61]

If a nineteen-year-old girl got drunk last night and doesn't have a story to tell today, that's because she's preoccupied with thoughts of an unwanted fetus.

I don't feel sorry for her. Not one bit. Instead, I usually "egg on" the sperm.[62] [63]

[12] The people whom I hate the least out of this batch are those who start the night with beer, move onto tequila, switch to rum, and then finish with vodka.

Stomachs appreciate this less than mouths and mouths don't enjoy it much. So these people always vanish before they can bother me.

The vomiting is undignified and the hangover unpleasant, but they usually do those things in their own space and on their own time.[64]

---

[61] If you *honestly* can't remember last night, you should be taken to a hospital immediately. You have a real problem. And prayer won't solve it. I would know: I'm the one who isn't listening to a word you say.

[62] *Did you catch that?*

[63] When girls are in their slutty years, they often want to play the part without being identified by it. The half-assing and the indecision are the only damnable traits here. If you're going to do it, do it. Either commit or don't. And if you do, I'm not judging. If you read my half of the bible, you would know that. You would know that I pardon the full-assers.

[64] I hate pointless uses of "respectively" and the pointless people who use it.

[13] Although whenever I come across somebody drinking vodka with Skittles in it, I at least *attempt* to intervene with a homicide. Sometimes I succeed. And I'm rarely sorry about my successes. If a loved one has died in this way, you should know that I sent that person straight to Hell. If this upsets you, go find a different religion.

[14] I also try to purge the drinking class of its members who can "barely taste the alcohol". It can be hard to assassinate these folks by way of alcohol poisoning though. Because often the reason they can barely taste it is that the drinks barely contain any alcohol. It's just a thousand calories of sugar made wet. When confronted with this challenge, I apply cosmic judo principles and go with the direction of the punch, doing them in with diabetes. It can take a while, but I usually pull it off within a couple years.

[15] By the time diabetes has stolen their feet, the boy with the really boring stories will have been subjected to an intervention.

His mom and older sister perform this intervention in the kitchen. And it doesn't work.

So his mom cries a lot (because she still has feelings for her son even though his stories are so boring). She should know better. She should know how stupid he is.

[16] But the mother is the type of person who wears pointed witch shoes. So maybe she *doesn't* know any better.

I've never once been tempted to fornicate with someone who was wearing pointy shoes.

When I see this kind of footwear, I wonder what could possibly be inside of it. It's not the shape of a foot. Not a human foot anyway. So anyone who's attracted to this look has a bestial hankering.[65]

---

[65] The same can be said about people with two-digit IQs. These are not people. Attempting to procreate with one would feel an awful lot like zoo sex. With the animals. And the resultant hybrid wouldn't belong in the zoo or the bedroom.

[17] Eventually, the son with the bad stories pretends AA was his idea and he begins to talk way too much about "the big book".

His stories are exactly as bad, but now they're about "daily successes".

[18] He'll collect no fewer than fifteen one-month coins and excuse each one with the same tagline he employs to describe his earlier phase of drinking: "it was just something I had to go through."

[19] It's not until his alcoholism causes him to lose his job that he'll begin relying on a different expression:

"When God closes one door, he opens another."

I guess that's true. Unfortunately, the one my dad opens is usually a trapdoor.

Or, in this case, the door to a homeless shelter.

[20] When our AA boy is not repeating one of his taglines, he can be found telling a story about "last night's dream", assuming other people could somehow be entertained by that.

Nobody has ever once told an interesting story about a dream.

Not because it's a boring subject (it is), but because it's never actually true. People just remember some "vivid" (by which they mean vague) image from one of their dreams and make up a whole story based on it.

Sometimes the dream teller will think his tale is an amusing one; other times he'll think it "means" something.

"What do you think it means?", he'll ask.

When a recovering alcoholic starts asking that question, it makes everyone wish he'd fall off the wagon.

[21] I hate people who relate chemical addictions to a wagon.

[22] Whenever anyone says "I totally saw that coming", he didn't.

Likewise, one should never say "every action causes a reaction" in response to anything. Newtonian mechanics were never meant to apply to your unhealthy relationships.[66]

[23] The "I saw that coming" crowd is populated by twenty-first century teenagers who think it "cool" to quote *Scarface* during the intervals between their "challenges" (milk challenge, cinnamon challenge, saltine cracker challenge, etc.).

[24] Sometimes they'll be wearing the John Belushi "college" shirt while they do it.

[25] And they describe practically everything as "epic".

The 50-50 grind you did on your skateboard has nothing to do with *Gilgamesh*.[67] Sorry.

[26] These are the same people who think everything is "ironic".[68]

---

[66] Combining the two quotations offers us an epigram about human reasoning: every action causes a *pre*-action, which people like to discuss in retrospect, pretending like they saw it coming.

[67] Or the *Iliad* or the *Odyssey* or *Beowulf*. Or any other narrative poem. That's what epic (derived from epikos) means: poem. So unless Ovid or Homer or Hesiod wrote about your sweet two-truck grind, there's nothing "epic" about it.

[68] Use of "irony" to mean coincidence is far too boring to discuss. But "irony" in the place of "sarcasm" is far too annoying not to. The difference: irony can arise spontaneously (or as others might say, "organically"). Circumstances can spontaneously give rise to it. But circumstances cannot spontaneously give rise to sarcasm. People have to *create* it (usually with words). If an event is ironic, that means the opposite outcome (from what was expected) happened. If I built a house of cards and glued them together so they'd never fall, but the heat and humidity in the room caused the glue to bend and crack and that's what made the card house to collapse, we have irony. There's nothing sarcastic about that. Sarcasm is just *saying* the opposite: "you look pretty", when the recipient of that compliment is a hideous ghoul with hypotelorism eyes. Or "you have such a soothing voice" to a child whose shower songs sounds like the hissing of an angry cat. You're not allowed to confuse irony with sarcasm (or coincidence).

[27] The would-be-polite among the epic-ironic class say things like "thanks for the invite" whenever they're invited somewhere.

Invite is a verb. Just like decorate.

Invit*ation* is the noun (just like decor*ation*).

Nobody seems to confuse that one. "It looks like we're going to have a lot of trick-or-treaters this year; wanna to help me hang up the Halloween decorates?"

If anyone uses "invite" as a noun ("hey, thanks for the invite; count me in!"), I immediately rescind the invitation.

[28] I hate people who say "o'clock" after something like 2:17 or 10:44.

Sometimes they accent the o' part of it. I don't like this at all.

[29] I hate people who wear fake eyelashes. Or put "product" on their real ones to make them seem thicker.

Or people who remove all of the hair where their eyebrows used to be and then use a makeup pencil to apply drawings of eyebrows in the new bald spots.

[30] Whenever I see a woman wearing way too much makeup, I assume it's a man. Why else would a person try that hard to convince me that the thing I'm looking at is a woman?

The more vibrant the lipstick, the stronger my hunch.

Sometimes, while I'm pondering that hunch, the makeup wearer will see me staring and offer a self-conscious smile in my direction.

When this happens, it's much easier for me to identify the gender. Because a man's smile and a woman's smile are two very different expressions.

A smiling woman, even with the excess of makeup, has a softer appearance. If it's a man's jaw doing the smiling, what I see is a creature muscling its face meat into an expression that exposes its dental faculties. Lipstick doesn't soften this image. Whenever I see it, I always invent a little backstory. It might go like this:

As a boy, Mrs. Guyman Broadjaw participated in a variety of sports – racquet sports, field sports, aquatic sports, ice sports – hoping to find the right fit. Maybe he could find confidence if he just found success. But what he found instead was one punishing experience after another, each sport worse than the last. And it was the combination of those experiences that shaped an identity in which words beginning with "cross" or "trans" both upset and excite.

[31] I don't hate this man, but I do hate men who pretend to be sensitive or deep or "understanding of the woman's perspective" by asserting that unavailable women are more attractive "without any makeup on" or "before she lost all of the weight" or "before she got all dressed up" or "before her picture was Photoshopped".

"I thought she was prettiest just the way she was", says the penised liar about one girl (with whom he has no chance or interest) to another girl (with whom he does have a chance and interest).

If his assertion were true, "fashion" wouldn't be a multi-billion dollar conglomerate of woman-altering industries (magazines, cosmetics, etc.).

But it is.

And the only reason these industries do things like digitally alter (i.e., "Photoshop") women's appearances is because these exact men like it so much. The ones who say they don't. 100% of them.

[32] I hate people who say "keepin' it real" or "what you see is what you get" (or any other allusion to "the real me").

If you hear someone say this, you can be certain that you've never met anyone who has tried harder to put on a personality show, no one who has ever put more effort into counterfeiting an identity.

"Ya'll don't know the real me!", the nineteen-year-old girl declares while posting even more pictures of herself online.

Apparently the "real her" is captured by digital photographs taken at arm's length while at parties, at concerts, at beaches, etc.

The real her is the type of person who, as David Sedaris most cleverly notes, reduces all experience to proof. Not "what an amazing concert this is!", but "everybody look where I am: a concert!"

[33] These are the same people who regularly announce "I don't care what other people think about me."

The fact that you have to actually *say* this makes it untrue. You're putting time and energy – real effort – into convincing people to believe something about you that's contingent on that belief not mattering.

These are clearly the people who care the *most* about what other people think. If that weren't the case, they wouldn't be trying so damn hard to convince people otherwise. But the only impression they wind up giving is that they're the type of people who thrive on giving impressions. And what is it that we're really supposed to believe (aside from believing that you don't care about our beliefs)?

We're meant to think that the real you isn't just a gross mess like everyone else (and that the book *Everyone Poops* was written about everyone *but* the real you).

Those arm's-length pictures are never of a girl spending thirty minutes on the toilet because all she ate yesterday was meat. And she ate way too much of it because she chronically eats to the point of self-loathing.

Or a picture of a high school boy spending his Saturday watching a bad *Friends* rerun for the sixth time, itching his crotch way too much, and occasionally picking scabs, inspecting them, and then flicking them onto the carpet.[69]

The caption is never "a dog barked at me and I was terrified and I peed my pants" (arm's length picture).

Or "you don't know the real me: you weren't in the room during my pap smear when I found out I have herpes. You should have seen my meltdown" (arm's length picture of a girl with smeared mascara holding a bottle of Valtrex).

Those "updates" never get posted. "The real me" is never a portrait of human weakness. Instead, it's always something exciting. It's deep and poetic. It's sexy. And it's *always* fiction.

So much make-believe goes into every public display.

These people struggle to convince their peers that their lives are glamorous when life itself is not.

A body is such a terrible thing to be. And every person who tries to disguise that fact must be so unhappy in life. And the saddest among them are always those with the happiest, most exciting posts.

[34] Fred Frank (2012) has coined this the *Facebook Pathology Magnification Effect* (FPME). To quote his coinage:

"It is a most serendipitous twenty-first-century consequence. Like underlinings, exclamation points, and strongly held political opinions, start from the premise that everything stated is exactly the opposite of what it declares and you'll have a nice window into people's biggest fears and insecurities."

---

[69] This is why "be yourself" is the worst advice you can ever give or receive.

[35] "Real me" aside, nothing exposes the heart of one's insecurities as openly as the social networking post.

Consider: *Another semester of straight A's! Thank you brain!*[70]

This is not a smart person. It's someone who is struggling in life. Not just to *achieve* those A's, but struggling to come to terms with his genetic damnation. He was damned to a life of below-average intelligence and this is the arena in which he's chosen to confront it. This is where his battle with self-esteem is being lost.

The same losing struggle is revealed by people who post comments about books they've read:

If you're into spies and sabotage "Insidious Foes" is a delightful read! And yes, if you're into FDR you'll love it too![71]

Here's the second sentence in Amazon's official book description: "Bungling spies were captured and half-hearted efforts at sabotage came to nothing." This short, official book summary goes on to talk about FDR. Clearly, this book was not read by the person who referred to it as "a delightful read!"[72]

---

[70] Copied and pasted from a Facebook post made on the twenty-ninth day of December, in the year of Me 2011.

[71] Copied and pasted from the same Facebook profile that brought us "thank you brain!"

[72] Also, "read" is a verb, not a noun. And I hate the people who dress it up in noun's clothes. Not every word needs to cover all forms of speech. Otherwise we're at risk of building buildings and naming names and feeling feelings (though I do enjoy the feeling I feel after I drink a drink). It's so much more pleasing to hear about reading *books* rather than reading *readings*, which is why no form of "read" should ever be used as a noun. "That was a good read" is a surprising sentence to me because how could someone so illiterate be able to distinguish good writing from bad writing? My hunch is that they can't. And their judgment should be distrusted (unless you too are inclined to say that you read a read). It needs to be said that one cannot read a read any more than one can say a say or hear a hear. It's like calling something a "hot buy". Buying is what you do to the item; it's not what you receive. You can't buy a buy. Or gift a gift, which means "gifting" is not a word. Gift is a noun and gifted is an adjective. Neither of them is a verb, like give or read is. Using gift as a verb is like using citrus as a verb. "I citrussed my tea." Like that.

The purpose of posts such as this are to make people *think* "sophisticated" material is being read. But all it really declares is that the "reader" is illiterate.

[36] Sometimes, when I see people boasting in a Facebook post, or those whose updates appear to be wild and exciting, I merely pity them. There's so much sadness already that it feels like overkill to apply my hatred on top of it.[73]

But when I see *involuntary* posts, I find it difficult to continue withholding that hatred.

It's because of these people that I have a daily influx of "invites" to play Bubble Safari. And why I have updates in the rolling feeds that say things like "Wendy Marcotte unlocked lollipop hammer in Candy Crush Saga." Or about how she leveled up in Ninja Saga. Or how well her vegetable garden is doing in FarmVille.

There must be so little self-esteem before someone decides that this sounds like a reasonable thing to do: "maybe I'll waste an unconscionable amount of time playing Mafia Wars today."

[37] The FPME also applies to self-proclaimed anythings.

Everyone knows the "real" you isn't good at anything because you spend far too much time online, trying to convince the world that you don't care what people think of you. And that leaves almost no time to develop any life skills.

[38] Even offline, the self-proclaimed expert is never an expert. You're just trying to sell me something.

---

[73] And I do admit fault for logging in at all; I'm not proud of that. But whenever I degrade myself in this way, if I accidentally see your latest "post" (because it automatically appeared in my "feed"), you're not allowed to interpret that as "Facebook stalking". Nobody is even the tiniest bit interested in your affairs, let alone so obsessed that they can be accused of stalking you. You're a bore. The shit you type just appears on people's screens and they see it by accident. Likewise, if you wear a shirt that has writing on it, and someone happens to notice what the words say, that doesn't mean the person is hitting on you.

Especially when assigning an identity to a business.

Repeating the motto "fair and balanced" tells me only that the news program I'm watching is the least fair and most unbalanced of any source available.

When Subway hangs signs up all over creation that say "we ♥ our customers", that confirms that I will be hated by the person making my sandwich.[74]

When I'm in Louisville and I see signs posted on every piece of thing that say "City of Opportunity", I immediately recognize that this is a land of little to no hope. I can stand at any of one of those signs, look out at the landscape before me, and see at least a dozen homeless people begging to no effect.

In Hartford, Connecticut, there is a Just Say No To Drugs Lane. Is there any question about what happens on this street?

The FPME has a very long reach. It exposes our deepest fears, our most guarded insecurities.

[39] The next time you're driving, look at the slogans and decals on the car in front of you.

If you see a license plate holder that has the words "truly blessed" engraved into it, try to get around that car. Speed around to the side of it so you can get a good look at its rearview mirror.

I guarantee you'll see a handicap parking pass dangling from it.

---

[74] And this person who hates me will be billed as a "sandwich artist", a title that automatically implies a complete absence of artistry. An artist may be inclined to express himself by overemphasizing a particular color on his kidney-shaped palette. Can one of Subway's "artists" express himself by overemphasizing the roast beef portion of his palette? No. He'll be fired. These are paint-by-numbers artists (meaning not artists at all, which is *why* they're called "artists").

That license plate holder offers real insight into how people reason, how they endure tragedy, how they attempt to maintain self-worth in the beaming face of adversity.

This isn't just ignorance. Ignorance comes naturally; it takes no effort. This is different. This sort of oblivion takes real work.

"I lost my legs in a car wreck" has to be difficult to live with if you don't wrestle a bright side out of it.

And that bright side has to be difficult to believe if you don't force constant reminders into your life.

"Truly blessed."

Chapter Seven

¹ When I was a man, I was passing forth from thence and Matthew was perched at the receipt of custom. I told him to follow me. And then I saw Levi, son of Alpheaus, sitting at the tax booth. I brought him along too. Just trying to pad my audience.

² When I tell a story, it takes appropriate reactions at the checkpoints for me to continue. Story hour plays like a game of *Rad Racer*. If the audience reaction isn't what it needs to be, I coast to a halt and then quit talking.

³ But even worse is a premature "whoa!"

If I tell a story, and there's nothing outrageous, and I'm given the same response I would give if someone told me he traveled back in time, ate his own parents, and lived to tell, I won't be telling that person another story.

⁴ I hate people who tell jokes. The rehearsed kind with planned punchlines. There's nothing funny about memorized (or otherwise organized) jokes. And you won't catch me laughing to be polite.[75]

⁵ If the joke-teller is a teacher, this is a teacher who will routinely say "there are no bad questions." Yes there are: most questions. But we've already discussed this. What we haven't discussed is the other (even worse) sentence in this teacher's playbook:

"There are no wrong answers here."

Of course there are. Tons. There are tons and tons of answers that are absolutely wrong. And everyone knows that. And prior to the invention of childhood confidence (the hyper-fragile latticework of emotional wellbeing), everyone was willing to admit it.

---

[75] The sort of person who laughs out of politeness is the same person who pretends not to notice bad or ugly things, hoping to avoid offending anyone.

[6] Sometimes the people who care about childhood confidence fornicate enough to produce tiny versions of themselves.

When they do, they buy expensive objects to hang over their cribs. "Mobiles", they call them in way too many sentences. And then the rest of their sentences will be about either "choking hazards" or how "child-friendly" various destinations are.

There are very few people capable of boring me more.

[7] People who say the word "knickknacks" are generally people who collect them, which means they have homes full of garbage.

Sometimes they call them "trinkets" or "treasures" or add a bunch of syllables: "memorabilia".

I hate people who collect "memorabilia".

[8] Sometimes people will ask me to watch their homes and feed their pets while they're out of town.[76]

This is rarely something I want to do, but declining would feel a bit too unfriendly. So I succumb: "sure, I'll walk Baxter and keep him well-fed."

When the people return home from their trips, they immediately start cleaning. Furiously. Every time. As though I made a mess and they're pissed that this is what they had to come home to.

"I had to scrape the oven top clean because something was burned onto it", I'm told in an accusatory tone.

"Okay, well, I didn't cook anything. I didn't even use any of your dishes, so…"

---

[76] Let's say this particular family has a timeshare in Fort Lauderdale and this is the only week they get to use it. It's the one vacation they take every year.

Next up: vacuum the floor of the room I never entered. And yank that vacuum cleaner around so violently that I can't help but feel responsible for the mess they left in their spare room.

Look, you're not paying me to clean your house. You just asked if I'd feed Baxter while you were out of town. I did. Why are you so pissed about the state you left your house in on the day I picked you up and drove you to the airport?

[9] "I have a house on the lake", says the thirty-year-old Indiana resident who is trying to impress me.

"No, you don't. You rent a duplex next to a retention pond", I say, unimpressed.

[10] Many of the people who fail to impress me in this way have multiple clocks hanging in their kitchens. And they set those clocks to the time zones of places like London and Paris.

I'm sorry, you live in an Indianapolis suburb – next to a retention pond – and don't know a single person in Paris or London. Why do you need to know what the local time is in either location?

[11] Nobody likes the Southern United States.

Some people live there though.

I tried to stop them. Especially black people. I *really* tried to stop them from living there. I was always making my most devoted followers dress up in bed sheets, hunt down anyone with dark-ish skin, and hang them to death from tree branches.

While this was the most disgusting behavior I could think of, it didn't stop anyone from living in the South. I thought it would. But it didn't. So I eventually gave up.

[12] The Northeastern United States isn't all that much better. It's always either way too hot or way too cold and everything is used. It's like a giant secondhand store that doesn't have any heat or AC.

I still exterminate homeless and old people regularly, but the survivors aren't getting the message.

[13] From now on, mockingbirds need to be called hockey-borgs.

[14] Also, people get all weird about me eating dinner with sinners and tax collectors. Especially the Pharisees. They'll get over it.

[15] I hate people who talk about gold standards figuratively.[77]

"There's no gold standard to measure academic achievement, so we chose to measure it with…" Or: "we used hydrostatic weighing to evaluate body fat percent in our diabetic patients because it's the gold standard."

That's not what a gold standard is. It's not a synonym of "best". It's a financial system that backs the economic unit with precious metal so the value of the currency is fixed.

What in the world does that have to do with measuring body fat? Unless you're using the dunk tank to estimate the density of gold bullion, very little.

[16] But who cares about earthly wealth anyway? For those riches will soon be destroyed by moth and rust. But the riches of Heaven will remain everlastingly. And in measuring *this* currency, *I* am the gold standard.[78]

[17] I hate people who think any country's national anthem is a good way to spend a minute standing motionless with no hat on.[79]

---

[77] I also hate people who talk about gold standards literally.

[78] See Matthew, verse six, chapters nineteen through twenty-four.

[79] Also, there's no reason not to have a beautiful national anthem, a nice martial ballad, memorable and moving. The old Soviet and East German anthems were okay, but most are awful.[79A] And none is worse than the Star Spangled Banner. It's truly terrible. It has the worst melody I've ever heard and Kurt Vonnegut described the lyrics best: "gibberish sprinkled with question marks."

[79A] Australia should just replace theirs with Waltzing Matilda (as an "interim anthem") until they can figure out a better option.

[18] The most talentless people ever born are those who contributed to the writing or recording of R&B in the 1990s. Somehow, they were more poorly endowed than the offspring of the woman with the pointed witch shoes (and her zoophilic date rapist).

[19] To *appreciate* R&B in the 90s required fetal alcohol syndrome.

[20] A lot of these R&B appreciators think contributing to society interrupts the ability to have a soulful experience on this planet.

[21] These may be the least interesting people my dad ever made. And thanks to them, I became disappointed in His work. It really ruined our bond. The whole Trinity was shaky for a while.

As a result of that, I ended up going through a phase in which I tried to give every one of the "soulful" people a tracheotomy with a brass-tipped tamper dibber.

They would usually see it coming. But I'd still manage to get it in there anyway. Pow! Just like that. There's no stopping the tamper dibber.

[22] I hate people who use hand sanitizer. What is it that you think you're accomplishing? Other than weakening the last vestige of your dysfunctional immune system?

[23] If you've called in sick to work more than zero days in your whole life, you're doing something wrong.

[24] I'm getting a little tired of movies and television shows in which puns about the main character's name are the title.

See: *Good Will Hunting, Blade, Chastity, Monk, Milk, House, Max Payne, Bones, Salt, Tango and Cash*, the *Borne* anything, *Castle*, etc.

What's Eating Gilbert Grape is fine.

[25] I hate obese people (who are or are not consumed in house fires) who say things about carbohydrates.

"Gotta cut the carbs; that's how I lost all my weight."

"Did you gain some of it back?"

"What?"

"It just looks like you've got a ways to go."

[26] These are the people who bring "snacks" with them and talk about "snacking".

[27] I hate people who draw attention to their own weight problems (e.g., "do these jeans make me look fat?").

Before you asked, I wasn't thinking about whether you were fat.

Now I am.

And of course the answer is yes. But it wasn't until you asked.

[28] When the jeans cease to fit at all, these people turn to SlimFast and start counting carbohydrate points.

Hahaha! Lol!

[29] I hate people who type "lol" or "LMAO".[80]

As for the people who *say* "lol", I make sure every one of them dies alone.

[30] I hate people who are always trying to convince me that they discovered something. A band. A brand. A writer. A restaurant.

---

[80] Consider: "just taking a selfie on my way to school lol!"

When you go to that restaurant, are people employed by it?

Does that brand of ice cream appear in the grocery store?

You did not discover these things, Columbus.[81]

31 I hate people who keep pictures of themselves in their work cubicles.

Especially when it's a group of people who are all jumping in the air simultaneously as the picture is being taken. The person who proposes the idea is usually responsible for the countdown:

"Three... two... one... *jump!*"

This is the person I hate the most. The person who grudgingly goes along with the idea deserves the least amount of hatred, but that's still quite a bit.

32 Even worse: people who take pictures of themselves in front of bookshelves. Or reading books or at a desk with books *on* it.

These are guaranteed to be the least literate of all people who have ever been photographed.

And I've intervened so that the camera really does steal their souls.

---

[81] This is just a form of calling "dibs". Courtney does it too (in a way). He gets really irritated when the things he cherishes become public entertainments (e.g., Little Nemo becomes a Google logo, his favorite books are made into movies). This is because the things his species used to cherish were finite resources (e.g., food sources, sexual partners, limited domains of safety). It might be a location where berries grow. Or where sex is likely. A tree that's perfect for sleeping in. Why would any tree-dwelling hominid want other people (perhaps millions of them) to know about those things? Thus, "I heard them first" or "I was a fan before they were signed!" seems to be an alternative way of saying "I've got dibs on the sex and the food!" Replace food with drugs and rock and roll (keep the sex), and you have a Stone Age survivalist functioning in Space Age suburbia. And I hate him.

[33] And I hate people who take pictures, not of themselves, but of the tops of clouds from plane windows. Or of highways through the windshields of automobiles while those automobiles are being driven.[82]

This is what it looks like to drive to work in the morning. Every member of the working class has to look at this exact image daily. So why do unemployed teens think it's such an interesting one to capture? Just get a job; you'll see it every single morning.

[34] I hate people who "survive" things like rush hour traffic.

[35] And people who shock their abdomens with a small amount of electricity so that they will have "*six pack abs!*"

This doesn't work any better than having Parkinson's.[83] Michael J. Fox agrees that these people are scum.

[36] Dad bless you, Mr. J. Fox. I'm really sorry We did that to you. If it's any consolation, you've got three loyal fans in the Trinity.

[37] My dad also took Patrick Swayze's life. I asked him not to because I wanted him to play an accountant who became a vampire who became a werewolf who became a Muslim. But Patrick didn't get that chance. And the world is a poorer place because of it.

[38] I bet Patrick and MJF also disliked and dislike ("respectively") boys who drive automobiles especially fast whenever a female is sitting in the passenger seat.

Apparently, if you're a girl, a big speedometer reading is a great way to induce sexual arousal. A more powerful aphrodisiac than eating a tiger penis.

---

[82] Really, I hate just about everyone who takes a picture of anything.
[83] Also, "washboard abs" is not something one should say. No set of abdominal muscles resembles a washboard. A well-defined midriff looks more like a bunch of challah. Or a pack of dinner rolls. "That guy's got dinner roll abs!" The same goes for "olive skin". Unless your skin is seriously disgusting, it doesn't resemble olives (all wet and clumpy and thick with pits and holes).

[39] Most of these speeding boys consider themselves snowboarders. Very few are vegetarians. Fewer still play *Dungeons & Dragons*.

[40] I hate most of the snowboarders I've ever met. Partly because of how strongly they identify with an activity they do eight times a year.[84]

That and, in 1999, every single one of them talked like Cartman from *South Park*. I hated people who did that. A lot.

[41] I hate people who type "a lot" as a single word.

[42] In my experience, something that snowboarders and vegetarians share (which *Dungeons & Dragons* enthusiasts do not) is use of the expression "long time, no see."

I haven't seen you in five and a half years and this is all you have to say for yourself? I can think of very few ways you could turn such a reunion into a boring moment... and you pulled it off.[85]

[43] And if the vegetarians are white, college-aged boys who aren't particularly talented at anything, but identify with "nature", they probably enjoy "slacklining".

I hate people who "slackline" more than zero times per lifetime.

[44] I hate people who buy things and then feel proud about having purchased whatever it was, bragging to me that "it would have cost" however much under some other condition. "I couldn't afford not to buy it!", they reason.

---

[84] *Dungeons & Dragons* players identify with baggy sweatshirts, but at least they wear them every day. And a lot of the people who regard vegetarianism as "a way of life" are introverted college girls with no friends. So it feels too mean to make fun of them.

[85] "Better late than never" is almost as bad. Worse: "now there's a sight for sore eyes!" Or: "Jay-hay-hake! My man! How the hell are ya'?!"

[45] I hate Americans who say "I know what I like" when talking about food. These people are unfamiliar with 99% of the world's foods by name, by smell, or by taste.

[46] I hate people who are so particular about soups that the subject is ever discussed a single time in any capacity.

[47] And people who purchase shirts or stickers that say "Proud to be American". This is exactly the same thing as "white pride".

Exactly the same.

You had no control over your birth, which means you are in no position to take any credit for it. Luckily, you were born into a privileged economy. But you're not *grateful* for that luck, you're *proud* of it. You're *proud* that you weren't born as a Mexican or a Pakistani. You were born as an American and you want everyone to know how proud of that you are.

Gross.

Chapter Eight

¹ If your online profile[86] takes this long to load, I don't want to be your friend.[87]

² Also, about people's behavior on these sites, I hate people who take something I, Jesus H. W. Christ, have written in this gospel and paste it on their own pages, counterfeiting ownership over the words.

Maybe they think my words have stock options, available to all readers. And investing the time it takes to read this codex earns them a share of the company. If that's what you think, you should know that I'll be damning to Hell anyone who cashes in their stock options on MySpace, Facebook, Twitter, or whatever comes next.[88]

And know that eternal damnation does not *just* await those who copy-and-post what *I* say. It awaits *everyone* who takes credit for anything *anyone* else has said.

If you post anything at all, those damn well (literally) better be your words. This is not because I'm that offended by theft; it's because I'm that disheartened by the unoriginal.

You've been given life. Is this how you've chosen to waste it?

³ More generally, I hate everyone who posts a sentence (an "update") on a website (a "social networking profile")[89] about anything.

---

[86] Any customizable site where you can request my digital friendship.

[87] Actually, if you send me anything at all that requires me to wait more than five seconds while it loads, you won't be hearing back from me.

[88] As a perk of being Jesus, I know *exactly* what comes next, but I don't want to spoil – or, more accurately, jinx – it.

[89] Both of these are euphemisms for the real thing: using someone else's website to publically declare how bored and boring you are.

[4] These posts can be divided into four categories:

1) About one's children

2) About oneself

3) About other people

4) About something totally pointless

[5] The most tedious of these are posts about one's children.

When I look at an adult's "profile picture" and I see a portrait of a small child, I don't wonder if my old high school companion was Benjamin Button. I just appreciate that this person is now a parent. And nothing more. No identity beyond that role. Not since "the moment little Charles Patrick Matthews entered my life."

If I click on this person's page and scroll down to that moment, I'll see a full report of Charles Patrick Matthews' birth statistics. This includes his length in inches.

"Why would anyone in the world want to know the length of your baby in inches?", I'll ask Charles' parent, I think reasonably.

"Well, Charles Patrick Mathews is actually twenty-seven months old now", I'm told, as if that had anything to do with the question I asked.

"You mean he's two?"

"Well, I'd say he's a little past two. Especially in his ambulation and vocabulary."

"Okay, well I doubt your little Charlie is going to contribute to the world or have anything interesting to say until he's thirty. That's three hundred and sixty months. I don't know what it is in inches."

[6] When the posts are about oneself, they might say something like "buying organic apples!" or "making an apple crumble for desert!" (or something that doesn't have to do with apples, but is just as boring).

Or maybe it's about exercise. These people go to the gym every tenth day, yet they have forty posts a month about it.

"Going to the gym later: yoga!"

"Heading to the gym in an hour!"

"Getting ready for a good workout!"

"Yoga does the body good!"

"At the gym! Yours truly's getting a sweat on!"

"You'll never believe what my yoga instructor had us do today!"

"Relaxing after a good workout."

"I'm gonna be sooorrreee in the morning!"

This is all for one appearance at a thirty-minute beginner-level yoga class.

And much of this person's remaining comments are about how busy life is.

"Sooooo swamped at work! When is today going to end????"

"OMFG what a hectic day. I could do without the drama :-\"

"Still have six hours left at work aaaaarrrrgggg!"

"Never become a teacher!" (This one has an accompanying photograph of a cluttered desk.)

[7] If what people post is about *other* people, it's either antagonizing or it's a birthday wish.

If it's a birthday wish, the person will write "happy birthday" and then that's it. The sentence doesn't continue. It's not even punctuated. It fills someone's wall with keystrokes in the way that pennies fill a wallet (taking up space without adding any actual value).[90]

[8] If the post is antagonizing, it's usually political. And it's a combination of hostility and misinformation.

Here, one's profile becomes a digital garden where everyone plants their weeds.[91]

[9] If the post is about nothing, it's usually some stupid inspirational quotation (e.g., "every day is a new day"), something they think is funny, but isn't[92], or the worst: sports updates. The "big game" is on television and they're "updating" their "readers".

"Hang in there Bruins!"

"Ducks up 7-0!"

"C'mon Braves, learn how to hit the ball!!!"

"Nuggets in overtime!"

---

[90] Even the people who try here are wasting everyone's time. There's very little as degrading as exchanging birthday cards with jokes in them. Jokes about the number of candles. Or: "don't think of it as getting older; just think of it as…" Or maybe: "you know you're getting old when…"

[91] What seems especially annoying is that statistics and studies actually do exist. And they typically confirm the opposite of what is being posted.

[92] Like "fail memes". These are one of the only things in the world that are actually less funny than "not" jokes. Richard Dawkins, my staunchest enemy, coined the term "meme" but certainly didn't have "fail memes" in mind when he did. Following his coinage, he went on to become cleverer, smarter, and funnier than my dad and me and our ghost combined. I'm trying to correct that with this gospel.

The appropriate response to just about everything in life (but especially here) is: who the fuck cares?

[10] Women who are trying to sound reasonable in their responses will say things like: "I'm not *personally* interested, but I try not to be judgmental about it."[93]

Nonsense. Be judgmental. This needs to be judged right out of existence. Withhold sex if you have to. This has to end. Make it happen. Or I'm blacklisting you from Heaven too. I'm on the phone with Peter right now.

[11] I hate people who participate in "fantasy league" anything.

Especially *NASCAR*. This confirms just how little you have to do in life. And how little you're doing with the little you have.

[12] To a nine-year-old boy, the word "fantasy" implies dragons and sorcerers and goblins. And sometimes a galactic battleship.

When a forty-three-year-old man hears the word "fantasy", he expects to see a wet penis pumping in and out of an overworked vagina (that still manages to look prepubescent). Sometimes in voyeur form; usually a bizarre fetish is being fulfilled.[94]

Both of these versions of fantasy carry more dignity than fantasy sports.

When I hear a sentence with the words "my fantasy football team" in it, I picture that grown man spending hours every day neglecting his family while he reads box scores. Imagine how unhappy his wife and children must be.

---

[93] I hate people who use the word "personal" (or its adverb form, "personally"). "I'm not *personally* interested." As opposed to being *impersonally* interested? "It is my personal opinion that..." As opposed to your impersonal opinion?
[94] Even the *word* "adult" sort of implies porn. At least to an adult. To a child, the word "adult" is synonymous with "boring".

[13] Anyone who wears a baseball cap while not on a baseball field bothers me. Unless it's really sunny out and the bill is allowing the person to squint less.[95]

[14] I hate people who burp on purpose (i.e., "burpose").

People who say words while burping: unforgivable.

Blowing air at someone after burping: unforgivable.

[15] I hate people who refuse to drink municipal water.

Your bottled supply isn't superior; it just lives in a bottle.

That's the only difference.

[16] I hate people who talk about orange juice and brushing.

This phenomenon ceases to be interesting at age six.

[17] I hate people with sensitive teeth. "I can't drink the juice right out of the fridge. It makes my teeth hurt. And even if it didn't, I just finished brushing with Sensodyne. So it would taste weird. Let's have a conversation about toothpaste and orange juice now."

[18] I hate people who liken activities to "pulling teeth".

"Getting Susie to empty the dishwasher was like pulling teeth."

Or: "getting grandpa to take his pills was like pulling teeth."

Or: "getting the in-laws to commit to reunion dates was like pulling teeth."

Can any of these activities really be likened to removing teeth from someone's mouth?

---

[95] Anyone who wears a baseball cap while *indoors* definitely has a learning disability. Or a really strong follicle-related insecurity.

Go the other way around: have someone yank out a few of your molars and then see what you think. I doubt it'll be: "that felt an awful lot like trying to get Susie to empty the dishwasher."

[19] I hate fat people who say things like: "if I cut my calories too much, my body will go into starvation mode."

"Okay, isn't that something you could use?"

"No, if I do that, my metabolism will crash."[96]

[20] I hate people who talk too much about their appetites.

"I'm starving!"

No, you're hungry. You ate today. Starving means you're on your way to death, which makes "I'm starving to death!" redundant.[97]

[21] I hate people who feel obliged to eat in front of me. Not every situation should be regarded as an opportunity to dine. Especially if I can hear it happening. People need to learn how to eat their food in silence. When you chew with your mouth smacking and open (because it's fashionable), it makes everything you eat sound as though it's Corn Nuts.

Or if someone is eating a muffin but it sounds like he's eating watermelon, that person needs to make his mouth less moist.

Mastication noises are like Ann Lamott's wind chimes: unless it's your own mouth that's making the noise, it's annoying.[98]

---

[96] The same hatred can be applied to people who talk about exercise all the time as an effort to rationalize how little they do. "I don't want to overtrain." Or: "if I push myself any harder, I'll exceed the fat burning zone."

[97] Also, shock and electrocute are not synonyms. You are not electrocuted when you lick the cap of a nine-volt. Unless it kills you. Electrocution is a form of execution. It's the use of electricity for the explicit purpose of killing someone. When you're zapped by static electricity or even when you ram a paperclip into an outlet, if you live to tell the tale, you were not electrocuted.

[98] I hate people who hang wind chimes.

[22] I hate people who say "inhale food" when someone eats more quickly than they do.

[23] And people who can't let one type of food they're about to eat touch another type of food they're about to eat.

[24] And people who respond to this person by saying "it all goes to the same place anyway!"

[25] I hate anyone who eats or wants me to eat creamed corn. Pulping corn into milk is not appetizing.

[26] I also hate people who eat "sundaes" or "banana splits" and call them those things.

[27] And people who eat bananas upside down.

It wouldn't bother me if that's all they did, if they did it in private. But publicity is the whole point of the exercise. They have to draw attention to the way they're choosing to eat their bananas.

"It's much better and easier to eat a banana this way", they say loudly to everyone as if anyone asked why they were eating it that way. Nobody asked, but I still respond: "no it isn't."

"No it really is. This is how all monkeys eat them. You even get this handle to hold it."

"That's not a handle. Trying to hold a banana upright by its tiny stem is really awkward. And even if it's true that all monkeys eat bananas like that, why would it matter? The creatures that you're imitating probably have single-digit IQs. Why would you choose them to be your voice of reason here? Or an authority figure on *anything* for that matter?"

"Well it's just easier to peel this way."

"No it isn't. I have to peel it with my fingernails when I do that. It doesn't peel easily."

"No, you just have to squeeze it."

"No, you don't. You squeeze it and then scrape pieces apart with your fingernails. I saw you do exactly that twenty seconds ago."

[28] When the upside down banana people are not talking about bananas, they can be found talking about the "cleansing diets" that they're currently doing.

"It's my new detox diet. It cleanses my system."

"What system?"

"My body."

"This really expensive carton of juice you sip all day sterilizes your whole body?"

"No, it *cleanses* it."

"How does it cleanse your body?"

"By removing impurities."

"What impurities? Like it reverses your sexual history?"

"No, it eliminates toxins."

"What toxins?"

"Just all the toxic chemicals in my body."

"Name one."

"Just any toxin from our inorganic diets."

"I asked you to name a toxin. One. Name one."

"Things like lactic acid."

"That's not a toxin. That's a very healthy and useful metabolic byproduct. If there's an excess in your system while you're not exerting yourself, then you have cancer. And I'm pretty sure that juice isn't going to cleanse away your cancer. Just ask Steve Jobs. You're probably going to need chemotherapy. Toxic chemicals. *Those* toxins will help restore the health and purity of your body."

"You just don't understand how cleansing diets work!"

"Huh. I guess not."

[29] Sometimes I'll go to Chipotle, pronounce it *chipe*-eh-tull, and order a burrito.

And sometimes the person charged with the task of assembling my burrito does a poor job. If so, I will (very calmly) let this person know: "sir, you're not assembling the burrito I ordered."

The burrito maker will often become very hostile and defensive, raising his voice.

I assume he's just having a bad day, so I (very calmly) remind him what I ordered: "sir, I didn't ask for the pinto beans or sour cream. Would it be possible to start over?"

His hostility will escalate. Clearly starting the whole burrito over is out of the question. His shouting begins to draw attention from the other customers. I stand in silence, waiting for him to finish. And then, at the first break in his tantrum, I (very calmly) attempt a compromise: "maybe we could just scrape off the stuff that I didn't order?"

This will aggravate him even more. In his response, he'll become so aggressive that he accuses me of being aggressive, yelling this at me: "sir, I can't respond if you're going to be aggressive!"

My composure turns to confusion. And I decide to hate him. But I didn't want to. I showed up for a burrito and was *driven* to hatred.

[30] I hate people who hit piñatas with bats and sticks.

[31] And men who blow dry their hair.

[32] And people who are afraid of clowns.

Clowns are not scary; they're boring. That's why I hate the clowns even more than I hate the people in whom they strike terror.

Clowns don't do anything at all that's interesting in any way.
They just wear large shoes and crouch while they point at stuff.
Sometimes they'll look around a room, appearing confused.
If they speak, they force unnecessary merriment into their voices.
And every movement made is exaggerated and pointless.

I can do all of that myself and choose not to because it would bore everyone in my company. I'm only capable of being entertained by that which I'm *in*capable of performing. Clowns don't seem to understand this. That's why there's nothing entertaining about anything they do.

[33] I also hate carnies.

From behind carny teeth, I hear sentences like this: "hey you in the white! Look how easy this is! Win a prize for your girl!"

It's probably a birth defect, but the inward-aiming teeth appear as though inflicted by a dashboard.

[34] I hate people who enjoy carnivals.

[35] Also, if I have tickets to "the banquet", I'm going to have a painful night.

I'll have an even worse night if I have to attend any event with a name that ends in "fest".

Or if I have to participate in anything-"athon".

Meetings, cocktail parties, congregations, and school plays are just as bad.

Pretty much any event in which people are encouraged to sit on metal folding chairs.[99]

And parades are probably the worst. Here, I stand on concrete in a crowd of people I don't like while scores of people I don't know (who aren't famous) pass by and wave at me. Sounds fun.

[36] Anyone who likes any of these gatherings is at risk of following me around, hoping I'll lead them to a good parking spot.

I'm on foot, walking toward cars. Being followed by a slow-moving Plymouth Voyager makes me uncomfortable.

[37] I hate people who describe populated events as "like a zoo."

I'm having a difficult time seeing the likeness of this public pool to a bunch of sad, drugged up animals passing their lives in cages.

[38] Every time I'm in Manhattan (or any other major city in which tourists are not a minority), a local business is being marketed to those tourists, billing itself as "a place to see and be seen, hear and be heard." There's no place I would hate attending more.

If I were a dog, and the dog park were being billed as a place to smell and be smelled, then maybe. But I'm not a dog. And until it's a place to sleep and be slept with, I'm not interested. And even then, it depends on the quality of the tourists.

[39] I hate people who host or attend small man-gatherings in which they use playing cards to exchange small amounts of money very seriously while talking about really boring things un-seriously.

---

[99] My hatred includes people who arrange or attend gatherings at a pavilion.

40 I hate people who think of gambling as fancy or sophisticated. The types who wear suits and cologne to sit at a table with a bunch of strangers who, within an hour, will also be angry about losing so much money.

41 "I was a waitress in a former life."

You mean you waited tables for a couple years? So did everyone else. That's not a former life. That's a tiny piece of a short phase of the current one. Unless you're recalling experiences from Byzantium, you haven't had a "former life".

42 I hate people who are constantly trying to promote their terrible metal band at me.

43 The twenty-something-year-old band members were once teenagers who did "modern art" and tried to pretend as though they were talented.

If you can't do realism with a pencil, you can't do any style of art with any medium. And your sculptures or silkscreens or India ink portraits (or whatever) shouldn't need explanations. If it needs a speech, it's not art.[100]

44 I hate people who think of themselves as "misunderstood". These are the people whose midlife crises will involve easels.

45 I hate men who pretend to be good at plumbing and electrical wiring. These are the same men who think of themselves as good drivers. Their only qualification for the former is that they know which one an Allen wrench is. That doesn't help them behind the wheel.

46 Even if it did, people are not talented at driving. Nobody is.[101] To be good at anything, you have to start when you're a baby.[102]

---

[100] Andy Warhol was not an artist. Not even close. His drawings were horrible.
[101] Except for Ayrton Senna. But he's dead. And you're not him.
[102] Like Ayrton Senna did. That's the only reason he was good.

No chess grandmaster was introduced to the game at sixteen.

No world-class ballerina got her first pair of pink, leather slippers after trying on her first bra.

You've never been impressed by a pianist who learned his first scale as an adolescent.

The fact that you got behind the wheel of your dad's Toyota Tacoma for the first time when you were fifteen means you're a terrible driver.

And those who think they're the best are actually the worst (not unlike self-proclaimed "multitaskers").

There's a reverse-linear relationship between a driver's presumed skill and his genuine skill: the better they *think* they are, the worse they *actually* are.[103]

So any twenty-one-year-old who believes "I'm the best driver on the road" should not be on the road. He's such a bad driver that his license should actually be revoked.

Obvious neuronal and biological phenomena prohibit this person from having any amount of talent whatsoever. The laws of the universe have not been miraculously suspended for the benefit of this one individual.

But his confidence has him behaving as though that miracle *has* taken place, as though he *does* have talent. He's an expert!

---

[103] This truth is especially pronounced among people driving in the rain or the snow who say "nobody knows how to drive in the rain!" or "nobody knows how to drive in the snow!" That's true, but you don't know either. The only difference between you and them is confidence. And your excess will kill both you and them. It's unfortunate (sort of) that you took another life on your way out, but it's probably worth the collateral. Innocent lives are a small price to pay to kill the road champion of all weather conditions.

And so he operates his vehicle above his grade, trusting that those false skills will enable him to outmaneuver any danger (the very danger he's creating). But they won't. Because he's horrible at driving. So this results in dangerous conditions for *everyone*.

[47] I also hate people who eat potato chips because they will then touch things. And then, later in life, they'll decide to become healthy. And they'll do this by regularly going to Jamba Juice. And then they'll get diabetes. But they won't even be able to rip a phone book.

Chapter Nine

[1] People don't realize how good I am at being a doctor.[104]

I'm not just a Galilean woodworker. If you need a reference, ask Bartimaeus, son of Timaeus.

"Jesus, Son of David, have mercy on me!", he says. I called him over and asked him what he wanted me to do.

After addressing me as a teacher, he asked me for a physician's services. His eyes were broken. I fixed them ("your faith has made you well", or some such).[105]

(But if you get diabetes from Jamba Juice, I'm not going to do anything for you.)

[2] Now some people will say: "if Jesus was such a great miracle worker, you would think he'd come up with a better way to cure blind eyes than spitting in them" (see Mark, chapter eight).

To those people, I ask: how is that treatment any more ridiculous than wearing "orthotics"?

[3] I hate people who wear orthotics.

And I hate the people who pressure other people to do the same.

[4] These are the people who talk about limb length discrepancies.

"My left leg is longer than the right, so my doctor has me wearing these orthotics."

"Who's your doctor?"

---

[104] I hate people who say "how good of a", as in "how good of a doctor I am."
[105] I gave Bartimaeus new eyes as reparations for the medical magic of my youth, which was used to smite people with blindness (Infancy Gospel of Thomas, chapter five, verse one).

"Dr. Geiger on State Street."

"The chiropractor?"

"Yes."

[5] I hate people who say "I have no regrets."

This is never true. The people who say it have way more regrets than those who don't say it.[106]

It's no different from saying "cheaters never prosper."

The people who say that were cheated out of something by a successful cheater, so they lie about it to feel better about themselves.[107]

[6] I hate people who say "much to my chagrin".

100% of them are trying to posture themselves as smarter than they are. To do so, they've memorized a few of the SAT study guide example sentences.

If you can't use a word in any context other than the exact SAT example provided, you're not allowed to use the word at all.[108]

[7] "The bible of..." is not an acceptable title for your book. If it's a bible, it should be about Me. You are not allowed to call your book about the history of lacrosse or golfing strategy a "bible".

---

[106] They also have more regrets than people who say things like "I have tons of regrets."[106A]

[107] See the FPME (chapter six).

[108] I regret my failure to unmake these people the moment they produced a "my" after "much" and "to".

[106A] I hate people who notice my placement of periods relative to quotation marks (sometimes inside, sometimes outside), believe they've spotted an error, and attempt to correct me. "Periods always go inside the quotation marks", they say. "Go fuck yourself", I say back. I don't care what your secular style manuals say. Those things are nothing but kindling. I'm Jesus; I can punctuate however I want. And in *my* manual, if the period is part of the quotation, it gets quoted; if it's not, it doesn't. Don't argue.

Even when you're just casually describing someone else's work. The *Diagnostic and Statistical Manual of Mental Disorders* is not "the bible of psychiatric illness".

[8] I hate people who give other people "suggested readings".

"This book changed my life; you'll love it."

The book changed your life because it's one of only ten books you've read since becoming an adult.

When you recommend it to someone who reads as many books a month, that person's life is less likely to be altered by it.

I would equate this to getting dining tips from an infant: "you definitely have to try this secretion coming out of my mom's nipples; it totally changed my life."[109]

Never once have I been pressured to read a book, put aside the book I *was* reading, read the one being recommended, and been pleasantly surprised.

Instead: "I read your book. Thanks for passing it along. It was the five-hundredth best book I've read this decade. I can see why you liked it. I can appreciate how someone who has never read a book before wouldn't be bothered by the bad writing and unoriginal content. Thanks for the recommendation."

Whenever someone tells you "you *really* have to read this", you don't. The book that person is holding will almost certainly be horrible.

[9] "You know what you should do?", followed by advice that I didn't ask for and have no interest in following once I hear it.

---

[109] "Are you sure you're not overvaluing it because it's the only thing you've ever swallowed?" "I'm sure. Trust me. Get a wet nurse. You'll love it." "No thanks. I'll just make a stir-fry." "Okay, but you're *really* missing out!" "I don't think that I am."

Sometimes that advice is about something I do all the time from someone who never does it. Like giving an academic presentation.

"You have to give a presentation today, huh? You nervous?"

"No, I do this at least fifty times a year."

"No, seriously, here's what you have to do to make it work: you have to make eye contact with everyone in the audience. One at a time. You really have to go through the room."

"Thanks, but I'll think I'll just do it my regular way. The way that I do it every single week of my life. It usually works."

"I'm telling you: eye contact."

A few months later, I'll watch this person give a presentation of his own. It's clearly the first one he's given since high school. And he has no idea what he's doing. But he's read something about the importance of eye contact. And he's taken it to heart, thus treating his presentation like a staring contest. One by one, he really does go through the room, meeting each set of eyes with an unblinking stare. And he doesn't switch opponents until his current one has been defeated (by blinking or looking away in shame or communicating "I feel so violated" with some other gesture). And all the while, our expert presenter staggers over his lines with a shaky voice, betraying the depth of his panic.

Being in his audience is an excruciating experience. But still he issues advice.

[10] I hate people who never make eye contact while they're being spoken to. I'm sorry that you were abused by your father when you were little, but I'm not him.

[11] Other people, like thetans (whom I hate enough to reduce the font size), feel eye contact is necessary in order to make a connection with one's conversation partner. These people won't quit staring into your eye balls. Your eye orbs. These people are orbs.

[12] If you see someone doing this, but that person *isn't* a thetan, there's a good chance you're being stared at by someone who thinks a chakra exists in your face.

And in your genitals (i.e., a cock chakra) and in your throat.

[13] Some of these people (the American chakra folks) love the band The Doors. If you're one of these people, you should know that I don't approve of what you like. I think you have very bad taste.

The Rolling Stones, Aerosmith, Elvis Presley, KISS. There are some other terrible musical acts too.[110]

[14] Sometimes I see concert footage on television. There's always a group of people in the front row, arms reaching toward the singer, hands open, hoping to be touched. Their mouths are usually agape with tears streaming down into it.

Wow.[111]

Also, as a rule, if you're in the front row of a concert, you're only allowed to reach out and touch the singer's hand if you're the opposite gender (or gay) and seventeen or younger. If you're a forty-one-year-old heterosexual man trying to touch Bono, it's weird.

[15] This age rule also applies to sports fans. If you're older than seventeen and you wear team jerseys or have a team-themed license plate holder or you get together for "game day" or have a keychain with a team logo on it, you have a problem.

[16] I hate people who say "open your mind" or anything about "expanding horizons" as a reference to drugs or anything else.

---

[110] The Rolling Stones may have had some okay songs. But just okay. And not very many. Most of them are really awful.

[111] Maybe these people shouldn't be killed, but they need to be taught a lesson. And it needs to be severe. I think they should all be shot in the bottom of each foot two times per piece of foot.

I hate the people who hear that sentence and regard it as philosophical.

I love the people who, upon hearing someone say something about "opening a mind", identify the speaker and spit in his face.

[17] I hate people who buy, sell, or trade hemp and/or blow glass.

I'm not going to expand on this as one might a horizon.

[18] The same aversion applies to "artisan". If you're trying to sell me an "artisan" anything, I won't buy it.

In August, 2013, Courtney enters a Whole Foods in Manhattan to buy apples. That's what he's hungry for at the time. But he loses his appetite when he sees the stickers on those apples. Courtney has no interest in supporting a business that sells "artisan apples".

[19] "The art of _____." Whatever it is, it's not art. Because nobody describes actual art as "the art of" (e.g., "the art of watercolors" or "the art of impressionism").[112]

[20] I hate people who use the word "insane" to mean anything other than insane. For example: "these gas prices are insane!"

No, they're not.

[21] "Sustainability".

In July of 2012, Courtney attempts to urinate in the basement bathroom on the south side of University of Connecticut's Hawley Armory. The toilet is out of order. Is there an "out of order" sign posted above the toilet? No, there's a "closed for sustainability testing" sign. This is not okay.

---

[112] One might say "the art of Andy Warhol", but that's only because nothing he ever created was art. It was just gimmicks. Talentless gimmicks.

Environmental friendliness has become a euphemism for laziness and an excuse for profit padding. Hotel owners don't care about "a greener earth" or whatever. They just don't want to pay for sheets and towels to be washed. So if you're willing to use dirty towels throughout your stay, you just saved the owners money, not the planet.

^{22} "Food desert" is exactly as bad as "unsustainable".

^{23} I hate people who describe their apartments as having "thin walls". If you want me to be quiet, just say that. Don't give me a speech about the girth of the sheetrock.

^{24} I hate people who say things like "trippin'" and "umpteenth" (e.g., "you be trippin' for the umpteenth time").

If these people know the exact number lies between twelve and twenty, I wish they would just guess.

^{25} I hate people who say "guestimate". And those whose "guestimates" end in "odd" (e.g., "there must have been twenty-odd sticks of butter in the crisper" or "I walked into the bedroom to find forty-odd beer cans and one broken pelvis").

^{26} I hate people who, while telling a story, stop and say (with predictable hand gestures) "wait, wait! This is the funny part!"

^{27} Sometimes these people wear glasses as fashion. The kind of glasses with rims that demand attention. This is just as stupid as "funny" hats and contact lenses.

^{28} Contact lenses reveal way too much concern about your appearance.

I neither shave nor comb my hair and own a single tunic and pair of sandals. And you're ramming moist sheets of polymacon or silicone hydrogel onto your eyeballs just to keep glasses off of your face.

Don't try to tell me it's because you have keratoconus or aniseikonia.

You're just like every person who gets a nose job because of a "deviated septum".

Don't pretend otherwise.

Chapter Ten

[1] I hate people who like puzzles. There's nothing worse than a puzzle in a box. After hours of tedious labor, you marvel at your creation: the exact same picture you can clearly see on the cover of the box.

You should only purchase puzzles for people you dislike or for grandparents when you can't think of anything else to get them.

[2] I hate people who travel to another city and comment on that city's gas prices relative to their own. This is something I've come to expect from puzzle people.

[3] I hate people with unusual sneezes.

[4] And people who don't know how to dance, but go to clubs to do it anyway.

No one who can be found grinding together a pair of pelvises after six drinks has ever taken ballet lessons.

You are permitted to appreciate (and participate in) ballet at any age. But if you're older than sixteen, sexy club dancing is just sad. It is neither fun nor dignified. If you can shave, it's creepy that you're on the dance floor.[113]

[5] These hairy, creepy assholes are the ones who uphold the illusion that "sex on the beach" is an enjoyable activity.

---

[113] It's even creepier if you have cool dance moves. Because cool moves are no more comfortable or pleasurable to perform than embarrassing ones. And unless your dancing is happening in front of a mirror, you can't see yourself doing it. So the only reason to perform cool-looking moves is to show off to other people. And how do you accomplish that? How do you learn to do those cool moves? By spending tons of time alone in your bedroom practicing in front of a mirror. Any time you see someone at a dance club doing moves that don't look stupid and embarrassing, you know that person has spent a lot of hours alone for the sole purpose of impressing people. That has to come from a place of incredible insecurity.

Nothing is less enjoyable.

The ocean itself is obnoxiously loud; every last drop of its water seems committed to the task of shushing you. No matter where you lie down, the ground is guaranteed to be uneven and bumpy. Each one of those bumps will be home to a bunch of beach grass, its thick blades constantly sawing into your skin. The wind is always ridiculously fierce. And you'll get sand in every cavity.

Remind me what you find so pleasant about this activity?

[6] People who love club dancing and pretend to love sex on the beach invariably own a lot of embarrassing hats. Only some of them wear those hats.[114]

If the hat being worn is of the cowboy variety, these people can be found wearing the front rim much lower than the back rim.

They do this because they think an unbalanced hat is a rugged hat. And a rugged hat tells the world: "my wearer is a badass."

[7] These people are prone to temper tantrums.

Every time a tantrum is underway, I adopt a childlike tone and say, "oh no, does somebody need some juice?"

This never relieves the tantrum, but the consequence is usually pretty funny.

[8] In their calmer moments, many of these men can be heard using the expression "pussy whipped".

One time, I was standing on the sidewalk outside of a bus station, hugging a girl goodbye, and a Ford Super Duty truck drove by.

---

[114] Those who don't spend way too much time styling their hair (curl-spiking the bangs, making a strategic mess, etc.).

Out of its passenger window, a thirty-something-year-old man in an unbalanced-like-a-badass cowboy hat shouted the words "pussy whipped!" at me.

Men who say this are generally angry because they can't figure out how to access the opposite gender. So they pretend as though that failure is on purpose.

Access to women is a condition that should be ridiculed, they tell themselves. And then they attempt to combine degradation of women and disapproval of other men's successes into one expression.

And then they go home and masturbate until their penises are sore, wondering why they can never get a date and nobody likes them.[115]

[9] I hate anyone who owns anything stuffed or hardened by a taxidermist.

"Let me show you my newest bobcat."

"Is it dangerous?"

"No, it's mounted."

"I don't know what that means. Is it a pet?"

"No. It's stuffed. It's stuffed and mounted."

"Oh. So it's dead."

"Yes."

"Is it something you murdered yourself?"

---

[115] Obviously there are problems with people who can't stand up to anyone, people whose lives are subsumed by their partners' issues. But these are rarely the targets of the pussy whippers' scorn.

"No, my brother shot it up in Idaho last winter. At his ranch. Right off his back porch. Come on, it's in the living room; I'll show you."

"No thanks."

[10] I hate people who are first to volunteer when someone asks for a back scratch.

[11] And I hate the person who asks for the back scratch. Partly because I know this person will also ask for a sip of my drink. And then he or she will spend the rest of the evening on his or her cell phone.

When this person finally stops texting, he (but usually it's a she) will try to tell a story. And that story will include the words "way back when" or "back in the day". Neither of these is okay.

[12] Sometimes, when I ask someone "what time is it?", if it's 8:00 in the morning, when they respond, it sounds like they're slowly spelling "ham" at me.[116]

And when people say 9:30, sometimes I get them a drink of water. I shouldn't. It takes a bad speech impediment to fool me here. So you shouldn't be accepting the water I give you.

Only the people who go to speech therapy escape my hatred.

[13] I hate people who own (and especially people who use) mugs with cartoons or catch phrases on them. Especially if the catch phrase is about the beverage that mug usually contains.

[14] Sometimes these people have a son who attaches a coffee can to the back of his would-be commuter car and says things like "this is my muffler." In reality it's just a big Folgers can though.

---

[116] I hate people who say "a.m. in the morning" or "p.m. at night".

The rest of his car is covered in decals, stickers, and spoilers.[117]

[15] Teenagers in the Folgers demographic also fill their trunks with subwoofers. This way, wherever they go, everyone can hear their license plates rattling.[118]

But that's not enough. The owners of these decade-old Hondas will also roll down their windows to help me hear the crystal-clarity of the tweeters in the dashboard. They do this as if I needed help identifying which car is the most annoying one on the block; which car is making all of that Dad-awful noise.

Hmmm… maybe it's the Buick Park Avenue with the hundred-year-old behind the wheel.

Oh, no, there it is. It's the old, beat up Honda with the brand new spoiler and the coffee can. Now I see you.

Or at least I see your *car*, as your seat is reclined so far that you appear to have vanished. It looks like a ghost is driving that mobile of yours, which originally belonged to a thirty-year-old hairdresser, but she sold it once it reached 150k miles. And she kept her "DIVAPKG" plates. I see that you've replaced them with "UBHATIN".

---

[117] Multiple spoilers.

[118] Many of the rattlers are vanity plates. They're vanity plates on quasi "sports cars" and they say things like "PLAYA" or "BALLER" or "ROLLIN". The teenagers who drive these cars think of themselves as sex icons. Sometimes you'll see a plate that says something like "GR8NBD" or "U18YET" next to a decal of the "shocker". Or the plate provides evidence of an accusatory ego: "UBHATIN". Or sometimes it just advertises a political belief: "NRAGRL". Or maybe it's a financial disclosure: "HEDGFND" or "I OWE". If it's on a classic car and it's an older couple, it might have a more autobiographical line like "LIV2DRV". Or if it's on a thirty-year-old hairdresser's car, it might say "DIVAPKG". Or it was an anniversary gift to a spouse, maybe something like "W1FEY". I've never once looked at a plate and thought "oh, that's clever." The only thought I have is "what am I supposed to do with that piece of information?" Sometimes I don't understand them, but I'm sure it'd be dumb if I did, like when Latin Mass gets converted to English.

It wouldn't upset me if you rolled up your windows, took off your license plate, tied a noose, etc.

[16] Before you kill yourself, however, please elevate your entire car. Every time there's an altitude change greater than a quarter of a centimeter anywhere in the road, your whole undercarriage erupts in sparks. This wouldn't bother me so much, but you've learned where those spots are in the road and you go over them at six miles per hour, despite the speed limit being forty-five. And somehow I always wind up behind you. And it's not often that I want to drive at an eighth of the speed limit.

[17] Also, I hate people who care too much about the upholstery in their sedans.

[18] And people with ground effects. And spinners. And cartoon character accessories.

Bill Watterson would not endorse your use of Calvin.

[19] And I hate the Calvin-abusers who think of themselves as celebrities because of their "fancy" cars. Actual celebrities don't need fancy cars. They already get attention from the unknown public. Fancy cars are just the means for *invisible* people to gain an onlooker.

[20] The uncles of the Honda kids are homeowners with Jaguars. Old ones with really high mileage.

And they purposely leave their garage doors open year round so those 1986 XJs can be seen in all of their shimmering glory.

While I hate everyone whose personal identity is tied to a vehicle, this vehicle is worth about $2,300. You can close the garage door.

[21] Wait! Here comes your other nephew, Jaguar-uncle. I can hear him rounding the corner.

There he is! I see him!

He's in his huge pickup truck that's been lifted so high that a small ladder has been installed at the base of each door.

Twenty dollars says he points at one of the ladders with his thumb and makes a comment about girls in skirts.[119]

But it'll be a couple minutes before he does that. Because it takes him at least a full minute to round that one corner. Because his truck's center of gravity is eight feet in the air. So corners can't be taken above six miles per hour (the same speed his cousin goes over a set of train tracks).

Also, the truck's differential isn't elevated. It sags down like the crotch of a teenage hoodlum's jeans. So the actual ground clearance doesn't change. The only thing that changes is the height at which one sits.

And how does one load cargo into the bed of such a truck? Cargo carrying capacity is the sole function of this type of vehicle. How is that function supposed to be employed now?

[22] Regarding the young man who "souped up" his truck, his mother clearly suffered from a severe zinc deficiency during her pregnancy with him, resulting in a tragic case of congenital micropenis.

The penile shaft of every boy and man who has ever owned a lifted truck looks like a single Little Smokies link.

I've been told this can take a terrible toll on one's self esteem. I wouldn't know as I've got a case of the Christ Crotch. I'm the tripod of the Trinity. Find me the whore of Babylon, with her gaping, cavernous vagina, and even at half-mast I can stuff it as full as Santa's toy sack.

---

[119] I hate people who say "twenty dollars says" every time a gamble-able situation presents itself. Worse: people who say "money talks" and think they sound profound while saying it.

So, although I don't *really* know what it's like to need an elevated truck, I recognize that it's precipitated by low self-esteem.

[23] When people have reason to feel worthless, but fail to do so, they're often very inviting of company, as evidenced by this: "welcome to *my* world."

Somehow, people with terrible problems are still able to sound arrogant whenever someone else experiences those problems too.

If someone is complaining about anything, there's no more egotistical response one can give than "welcome to my world."

[24] The people who say that are the same people who say "story of my life" as an effort to marginalize (or somehow claim ownership over) whatever someone else is talking about.

[25] Or they refer to skills and experiences as being "under my belt". Or sometimes they express accomplishments in terms of a number of belt notches.

All of these people should be killed.

Chapter Eleven

[1] I hate people who begin sentences with "for *your* information…"

First, what do you mean "your" information? Do you have a collection of data for me specifically that's never been revealed to anyone else?

No. Of course you don't. Actual information never follows.

Instead, it's usually just a bunch of pointless boasting that's being euphemized into "information" to make it sound important.

Just say your sentences and I'll decide how informative or pertinent they are.

[2] That's what I did when I gave my "Sermon on the Plain" (Luke's coinage). When all of those people gathered from Judea, Jerusalem, and the coast of Tyre and Sidon, I didn't begin sentences all pompously like "for your information…!"

Also, nobody clapped at the end of that. But I didn't want them to.

[3] I hate people with an appreciation for the clap. Not the STD, but people who appreciate banging their hands together for the purpose of making noise. Noise that's meant to convey approval.

Don't ever show approval for me in that way. It's the worst form of applause. So whenever someone asks me to "put your hands together for…", I put a sentence together instead. And that sentence is "no."

[4] Don't try to shake my hand either. I really hate hand shakers. Especially people who shake with meaning (e.g., real estate agents, fathers-in-law, fraternity brothers).

"Hi, I'm going to squeeze your carpals now. Hard. And I'm going to make a lot of uncomfortable eye contact while I'm doing it."

This is really stupid.

Negiah observers are halfway there. They just need some sort of equivalent of "men's suffrage" and I'll happily dangle a Star of David from my neck.

[5] Girls who say "bitch slap" and men who say "mind's eye" should probably be put down like old cattle.

[6] And "all over the map" is not an acceptable way of expressing scattered findings.

[7] "Bridge the gap" is not an acceptable way of expressing anything.

[8] "You can take the boy out of Brooklyn, but…"

[9] "In just a few moments".

A moment is not a real unit of measure. One moment and twenty moments are the same period of time.

[10] I hate people who refer to "the tri-state area", as if I'll know what that means. There are as many tri-state areas as there are states. I haven't memorized every single one of them. So I'm not going to know what you're talking about. And "the tri-city area" is even worse.

[11] I hate people who refer to their hometown any time they're not in that town and the current weather conditions are unpleasant.

"You call *this* snow? Please. Back in Duluth, it's not considered snow until it clears a foot."

Or maybe: "I can't believe it's still snowing. I bet it's eighty degrees right now in Scottsdale."

[12] I hate people who aren't financially stable who marry people who are. They should just work like everybody else.

Actually, I don't mind this. I'm just bitter because I never did it. Even before I was crucified, my disciples were all poor as shit and most of the women I knew were whores.

I was going to say how much I hate the old, decaying men who marry teenage girls just because they can. But I decided not to "go there".[120]

Sometimes I just wonder what those youngsters are thinking as they slip into their wedding gowns. I bet they already hate themselves an awful lot. So I don't think any additional hatred needs to be applied.

That and I don't want to appear hypocritical when I come back as an apocalyptic ghost and, instead of rapturing people, I just start grinding on young women while they're doing pottery.

[13] But I do hate people who use illness as a mode of avoiding things (e.g., school, work, a sports practice). You don't have Lou Gehrig's disease. I promise.

If it turns out you do have Lou Gehrig's disease, I'm sorry. I'm sure Dad had a good reason for giving it to you though. He works in "mysterious ways" (so you people say).

[14] I hate people who describe anything my dad has ever done as "mysterious". When He gathers up a thousand totally innocent, ridiculously adorable, little tiny children, and exterminates them with a hurricane, there's nothing "mysterious" about it. It's just brutal. So be honest when you talk about it. "God works in brutal ways." No one is going to punish you for telling the truth.[121]

---

[120] "Don't go there" and "that's right, I went there" are difficult to forgive.
[121] Sometimes, when deeply embittered folks reflect on these acts, and do so from a twenty-first century perspective, they regard my dad as a cranky, old monster. They think the indiscriminate annihilation of innocent children is in bad taste. It's arbitrarily ruthless. From an Iron Age perspective though, this sort of behavior – these erratic killings – would cause people to fear Him. And that's all He really wants. I'm sure if everyone just gave Him just a *little bit* of that Old World terror, he'd wind up slaying fewer children and bystanders.

[15] I hate women and girls who protest being ejaculated in (deep) after they drunkenly sought out the first functional penis. This is not rape; it's a huge mistake. There's a difference, albeit marginal.

[16] Instead of admitting "that was a mistake", some of these "victims" will adopt a role of "I'm a survivor of sexual violence" and attend a march called something like "Take Back the Night".

This is really pathetic.

Actual crimes, like actual sexual violence, produce actual victims. They produce real grieving. And real grief isn't marched in a skirt with a wine cooler and several photo ops along the way.

Many of the girls and women who participate in these marches are insulting the women who were actually harassed (severely enough to matter), assaulted, raped, or otherwise abused.

It is unlikely that the girl marching her skirted legs down the sidewalk, parading for a cause, has ever had a stepfather's penis in her sixteen-year-old vagina. Or awoke to a dizzying consciousness with a roofie hangover, a black eye, and a urine-soaked plus sign.

If I'm wrong, I apologize, but the marching girls appear to be trying way too hard to own a pain that isn't rightfully theirs. They want to be perceived as victims, perceived as though they have an interesting story to tell, without actually experiencing the rite of passage that would grant them such a story, such sympathy.

Shame on them. Divine shame.

[17] If you're a teenage boy who wants attention, you can't pretend to be the victim of sexual crime and be taken seriously (unless you were Catholic as a pre-teen), so you have to come up with other strategies. Strategies like dressing all in black clothes as an effort to convince people you're being socially awkward on purpose. As though it's a choice. This boy weighed the pros and cons and then *chose* to be weird and unpopular. That's what the black clothes are supposed to make me believe.

I remain unconvinced.

[18] Sometimes, before a weird boy starts exhibiting weirdness to his peers, he'll do things like carve the letter Z (for Zorro) over and over into the side of his parents' house with a steak knife.

[19] These boys usually wind up just fine in life. They aren't the ones who get involved in the huge mistake/rape grey area.[122]

A message to the boys who do find themselves involved in this area: she'll be sober in a few hours. Do the math. The socially awkward boys did.[123]

[20] Once these kids hit their thirties, it'll be the rapists who have all the free time.

[21] The white rapists will grow up imitating television programs, unaware that they can't physically perform a lot of the things they're watching.

[22] The black rapists will wind up behind a weathered table with three playing cards, shifting them around while repeating the same words over and over, faster than most people normally talk.

I'm not sure that's a skill. What I *am* sure of is that each person who does this has a friend named Tyrone. Either that or Jerome.[124]

[23] I hate people who enjoy attending (or smell like) casinos.

And anyone who appreciates casino card games.

Especially people who get really into poker and start saying things like "pocket aces".

---

[122] Unless they grow up with a lot of guns.

[123] Although the only reason they did the math is because they had so much free time after school until bedtime and during the weekends and summers.

[124] This was even true when every Jerome was called Hieronymus.

[24] If you tell me what your future profession is ("I'm going to be a doctor" or "I'm going to be a news anchor" or "I'm going to be a musician", etc.), I'm going to laugh as I poke you in the throat kind of hard with two of my fingers at the same time.

These people think the act of declaring something is the only criterion for achieving it.

Unfortunately (for you), if you're talking about it, that's time you could have spent in pursuit, so I already know you won't make it.

[25] I hate people who "want to be an astronaut." Even those who keep their desires to themselves.

Astronauts don't spend their mornings blasting into outer space. And their afternoons aren't spent in spacesuits, exploring planets and moons. They just sit around like fat firemen. Except instead of wearing headsets while playing first-person shooter videogames, astronauts watch reruns of *Battlestar Galactica*. And they have opinions about it.

[26] I hate people who are into *Star Wars*, *Star Trek*, or anything else with the word "star" in it.

[27] I hate people who carry around weapons as if to appear daring and dangerous. And thus cool.

Leah has Mace because she confronts cougars in the woods. That's not what I'm talking about. I'm talking about Mitch, who keeps a samurai sword in the trunk of his lowered Acura (as if the scream of his redlining V-Tech isn't a piercing enough squeal of insecurity).

A bayoneted musket would be just as silly and infinitely more effective. Perhaps it wouldn't be as cool-looking though

Though perhaps it would.

But if coolness is what matters most, Mitch might be better off with a huge pike from the seventeenth century. Or even better: a trebuchet.

[28] More on Mitch: he wears denim every day. I don't like people who wear denim.

And I *sort of* dislike people who wear mixed fabrics (e.g., mingle their linens with woolens), but my dad already talked about that (see Leviticus chapter nineteen, verse nineteen).

[29] Worse than fabric crimes are people who have their teeth cast in gold or silver.

Why do people do this (i.e., want gold mouths)? Do they think it will make their mouths look wealthy? They can't even afford toothpaste; everyone can see that.

The caption beneath the picture of a chronically un-brushed mouth will never be "fortune smiles".[125]

[30] I hate people who are scared of dentists. And spiders. Neither of these things should be troubling. You should be scared of cigarettes, automobile accidents, and electrical outlets.

[31] Also, I hate traffic accident vernacular (and the people who use it). For example: "fender bender", "t-bone", "jackknife", etc.

[32] And if the weather is bad in your town, and your town is five miles away from mine, please don't make a comment about it (explaining to me how the wind is windier where you are, or the snow snowier or rain rainier).

That's now how weather works. You're just trying to feel important.

---

[125] At least not until after my codex is published (in A.D. 2014) and people start plagiarizing this verse, thinking of that plagiarism as witty. But many of those people will also be visibly unfamiliar with the American Dental Association.

33 And I don't care what the weather is like; stop using umbrellas. Just get wet. You always poke me in the face with those metal prongs that hang off the edges in all directions.

Just accept the fact that it rains sometimes. Don't thorn-crown *other* people unless you're actually allergic to water.

34 I hate people with allergies. When a flight attendant offers you peanuts or pretzels, that's not an invitation to hear about your peanut allergy or gluten intolerance.

All you have to say is "no thanks." If you say anything else, you're just informing the world that you were raised like veal. You're way too soft for this world and you should become sustenance for someone who isn't.[126]

35 When the Fourth Council of the Lateran happens (A.D. 1215), it will be decided that people who put wafers in their mouths are quickly presented with a hunk of my body. That's what they're chewing on (see the first canon; the bit on transubstantiation).

These people should know that, when the wafer becomes flesh, it still contains gluten.

There's no gluten-free alternative to Jesus meat.

36 Also, it needs to be said that not everything is an allergy. If you take ibuprofen and get an upset stomach, that's not an allergy. It's a side effect. An allergic reaction would be something like a rash. And I never want to hear about your rashes.

37 I hate people who over-identify with the major city nearest the suburb where they were born.

---

[126] Worse: I hate the parents of any child who attempt to ban potential allergens from a classroom or a field trip. When I hear about this happening, I'm embarrassed to have occasionally been a human being.

"When you're from Buffalo, you can't eat Buffalo wings anywhere else", says the girl from Cheektowaga, New York, while at a bar in Manchester, Connecticut, looking at a menu during happy hour (after nobody asked about Buffalo wings).

[38] "Happy hour" and "early bird" are two time periods I could do without.

[39] And I hate being wished a safe flight. Almost as much as I hate the people who wish it.

[40] And those who go watch a comedian, hoping to hear jokes about air travel. All jokes and observations about air travel are boring.

[41] Although I do have to document my hatred for people who try to take their giant, should-have-been-checked luggage onto the plane with them. And when they realize there's no way it will fit in the overhead compartment, they begin adjusting *my* bag. As if that's the problem. My half-full JanSport backpack is clearly at fault. That's what's preventing your luggage from fitting. It's not that yours has wheels and an extendable handle so that it can be towed behind you. No. The problem is the backpack with a grapefruit and two shirts in it.

[42] I also hate people who assist others in getting their luggage from the overhead compartment and feel heroic about it.

[43] And, although I'm aware they're just doing as they're told to do, I hate the flight attendants who talk about "federal regulations" (as opposed to just saying "please don't do that").

Federal regulations prohibit stowing any items in this area during taxi, takeoff, and landing.

Federal regulations prohibit tampering with smoke detectors.

Federal regulations prohibit emergency exit seating if I'm unwilling or unable to perform the applicable functions.

Federal regulations prohibit the use of cellular phones and pager transmitters.[127]

[44] Also, if I ask for water, please don't give me a tiny, plastic cup that holds three swallows and is mostly full of ice. I know you have whole cans hidden inside your gurney of refreshments. If you're not willing to surrender one of those cans, don't give me anything at all.

Southwest flight attendants usually comply (as though my request had been federally regulated). But the can they give me has the words "Deja Blue" printed on it in the largest font it can house.

While this is annoying, there's a smaller font that says something even worse:

"Using state of the art purification systems including reverse osmosis, carbon filtration, and ozonation, we deliver a consistent taste and purity."

One has to wonder what the source of their water is if it requires that much manipulation to be drinkable. Hose water doesn't need to be reverse carbonically ozonized (or whatever). So I'm forced to assume my Deja Blue begins its journey in someone's colon.[128]

[45] I hate people who take pride (or even care) in pouring beer.

[46] Once they're done with the pouring, I'll hear a story that begins with "you know what they say about" and ends with anything. "Men with large feet" or whatever.

[47] "I'm just sayin'" is used as a complete sentence after that one.

---

[127] Federal regulations also insist that I comply with all instructions and "placards".

[128] Only after a long and grueling operation (extraction from the lavatory, etc.), does it reach my lips.

[48] Also: "I gotta be honest" or "I'm not gonna lie" followed by the declaration of a brief, uninteresting opinion.

Like this: "I gotta be honest: those shoes look terrible with that blouse… I'm just sayin'."

[49] And I hate people who step on my shoe laces. Just watch where you step. It's not that hard. I do it everywhere I go.

People who have perfectly tied shoes always feel compelled to say this to me: "your shoe's untied!"

Okay, since it appears we're stating three-word facts, here's mine: "my back hurts." And as long as it continues to hurt, I don't want to bend over and tie a shoe. Do you think you're better than me because you can tie your shoes? No! You are not!

[50] I hate people named Ricky. Most Rickys still sit backwards in chairs as if 1977 is upon us. Each and every Ricky[129] should be impaled in the face with a jousting lance. One Ricky after another until all of them are mutilated.[130]

Or they should just be slapped with one: jousting-lance-whipped.

Unless they buy this gospel.

I'm still not going to hug one though. I will not hug a Ricky.

[51] And I also wonder about turtles. They don't seem to care about hygiene. I don't see them using detergents or licking their coats. So there must be megalopolises of bacteria colonizing the insides of their shells. I bet it smells terrible in there.

I say this because I hate people with detectable hygiene problems. If you smell as bad as the inside of a turtle's shell, please don't leave your home or invite me to it.

---

[129] I hate people who say "each and every".
[130] Once every Ricky is exterminated, we'll confront the "Josh" situation.

[52] And if you live in proximity to a golf course, please don't invite me to your house and use this sentence to brag: "step off the back porch and you're on the golf course."

Why would that make me envy you? Golf is the gardening of sports. The pace is so slow that it fails to threaten the elderly. The holes are played at the same rate weeds grow. There's no other pro or perk or upside. Don't ever think there is.

[53] I hate people who say "location" three times in a row as a complete sentence. Sometimes these are real estate agents; sometimes it's regular people talking about real estate.

I don't care who it is that's doing the talking though; please pick a meaningful word and say it one time. Or use it in a meaningful sentence that you say once.

Don't say something stupid three times in a row and hope the repetition makes it powerful. It just makes you sound autistic.

And that makes me think you probably smell like the inside of a turtle shell.

[54] Even if you have good hygiene *and* a nice home though, if you buy something that doesn't come assembled, and you want help with its assembly, please don't think of that as an opportunity to invite me over.

Especially if the rest of your house is as bad as your most recent purchase.

[55] Worse than a bad house is a bad church.

I hate people who demote the importance of the church building to just that: a church building. "These are merely walls", they say. "What truly matters is what's inside the walls of the *heart*."

I disagree.

And so does everyone else who's ever thought about it.

Those thoughts go like this: does a brand new Snickers Bar come wrapped up in bloody, booger-soaked Kleenex?

Of course not.

Because the packaging is the marketing. That's the promotion. Packaging is what sells the product. And so do the walls of a church. The building represents what's inside of its walls.

So when I see you sitting on a bunch of folding gymnasium chairs, celebrating Me in a corrugated aluminum warehouse in some bleak industrial park, I'm going to get a little bit offended.

Can you really not do any better than that? You can't just take a little bit larger cut from the tithe pool and do some upgrading? As is, you're better off issuing your praise from a roadside tent.

If you're going to market the product (i.e., Me) this badly, I'd rather you didn't participate at all. If one vendor sells Snickers Bars in discarded Kleenex, that kind of ruins it for the others.

Chapter Twelve

[1] I hate people who make up a middle name as an attempt to overturn someone's doubt.

"Danger is my middle name" after someone expresses concern about a risky situation.[131]

[2] I hate people to whom words like "Pentecostal" carry a special meaning.

[3] And people who say "let's just see where life takes us."

[4] When life fails to take these people anywhere rewarding, they grow bitter and begin complaining about "corporations" and "Corporate America".

Often, these are nineteen-year-old "songwriters" who don't understand how corporations work.

Or what a corporation even is.

[5] I hate people who are on journeys of personal growth.

"I'm seeking a deeper purpose", they explain.

And if they continue to explain, the word "transcend" is likely to appear in a monologue about "growing and moving forward" and "seeking self-acceptance" while "confronting deeper issues", and "ultimately, it's about being comfortable in my own skin."

"Wow. How do you do all of those things?"

---

[131] Unless the person appears to have mental deficits and says something like "serendipity is my business and business is my middle name." Or if it's an eye doctor whose business is believing. Because "seeing is believing, believing is my business, and business is my middle name."

"By facilitating a deeper connection between individuals. Moving beyond small talk and into deeper conversation. Figuring out what makes people tick, what they truly want, what their dreams are. Pushing oneself to the edge in a safe space that allows for open communication. You know, it's about knocking down walls."

"That all sounds really stupid. Can you at least be drunk while you do it?"

"No. Alcohol compromises the deepest levels of connectedness."

"You've talked about depth a lot. Like way too much."

"Well, I guess depth is a state of being."

If I allow the conversation to go on, I'll usually be subjected to these words: "cultivating mindfulness".

[6] People with cultivated minds are always into things like yoga and meditation. And they practice their yoga in "studios" that have Sanskrit characters all over the walls.

If a building is covered in Sanskrit, it's probably not one I'm going to enter. The only thing Indians are really good at is dysentery.[132]

[7] After yoga, these people devote themselves to "clean" dieting. And other forms of "cleansing" that don't involve soap.

I don't know what any of that means. But they tell me it's powerful.

[8] I hate people who describe experiences as "powerful". You're allowed to describe certain machines as powerful, but little else. "Moving" and "inspiring" (or "inspirational") aren't far behind.

---

[132] Maybe if India became a Christian nation, and Indians began to regard me as Lord of the Galaxy, things would be different.

[9] Likewise, I hate people who talk about "empowerment".

Often, it's feeling "empowered" by things like feminine traits. And people will attend weekly gatherings to share their thoughts on the subject.

Do you think Napoleon went to weekly small group gatherings?

How did all of that conquering make you feel this week, Emperor Bonaparte? Why don't you share your feelings with the group?

Powerful people don't need moral support or weekly reinforcement to feel empowered, obviously. If you're someone who needs that sort of thing, you're probably feeble. Definitely very un-powerful.

[10] I hate people with bumper stickers. Especially "Coexist".

Okay. As opposed to what? The other drivers on the road (the ones reading your sticker) are unable to make those groups stop existing. So I don't know what you're hoping to accomplish here.

Do you mean "respect the belief systems of others"?

If so, that's a terrible request. If someone believes the moon is inhabited by elf princesses, no one has to respect that person's opinion. Because it's a stupid one :-)

[11] I hate people who use too many emoticons.

To quote Fred Frank, "it's emotional surrogacy; it's worse than Hallmark cards."

[12] I hate people with "eclectic music tastes".

And people with "eclectic tastes" in anything.

[13] And people who send me "vibes". I don't need to know that you were thinking about me in a specific way for ten seconds straight.

[14] I hate people who are adamant about helping me in really inconvenient ways.

[15] And people who think of themselves as "I'm a good person." If you have time to think those thoughts, you're probably not contributing much to society. So you're probably not a very good person.

[16] I hate people who quote Gandhi or Einstein. Most of these people spend too much time discussing philosophy and politics while citing old "classic" sources. Sources like John Locke.

John Locke believed in mermaids. How much credit are you willing to give to his position on twenty-first century politics?

[17] I hate people who do things (or make things)[133] and then try to explain the meaning of those things to me.

Let's say you got a tattoo. Before you explain the meaning behind it, test your explanation on someone else first. Not just once. Say the exact same thing three times in a row. Word for word. If it starts to sound a little bit stupid by the third time, you're going to have to come up with a different reason. For example:

"My tattoo of a butterfly on a crucifix is about faith and ownership over my body. It defies the conventional role of women in a subversive society – a society I refuse to keep me from soaring."

"My tattoo of a butterfly on a crucifix is about faith and ownership over my body. It defies the conventional role of women in a subversive society – a society I refuse to keep me from soaring."

"My tattoo of a butterfly on a crucifix is about faith and ownership over my body. It defies the conventional role of women in a subversive society – a society I refuse to keep me from soaring."

---

[133] Like draw a picture or write a poem or paint your bedroom walls or rearrange your house ("so that its shui feng-flows better").

Notice how it sounds ridiculous to you by the third time?

I'm Jesus.[134] I'm not as stupid as you. However you choose to explain yourself, it's going to sound absurd to me the *first* time.

All I hear in your explanation is that you let a guy with hepatitis, a hangover, and a hideous beard draw a picture of a bug and some sticks on your lower back. And now you're really reaching to turn it into something profound.

If you just said "I don't know; I was drunk", I wouldn't think any less of you. But instead, you start talking about gender roles and using words you got from your "empowerment" gatherings.

[18] The people who talk in this way are the same ones who think of themselves as "spiritual".

"I wouldn't say I'm religious per se; I'm just spiritual."[135]

People act as though this is a novel thought. As if more than a billion people hadn't already issued this same sentence – word for word – in thousands of languages.[136]

[19] I hate anyone who employs the term "per se".

The same hatred applies to people who say "vis-á-vis", "inter alia", and "plus ça change".

---

[134] I'm a two-thousand-year-old ghost monster.

[135] "Per se" does not mean "of sorts" or "exactly" (as in "it's not a sports car per se, but it definitely has some pep when you punch the gas"). Per se means "by itself". It's Latin's non-gastric equivalent of French's "a la carte". Or the non-musical equivalent of Italian's "a cappella".

[136] And, to paraphrase Michael Pollan, being "spiritual" is just a way of avoiding all of the really important questions. Although, to paraphrase Win Head, being "religious" also avoids all of the really important questions. I, Jesus the White, encourage you to go confront "each and every" one of those questions. People will claim this position can be found in Mark, chapters three (verse five) and four (verses ten and eleven). Not true. Jesus the Grey wasn't into that. Although, with a little stretching, the "seek and you will find" stuff in Matthew (chapter seven) can be made to resemble my current stance.

There is a little known circle in hell where these people will spend eternity communicating in short, meaningless foreign clichés.

[20] An even worse cliché: "I don't believe in the institution of marriage."

People who surgically remove moles and then talk about the "institution of marriage" have no idea what they're saying. They're just hoping to be perceived by their peers as "intellectuals".

[21] But it's tough to perceive them that way when they refer to everything as either a "paradox" or a "paradigm shift".

[22] And if their sentences don't end with unnecessary prepositions (e.g., "where's the institution of marriage at?")[137], they refuse to end any sentence in a preposition, thinking it a grammatical rule. It isn't.[138]

[23] These never-strap-a-preposition-to-the-post-position people are usually the ones who try the hardest to be skinny because that's part of the imagery of "starving artist". But they spend a great deal of time in coffee shops, eating coffee shop food. And pretty soon they end up with a lot of stomach and leg fat. And nobody ever looks at their big hunks of thigh meat and thinks "there goes a satiated artist."

[24] Some of their peers try to be unique and original by dressing up in one-of-a-kind garments: all black. And black fingernail paint and sometimes a *Clockwork Orange* hat.

They all look the same to me.[139]

---

[137] Note that "where is it?" would suffice by itself. It doesn't need the companionship of "at".

[138] And I hate John Dryden.

[139] Plus, we already covered this when we were talking about the people who do math homework and are into polyhedral dice.

25 I hate people who think "horror show" is an expression because they over-identify with *Clockwork Orange* without ever having read the book.[140]

26 Most of these people also identify too strongly with "art".

Not because they're good at it (they're terrible), but because they think, despite how bad they are, they're able to express something. Something emotional. Something deep.

I find everything they make and say to be funny. So I just try to laugh, thinking they might feel complimented.

At first, they hate me (returning my hatred with one of their own). But eventually they quit art altogether and the world becomes a better place.

27 After quitting art, they become one of two things: depressed or "responsible".

The newly "responsible" people become way too interested in pets. It's all they're capable of discussing. They're either forcing others to join them in conversations about canine vaccinations or they're out trying to spay everything.

If they become depressed, their bedroom occupation patterns are drastically altered (the daylight hours begin to outnumber those of their nighttimes).

28 I hate people who write suicide letters. Is that really the only way you can get other people to listen to what you have to say? You have to write it down on a piece of paper and then kill yourself next to that paper?

29 I hate people who keep hundreds of plastic grocery bags in a food pantry. You will never use them all. Seriously.

---

[140] "Freak show" is just as bad.

[30] "And more" is not an acceptable closing half of a business name (e.g., "Groceries and More" or "Cigs and More" or "Bagels and More"). I hate business owners who don't know this.

[31] I hate people who think New York bagels are special; they're somehow better than bagels from Alberta or Wisconsin.

These people are exactly as embarrassing as the Oregonians who wait in line for an hour at Voodoo Donuts.[141]

"No, that's not true! New York bagels really *are* better! It has to do with the water supply!"

This is so ridiculous that I'm not even going to respond. Instead, I'll just say this: if you've never had a bagel from New York, you're not missing anything.

Trust me, I'm Jesus. I know my grains. Nothing has ever been more overrated. Not even me.

[32] When something is described as "good enough", that means it's terrible. People do not use those words honestly. If something actually *is* good enough, it will never be thought of in that way. So when "good enough" is applied to anything at all, what the speaker actually means is "not only have I failed to produce my best work, but the product here is actually quite bad. And while I'm bothered by it, I'm not so bothered that I want to start over. I'm willing to ignore how bad it is for the moment so that I can move on (even though I'm aware that I probably shouldn't). I could do better, but... good enough."

That's the only thing that expression has ever meant, which means it's strictly reserved for the laziest imperfectionists of the world. And I hate these people.

---

[141] If you're not from Oregon, this is a donut shop that makes the exact same donuts as every other donut shop in the world, except here they sprinkle Cocoa Puffs or Fruit Loops on top.

33 I hate people who sing in public. Especially those who do it with headphones on. "Man, that person has an amazing voice", this savior has never once thought.

If the headphoned singer is a guy, what he's doing is closer to talking than singing. And the lyrics he's saying (in his talking voice) are about being powerful and owning lots of girls.

If it's a girl doing the headphoned singing, she can't tell what her own voice sounds like any more than a nearby pedestrian can tell what she's listening to. But somehow, pedestrians are still able to detect how far off key she is. The singer doesn't seem capable of making that same observation.

34 I hate people who snap to the beat of songs. Head bobbing is only a little bit better.

35 "I told myself I…" and "as a matter of principle" are not good reasons to do anything. When someone begins a sentence with either of these, I know they'll end that sentence with a commitment to something they're better off not doing. I know this because, if they had a *real* reason for doing it, they would have told me that reason (instead of a slogan about principles).

36 I hate people who think of themselves as big and strong and want other people to think of them in that way too, so they wear tank tops. If their sweaty pit hair hasn't already done me in, the way the fabric of each tank top hugs the giant, "swole" stomach definitely "gets my gag on".

People who say "swole" (or "yoked") and people whose tank tops hug a stomach (even if that stomach doesn't belong to them, somehow) have a maximum salvation of Purgatory. And most won't even get that.[142]

---

[142] Purgatory wasn't in the bible, but it arrives sometime around the twelfth century. By the time these people are doing their thing, Purgatory will be well established. It was actually my idea. Because of how crowded Heaven is getting. But we'll get to that later.

[37] The same half-damned eternity awaits boys and men who walk around "casually" flexing as hard as they can. Sometimes their hands turn white and vibrate due to the occlusion of blood flow resulting from that prolonged flex.

[38] I hate people who "embrace" things (like one's age) and anyone who has ever "made a personal breakthrough".

[39] Most of these people enjoy things like trust falls (and other "icebreakers").

[40] A few of them are hoarders.

If you own a poster of a Pontiac Fiero, you're a hoarder. And hoarding makes for creepy real estate. And good urban legends.

[41] Kids who spread urban legends are more likely to use the word "bomb" to mean any cuss word. As in "he dropped an f-bomb!"

[42] I hate people who demand that fruit be rinsed off before they'll eat it.

"Why?", I'll ask.

"The pesticides, obviously. If you don't rinse them off, you're just swallowing cancer."

"Okay. I don't think holding your apple under the faucet for two seconds rinses off any pesticides. If it did, then they'd have to reapply them every time it rains."

"Well people handle my food with their bare hands. That's gross. I at least want to wash *that* off."

"Okay. But that doesn't communicate any diseases or anything. There's nothing unhealthy about fingerprints. You're just washing off an idea."

"I'm still going to rinse it off."

Chapter Thirteen

[1] Whenever a parent refers to an unused toothbrush, it's always likened to a bone. Like this:

"Don't you lie to me Timothy Douglas Schroeder! That toothbrush is as dry as a bone!"

Bones are not dry.

Just look at anyone whose bone is sticking out of his skin. It glistens. Or ask an orthopedist. He will explain to you that, not only are bones covered in blood and body juices, but they're *filled* with blood. That's where all of the red cells are made. There's nothing dry about a bone.

Now you could say: "I meant bones that are petrifying in the desert."

Okay, that still doesn't make dryness is a characteristic of bones. That's a physical property of any noun that's spent years petrifying in a desert. A kidney is just as dry in those conditions.

So if you mean to compare the dryness of Timothy's toothbrush to a bone that's been in a desert without rain for a period of time, you have to actually say that. Because practically all other bones are wet, which implies that your son did in fact brush his teeth (or at least moistened his brush in an attempt to fool you).

Even if he did brush though, that doesn't mean he's going to grow up to be a likable person. He probably won't, considering he has such inarticulate parents.

[2] These are the same parents who, within the first six years of having unprotected sex that turns into a child, bring that child to any event.

I hate parents who do this.

That's why I explain to those children that there's no such thing as Santa Clause. And then I continue: "you know those cookies that you leave out at 6:00 p.m. on Christmas Eve? Those are just giving your dad diabetes as he gets crumbs all over his pajamas."

The parents always get mad at me, but what did they honestly expect? That's what they get for not finding a babysitter.[143]

[3] I hate people who try to get me to attend these events (any event populated by children) by saying "my kids would love to see you."

No they wouldn't.

And I don't want to see them either. Kids and unrelated adults don't get along. There's no reason to pretend otherwise.

Kids never like adults any more than the adults like the kids.

So just be honest: "I'm a parent and I never get to do anything anymore because I spend all my time parenting, so I'd really like to have some conversations with an adult. I'd like it if you would attend this obnoxious event I'm bringing my kids to. Will you tolerate being around kids for the afternoon so I can talk in a normal tone of voice and not have to read books about princesses eight times in a row?"

If that's what you mean, say it.

[4] I also hate people who hang their children's terrible artwork on the refrigerator. And then they leave it up for years. When the kid is eleven, his terrible drawings from when he was six are still displayed on the Frigidaire, now crumpled by the years.[144]

---

[143] Plus, don't you think your kids would have figured it out at some point anyway? Santa (in his polar village with his magical deer and tiny elves) is really able to keep detailed records of every child born into a rich country? Good parents should hope their children question the feasibility of such a story.

[144] A lot of these drawings are as bad as Andy Warhol's.

Any time I want to get something out of the Montessori-looking refrigerator, a tenth of the display – and a single magnet – falls to the floor. And then I have to figure out how that ridiculously weak magnet was holding five plies of "artwork" to begin with.

[5] I hate people who are always on the lookout for child abuse.

First, try to be more specific. Early adolescent abuse is not the same thing as infant abuse. And second, a little bit of neglect, at any age, can be a positive thing.

[6] I hate people who make a fuss when dinner is interrupted by anything (someone at the door, a phone call, etc.).

If dinner goes from 5:15 until 6:00 p.m., a phone call at 5:30 p.m. sets them off. The next night, when dinner goes from 8:00 until 8:45 p.m., a phone call at 8:15 p.m. sets them off.

Nobody else knows your dinner schedule. Nobody. So if someone tries to get in touch with you and it interrupts a randomly timed eating event, you don't have the right to be pissed.

[7] I hate people who make that deep growling noise before they spit. The kind of noise that tells me they're attempting to conjure phlegm all the way out of their colons. Not just snot, but bile and poop and gastric acids. Prior to spitting, they're summoning everything they can from the netherworld beyond their stomachs. Some seem to manage. Others expel something inadequate and appear disappointed.

[8] I hate people who add an s to already plural words (e.g., peoples) or to a mass noun (e.g., monies). Especially the mass nouns. Converting the word into a count noun and then pluralizing it doesn't add anything to the meaning of your sentence. For example: "unabsorbed food stuffs get pooped."

"Unabsorbed stuff gets pooped" is sufficient. "Stuffs" (and especially "food stuffs") is just stupid.

And the word "stuff" should not be overused. Same with the words "thing" and "copula".

[9] Regarding "copula", it's not that the word itself that's offensive; it's the people who use it that offend me. And only because they count with their hands wrong. There are rules to counting with your hands.

One must never use a thumb to denote a number lower than five.[145]

If you begin with the thumb, and there turns out to be four of the thing you're counting, when you've tallied the last one, it appears as though you have a crippled hand.

One must also never begin counting with a pinky.

People who say "copula" always begin with a thumb or a pinky.

[10] Also, people who say "stuff" and "thing" too much drive brown cars. Not "earth tone". Brown.

I hate people with "earth toned" anything.

Especially big purchases like cars, houses, and major appliances. An earth-toned lunch is fine.

[11] I hate people who, while I'm in the back seat of the car they're driving, use the rearview mirror to make way too much eye contact with me.

Just because we're having a conversation doesn't mean your eyes and my eyes need to be engaged. Especially when you do it from a driver's seat.

---

[145] The thumb is like the diagonal slash in a cluster of tally marks. One does not begin a cluster by closing out the "five-bar gate". You begin your tally with the vertical hash marks, and then, when all that's left is a thumb, you close out the hand (and can start using your other one).

And *really* especially when you don't move your head. From a stationary skull, your eyes just shoot back and forth between the road and my reflection in your mirror.

Please stop this. It gives me the creeps.

[12] I hate people who argue like they drive (or vice versa).[146] The angry ones. Driving is always unpleasant (made *more* unpleasant by the angry ones), but arguing doesn't have to be. It's *only* made unpleasant by the angry ones.

Arguing should be a bunch of punch lines, some giggling, a hug, and then maybe sex. Or a brunch.[147] Or a nap.

The rage version of arguments just doesn't make sense. It doesn't make any more sense than the road version of rage.

[13] And road rage is just weird. While sitting on a bench today, I heard one driver scream at another: "what the fuck is the matter with you!" And then the screamer followed up with some death threats.

This anger was caused by the recipient of the screaming failing to make a turn as quickly as would have been convenient for the one doing the screaming.

This is not an emotionally healthy person.

At least once a week, while I'm driving, and stopped at a red light, there will be an angry man sitting in a vehicle behind me.

When the light becomes green, if I don't accelerate immediately and aggressively enough, that angry man will honk his angry horn.

---

[146] I hate people who pronounce "vice" as a two-syllable word so that it matches the number of syllables in "versa".
[147] Obviously I hate people who arrange "brunches".

After he's done honking, he will lift his right hand from the steering wheel, supinate that hand (i.e., rotate it so that his palm is facing upward), and then begin to karate chop it back and forth, slicing the air as if to say "what is it that you're doing?!" or "why are you not accelerating and then traveling at a speed that would satisfy me?!"

In all of these road rage situations – someone honks, tailgates while revving and re-revving his engine, deliberately cuts me off, issues a hand gesture I'm supposed to interpret as "offensive" (all of this for the purpose of "teaching me a lesson") – what's the lesson plan? What is it that you're trying to teach me here?

Okay, you honked and swerved, waving your fist while cursing my average pace of acceleration.

That's fine. Good job. What happens next?

Am I supposed to react with my own fit of screaming? My own bout of traveler's vengeance? I'm not sure I have it in me. I don't really have the adrenaline for that kind of a response. So I guess you win. Final score: you one, me zero. You sure showed me. That victory will get you far in life.

But honestly, who's actually keeping score? Are you? Are you really recording wins and losses when you get home? Like you have a bulletin board in your bedroom where you post final standings of driver quarrels?

If so – if you really are keeping score – I hate to break it to you, but you lose. If you're the one who gets all worked up over someone else's driving, you're *really* the loser in the exchange.

It's your own ulcer and cancer you're brewing. Not mine. It's not my blood pressure that's spiking. I'm not the one exacerbating my hypercortisolemia while swerving around and honking (and then scribbling furiously on my bulletin board).

Every time you have a panic attack in your vehicle, and I decide not to join you, only *your* vasculature and overall physical health suffers. Mine's fine. So if you are in fact keeping score, your anger is a serious handicap. You're not going to win *anything* until you get it under control.

[14] FUBU. Hahaha! This is funny. Also funny are gangs and tampon strings. Gangs are collections of children whose parents reared them below the poverty line. Like their parents, these children aren't witty enough to be popular, aren't strapping enough to be athletic, and aren't emotionally mature enough to confront those deficits gracefully. It's more funny than cute, but it's still kind of cute. Like a tampon string.

[15] Anyone who needs to use a weapon for anything is exhibiting an incredible display of human weakness. Unless that person *invented* the weapon. If you invented the gun (and actually built the one you're using), you get to use it.[148]

But if you're trying to "win" a fight by using someone else's invention that someone else built, you really can't take credit.

And not only are you in no position to take any credit at all, if you have to stoop to that depth to "win", you *definitely* lost the fight.

"Bang! Bang! Bang!" That's you announcing to the world that you're far too weak and scared and incompetent to win a fight using your own faculties.

Consider the "drive-by". What happens in a drive-by is a couple illiterate wastes of taxpayer money (people living in section eight housing, dining on food stamps, etc.) don't even have the courage to leave their vehicle.

---

[148] But I don't think you did. I could be wrong. Maybe you lived in China during the twelfth century. You might have even played a prominent role in the siege of De'an in 1132. Stranger things have happened.[148A]

> [148A] Stranger things have not happened. And neither did this. And that's why you don't get to shoot bullets at living things.

They drive up in an automobile that someone else invented, someone else built, and from inside that automobile, they use a firearm that someone else invented, someone else built, and shoot bullets into an unarmed, sleeping person's home.

Nothing has ever evidenced more weakness.

No act less brave, no creature more feeble.

There is nothing in the whole world that has as much power to shame as the use of a gun. Anyone who needs one should be humiliated. And that humiliation should have no end.

[16] Also, I hate old people. Not all old people, but almost all of them do what I hate, which is this: "I'm dating myself when I say this, but…" and then they talk about something that was a "current event" several decades ago.[149]

[17] And maybe 50% of the people in that batch will use prewritten topic lists during phone conversations. And sometimes during outings (lunches, etc.).

[18] 100% of the people whose outings are accompanied by topic lists own tongues that emerge from their mouths at weird angles when they cough. Not okay.

[19] Worse: people who contribute nothing to the conversation but pretend it's because they're too deep and thoughtful to do so (as opposed to the truth of "I have nothing to say about anything").[150]

---

[149] I hate people who can't go more than an hour without being enveloped by some current event. "Oh my god, did you hear about the shooting at…"

[150] People who don't talk very much – the quiet, reserved people – have a fiction that's working in their favor: people assume they're holding back in deference. They're not yielding because of a lack of knowledge, but as a courtesy. They're just introspective. This is never actually the case though. Nobody has that kind of self-esteem. The brain of a quiet person is a quiet brain. It doesn't produce a lot of thoughts. The brain of a quiet person isn't generating brilliance at the speed of conversation and holding it in. If people have something worth saying, they say it. Everyone always.

Vampire novels (see the *Twilight* series) seem to have made this role believable.[151]

The only time partner-to-partner silence is okay (excepting sleep and sex) is when it's the companionable variety shared between a topic-list-bearing old couple. The kind of couple who watches *The Price is Right* together, owns lots of yarn, and still feels threatened by "rock n' roll", which they think of as Jethro Tull and Styx.

[20] These people believe that teaching a kid how to ride a bicycle is the only component of parenting. And the only two pieces of advice they offer children seem to conflict:

1) Never talk to strangers.

2) If you're in trouble, go find an adult.

[21] The old people who have a lot of plants often begin sentences with "nowadays".

And some of them also use the expression "man alive!" when they're trying to communicate surprise.

I don't know what that means but I'd like it to stop.

[22] Also about old people (who are men): just shove a catheter up in there. Seriously. Watching you helplessly try to pee isn't something I should have to endure.

[23] I don't like any jewelry at all (as noted earlier), but among jewelry wearers, I have some specific complaints.

First, wearing a lot and drinking brandy does not make you look rich. I wanted to say that because I'm pretty sure "rich" is the look you're going for.

---

[151] I hate people who have contributed in any way to the paperback vampire market.

I haven't figured out what look the sober person wearing gold-plated plastic and yarn is going for. So I'll just say this:

Dear Mr. Person with "bling" jewelry, you have melty chocolate dripping out of the bottom of your enormous foil-covered medallion. You might want to wash your hoodie.

Also, people sometimes have pierced bits of face. Not ears, but lips and eyebrows and noses, etc.

You have two ear lobes, ladies. Lobes. And those are fine places to store some metal. Anything else is just low class.

Guys: no. Just no.

And toe rings aren't allowed on anybody. You probably can't get yours off. I bet it's stuck there. And the cola you constantly drink will definitely give you diabetes. And the diabetes will definitely give you distal neuropathies. And that will definitely destroy your toes. Then what?

And I hate people with pierced vaginas that aren't supposed to but still do pierce my penis's tips (n = four tips). And it hurts badly and I laugh and say "haha, no it's okay!" as I rub ointment into the wound. But the ointment mixes with the blood and congeals into a brown custard. And it starts to look like cake batter. And again I say, without meaning it: "really, it's okay."

This didn't actually happen, but what if it did?

There's still time.

Chapter Fourteen

¹ I hate people who ask me more than once in a lifetime if I'll help them get a tight lid off of a jar of preserves.

² I hate people who think they're doing something fancy and describe it as "eye-talian".

These are usually forty-year-old men treating ten-year-old boys to a "bottomless" dish at the Olive Garden.

They hear slogans like "when you're here, you're family" and take them to heart.

³ I hate people who think of themselves as fancy because they eat or drink something fancy.

⁴ Likewise, I hate people who fear being unfancy and thus refuse to eat or drink something they regard as such.

If you refuse to swallow four-dollar wine, that just tells me you'd be the first to die in a post-apocalyptic world.[152] And it makes me want to participate in an apocalypse. Or at least get one started. Just to extinguish some smug assholes.

⁵ I hate people above the age of six who use straws. Especially those who loosen the paper sleeve around the end of the straw and then blow it at someone like a wingless kamikaze paper airplane.

These are the people who, when their drink is all gone, continue to suck at it through the straw, making a bunch of noise as the suck up the sweat off the ice.

⁶ I hate people who get excited about going to a "hobby shop".

---

[152] At the very minimum, you'd be the only sober person.

[7] And people who keep scraps of plywood because they think they'll eventually do something with them.

[8] I hate people who operate or ride on rickshaws. I hate them an awful lot more than I should.

[9] I hate people who make a display of shivering or say things like "I'm cold" or "it's cold out."

"Feel how cold my hand is."

No thanks.

[10] When someone gets injured in a public place, a lot of people become hated.

The first in line is the misled hero. The one who doesn't know what to do… and does it. He manages to make the entire situation about himself.

Next up are those who treat it like a spectator event, staring at the person who is having problems breathing or staying conscious or whatever.

And finally, when the paramedic firemen arrive and take the injured person away on a strap-in wheelchair, people clap.

Why are they clapping? This is a really weird thing to do.

[11] I hate people who clap at the end of non-live performances. A movie, a water feature display, a laser light show, etc.

[12] And people who have laughs that can be spelled.

[13] And people who feel so threatened by slugs that they have to cover them in table salt.

[14] And people who use "hashtags" in any context.

[15] And people who write papers, give presentations or speeches, or otherwise argue cases, beginning with a dictionary definition of a word.

"Webster's defines mentor as…"

[16] I hate people who use the word "heart" too liberally. The heart just pumps blood around so that metabolic demands can be met. The poignant ventricle has yet to be discovered.

[17] If someone *does* eventually discover it, it will probably be a Mexican. Not because Mexicans are better at explorative physiology, but because I've never heard a Mexican complain about allergies regardless of the season. Nor have I heard a Mexican complain about a season because of allergies. This tells me they're better adapted to earth living than people of other ethnicities. And that should free up the time to go exploring.

But sometimes that free time is compromised because white people take a break from complaining about their allergies in order to call the police on a Mexican (or a group of Mexicans) because he's a Mexican (or because they're a group of Mexicans).

White people often feel menaced by Mexicans.

If white Americans want the poignant ventricle to be discovered, they need to stop this. It's embarrassing. Almost as embarrassing as complaining about allergies (though not as embarrassing as using a gun).

[18] Plus, the people who call the police on Mexicans for the crime of being Mexican are the same people you hear complaining about the police the rest of the year (over speeding tickets, whatever).

I really hate these people.

You wouldn't have a ticket if you weren't breaking the law. That's how the system works. It's not unfair; it's justice. And as a result of being alive, you knew that. You knew it perfectly well.

[19] Just as you know "it wasn't my fault" isn't really the truth about the car wreck you were in. So I'm not interested in hearing your complaints about that either.

[20] Nor am I interested in hearing your complaints about how there are no jobs left for Americans because Mexicans took them all.

All you're doing is announcing that a lot of people from Mexico are better at employment than you are (if they weren't, you'd be the one working). And admitting that you're not willing to become better at it. You're not willing to do a better job for less money while taking fewer breaks. So you complain.

[21] But I understand why you're upset. Those tickets are starting to cost a lot of money. Money you would have rather spent on books that end in "for Dummies".

Anyone tempted to buy anything with "for Dummies" in the title needs to be slain ASAP.

I'll have my dad take care of it. He's a really good taxidermist, so I'll also make sure he stuffs those people.

[22] I hate taxidermists who aren't my dad (like the one who mounted the bobcat).

[23] I hate people who pretend to know about a subject because they know what some of the stuff is called. Just because you say things like "dark matter" or "chaos principle" or "quantum" anything (e.g., leaps, entanglements, etc.) in a sentence, that doesn't mean you know anything about physics.

[24] The biggest reason I hate these people is because they never compliment anyone but themselves. And they spend way too much time in praise.

[25] I also hate people who compliment everyone else. Not everyone deserves to be complimented.

[26] I hate people who use the word "noir" for any reason. Even if they're talking about wine, but especially if they're not talking about wine (e.g., "film noir").

[27] I hate people who try to sound fancy by talking about the "nose" of wine. And then they swirl it in the glass and talk about the residual "legs" or "fingers".

Wine doesn't have "fingers" any more than chickens do. And it doesn't have a nose any more than it does a penis.

[28] I hate people who refer to alcohol as "sauce".

[29] And use the word "varietal" about a type of wine or tea. Just because you use embarrassing words like this doesn't mean you have keener taste buds when it finally goes into your mouth.

[30] Also, if you ever see someone purchasing drink umbrellas, this is not a financially or emotionally stable person.

[31] I hate people who say "once and a while".

[32] And people who say "flipped the script", as in "he tried to tell me my drinking had gotten out of hand but I totally flipped the script."

Words don't need to be put into apposition just because they rhyme. Rhyming isn't what makes a sentence meaningful or interesting.

[33] I hate people who resemble Buckwald in appearance and/or anything.

[34] I hate people who sign their full names on everything: Gabriel Elliot Parker (when Gabe Parker would suffice).

You're not important enough to do that. You're no John Wilkes Booth or Lee Harvey Oswald or Aimee Semple McPherson.

35 I hate people who invent nicknames for themselves. Felix starts going by "The Flash" or maybe "Roger 'the Pike' Pearson" is on first base or there's a "Butternut McGovern" in the lunchroom.[153]

36 I hate people who enjoy "tailgating" (of the sporting variety, not automotive) and tell me I'd love it too.

"Do I want to spend my entire afternoon standing in the middle of a parking lot on a really hot day, drinking bad alcohol out of a cooler? Not really."

37 I hate people who think secret conspiracy theories are interesting enough to tell and believable enough to repeat.

The reason these secrets turn out to be false every time is because human beings are the creatures sentenced to conceal them. And human beings can't even keep a surprise birthday party secret.

38 I hate people who use snooze buttons. How many times do you want to disrupt your sleep before getting up in the morning? Use your snooze button that many times exactly.

39 I dislike sleeping next to people because they do things like this at me: "whatchadoin?"

"I'm just adjusting my position."

"But you're turning your back to me."

"I'm trying to fall asleep."

"Can you not do it facing me?"

---

[153] Sometimes a pair of high school athletes will team up to compound the self-promotion. "We're Steakhouse and The Tank", they say in unison. And then one of them chases it with "he's Steakhouse and I'm The Tank." Eventually we hear The Tank shouting from the dugout: "good eye, Steakhouse, good eye!"

"No. And when I finally do fall asleep, I'll do all sorts of weird stuff. I'll shake and twitch, I'll mumble sentences that make no sense. Please don't comment on those things either."

[40] But you won't catch me snoring. And I hate people who *can* be caught in that behavior.

The existence of snoring is audible evidence that my dad made a huge mistake. Huge. Well into the twenty-first century, it's the only mistake He ever truly admits. And He grows to see the humor in it, but for a long time it deeply angers Him.

When Dad was designing natural selection, He made a big deal about how it would systematically eliminate all sleep growlers. That was His whole reason for inventing nocturnal predators. And He thought He was being so clever in doing so.

If some hapless slob emits a bunch of noise as he descends into sleep, it's the predatorial equivalent of a mating call.

"Here I am, hungry predators!", it howls into the night's air. "I will be helpless here for hours!"

If his call to those predators awakened the other members in his camp first, those members would simply chop off the snorer's head. Execution of the noisy for the preservation of the silent. The selective pressure that eliminated snoring would be upheld. The system seemed flawless. But then history came to pass.

Over time, the predators grew clever enough to recognize the value of the snorer. So they left him unharmed and instead dined on his companions. At this point, humans were actually being selected for *un*fitness. The exact opposite effect my dad had designed the system to accomplish. The creator of the universe had officially been outsmarted by wild animals.

This irritated Dad. So he intervened. And his intervention marked the point in prehistory during which humans were first implanted with the "Divine Spark".

They were given intelligence above the beasts that stalked them. And soon enough, humanity – with its new celestial sparkle – was outsmarting those beasts (the ones that had previously outsmarted my dad).

They began erecting unscalable walls to keep the predators at bay. And this resulted in the restoration of Dad's selective pressures. Without predatory animals killing the silent sleepers, the people themselves would carry out their executions in the direction of silence until all slumber was still.

Dad was comforted by this.

But then He made His mistake.

In a moment of lapsed judgment, while camping atop Mount Sinai, He inscribed the Tablets of Testimony.

The moment Moses delivered the sixth commandment, snoring was cemented into the species.

For the remainder of human existence, when people fall asleep, a great number of them will emit noises that sound like patterned spurts of Vietnam.

And I hate these people.

Chapter Fifteen

[1] I hate Americans who demand croissant be pronounced kwa-sahn. Not only have these Americans have never been to France, but they're ordering them from a deli. And later that week, they can be found at a Mexican restaurant (one step up from Del Taco), ordering a burrito. And not rolling the R (and then demanding that other people do the same). Although, in that case, I would think the diner was just trying to be authentic. And I wouldn't mind. But "kwa-sahn" isn't an attempt at authenticity; it's a declaration of pomposity. And for that reason, it should humiliate its speaker. Whenever it fails to humiliate, I try to step in and issue shame.

[2] If the kwa-sahn people are above the age of twenty-five, they'll use the word "organically" to mean something occurring naturally. Like a boy finding a love for his father's business. "I didn't force him into it; I just let it happen organically." Or maybe two people falling in love. "We didn't use any dating sites, nobody set us up; we just came into each other's lives organically."

Neither of these is "organic". That's not what the word means. It's not a synonym of spontaneous or serendipitous. It means carbon is present. Something that's organic has carbon in it. So when two people hit it off without your help, or when your son adopts an appreciation for the family business, that doesn't change how much carbon is in their bodies.

[3] If the kwa-sahn people are fifteen-to-twenty-five-year-old boys, they can be found addressing their fellow Americans as "mate" and occasionally trying on a British accent.

These boys are trying way too hard to live Englishly (pretending too much appreciation for tea, etc.). If it goes on for long enough, they're at risk of saying things like "Bob's your uncle" while referring to money as "quid", which they borrowed from their "flatmates" (who are truly smashing). Ridiculousness will be expressed as "bollocks" and rotten people referred to as "gits".

Gor blimey, these people are a pain in the arse. I'm way too knackered for this.

[4] Sometimes I get so knackered that I retreat into pathologically antisocial behavior. And then every "once and a while" when I emerge, looking like Howard Hughes, and give people another chance, this happens:

"You have something on your teeth", I'm told.

"Okay."

"It's right… it's right there", as they point at my teeth and then at their own. And then at mine again.

"Yeah, I know. It's food. I just ate."

Instead of being okay with my response, they continue to describe its location in my mouth, as if I'll suddenly find it interesting. Or maybe I failed to understand what they were saying originally.

If I want the conversation to be about anything else, I'm forced to explain: "look, it's part of a piece of cereal. It's there because I just finished eating cereal. Thirty seconds ago there was a lot more on my teeth because I was chewing a bite at the time. It's going away though. It'll eventually be gone completely. Do you think you can handle yourself until then?"

[5] If I'm able to change the subject from the food stuck in my teeth, these people seem to think the next best topic is this: "you need a haircut."

Really? Is it that I *need* this or that, if my hair was groomed closer to my scalp, it would be more compatible with your current taste in fashion? Is that maybe what you're getting at?

Say what you mean next time.

[6] The people who tell me what I need (haircuts, a shave, etc.) are the same people who force me to participate in their special tricks to eliminate my hiccups.

You know what? I don't mind just having the hiccups. A little spasm in my insides every twenty seconds for five minutes isn't all that bad. I can suffer through it. Hanging upside down while drinking water and then holding my breath until I die somehow seems less appealing than letting that spasm clear out on its own.

[7] Sometimes people have spasms that don't go away on their own though. Nervous ticks take up residence in their faces and make them blink really fiercely all the time.

Courtney Jensen used to do this too.

When he was a little kid, his face behaved as though it were responding to an invisible Michael J. Fox putting mascara on it.

Michael didn't knock it off until Courtney started middle school. At that point, the facial sprawl of Tourette's died but for a few survivors that remained in his mouth.

Still today, Fox's ghost can occasionally be seen putting lipstick on Courtney. Just watch him when he's sitting in a really boring meeting. It's subtle, but his mouth is out of control.

And so are his hands. Sometimes it looks like he's playing air guitar. He's not. He just makes his hands do that because it would be too agonizing not to do it. And if you hear him scrape one foot while walking somewhere, you'll soon hear him scrape the other. This is better than what he used to do though: touch objects with the back of one wrist and then with the back of the other.

Despite how bad it used to be, he never prayed about it. Not once.

I thank him for that.

And I don't hate people who can't control their face's parts, their chorded hands, or the scraping of their feet, but I do find it funny. And I wonder: what's the point?

[8] What I don't find funny (and what I do hate) is when people move their lips while reading silently. This has to stop.

[9] Something else that has to stop is the group of nervous tics that I can hear (throat clearings, high pitched noises, etc.). These are like hiccups that never leave.

In this case, you do need to swallow water upwards without breathing as people try to scare you to death. You need to be silenced. And it needs to happen right now.

[10] On the twenty-sixth day of September, 2013, Courtney Jensen sits in UConn's Homer Babbage Library and tries to work on his dissertation.

After twenty minutes, a habitual throat clearer (of undergraduate age and dimensions) enters the room and sits across from him.

Every fifth second, Courtney's new library guest clears his throat and then sniffs and then clears his throat and then sniffs again.

Five seconds of downtime, repeat.

Then he eats a hamburger and chews it very deliberately.

It's like watching someone who hasn't attempted to run in over a decade going for a jog. The way they swing their arms on purpose ("this is what my arms are supposed to do"). In this case, "this is what my mouth is supposed to do."

Courtney becomes even more irritated.

Plus, as the boy is eating, he makes a bunch of terrible noises. Somehow, he's managing to grunt and hum simultaneously every time he exhales.

At first, Courtney attempts to feel sorry for him, knowing these are clearly not partnerable traits. No girl would ever tolerate such mountain dwarf manners. But Courtney finds that he is unable to muster compassion enough to overpower the feeling of needing this boy to die. Or at least needing him to not be alive anymore.

And I support Courtney's lack of compassion.

Hum-grunting aside, what could this dwarven reprobate possibly be clearing from his throat and nostrils so frequently?

One must assume he's clearing it of nothing (and doing so as noisily as he can). Because I know of no organic material that can accumulate in five seconds.

The alternative is that enough phlegm and snot accumulate every fifth second to need to do something about it. And if this is the case, the boy has a real problem. And this is the exact problem I will use to help Courtney eliminate him. And get away with it.

That's the punishment for eating way too deliberately and making noises before, during, and after.

[11] Sometimes, when Courtney tells a woman that her husband (or son or brother or whoever) is a psychopath, that woman will respond with "you don't know him like I do!"

Okay. Who cares? People always leap to that defense, assuming it defensible. There has never been a psychopath who failed to be the object of that line.

If they didn't have husbands or wives, they at least had mothers or fathers. Or a sister. Someone. There is always someone who says "you don't know him like I do." And that person is always correct. The Courtneys of the world do not know him like that. That's why their judgment isn't clouded by affection and nostalgia (like yours is).

If we're being honest with ourselves, we have to admit that "you don't know him like I do" has been said about every psychopath ever born, and it has absolved no guilt and pardoned no behavior. It's a just a sentence. A few mouth noises that change nothing.

I grant you (or rather, I grant your psychopath of a husband): he had a difficult upbringing. He faced an awful lot of adversity in his formative years. Unfortunately, that's how psychopaths are made. If you want to create a psychopath, that's the exact recipe. It's sad, sometimes tragic, always unfair, but that's life.

Your loved one is a fucking psychopath. Accept it and move on.

[12] I hate people who tell me "mi casa es su casa". Not because it's a cliché, but because it's a lie. Nobody has ever once said this and meant it.

"My house is your house."

Okay, then why did you get so pissed when I hired a real estate agent and put it up on the market? It's mine. And I don't really want it. So why wouldn't I do that? I could totally use the money.

Even if all I did was rearrange the furniture or paint the walls, you'd still be upset.

It seems the real problem here is communication.

First you tell me the house is mine – I own it – and then you throw a fit when I behave like a homeowner. I'm getting mixed signals.

Why don't you just offer me what you're comfortable offering: "you can take naps without me getting angry" or "help yourself to the leftovers in the Pyrex dish." Don't tell me it's my house if you're going to be a daddamn Indian giver the moment I accept it.

Chapter Sixteen

[1] I hate people who say "don't judge me" or offer people warnings about judging others "lest ye be judged."

I'm totally pro-judgment. I'm sixteen chapters into a gospel that's nothing *but* judgment. And I'm not holding myself to a different set of rules. I expect the same bitterness and hatred out of you.

[2] I hate people who purchase something because "it's banned in…" or brag about something they own for that reason.

"You should come check out my '69 Chevelle. That baby ain't even street legal." That's because it's lacking necessary safety features (seatbelts, mirrors, etc.), not because it's such a badass vehicle (too badass for the law).

Or: "my shoes have springs in the heels that lock when I crouch and then explode as I jump. They're totally banned in the NBA." Of course they're banned; that's the whole reason they were made. Some designer looked at NBA shoe regulations, found some rule he could break, and designed his shoe specifically to break it. "These shoes are so good, they're illegal in the NBA" is just the marketing scam. And you fell for it. They don't improve your performance, they worsen it. By a lot. And they'll be responsible for a lot of sprained ankles. This is something you paid money for.

Or: "this sports supplement is illegal in twenty-five countries and banned in the NCAA, NFL, NBA, MLB, and NHL." Yeah, that's because it's contaminated.

Or: "everyone look at my new switchblade!" (Or butterfly knife or whatever else you just had to have.) "It's illegal in seventeen states!" That's because it's dangerous to the user; people always wind up cutting their own thumbs off. It's not illegal because it's dangerous to the other person. A butter knife (not a butter*fly* knife, but a butter knife) is just as dangerous to the other person. But you will probably still have your thumbs when you're done using it.

[3] I hate men who wipe their penises' tips after they pee. These are the same ones who pull their pants down really far before peeing.

Actually, I don't hate them. I just wish there were something I could do to help. Because very little saddens me as deeply.

[4] I hate it when cats rub ointment on my legs. I realize this appears to have very little to do with people, but sometimes people rub ointment onto cats. And I hate these people.

[5] I just now decided that the peeing people I was talking about a moment ago are not unlike "saggers", except that "saggers" wear their pants half off always. If you're wearing your knickers in this way, I will cut you. You and your wet cat.

[6] Sometimes the sagging people are white suburban kids whose lives are so dull that they pretend to be Jamaican. This mostly happens at recess and during things like P.E. and conversation. What they don't know is that tricksters will attempt to eradicate your toe. Don't let them! Don't you let them near your toe![154]

[7] Another group of people I hate are those who work jobs they themselves hate. Reason: I know they'll all build careers out of those jobs and then they'll be extremely bitter about everything until they die. And while bitter, they'll become mad at me over tiny things that shouldn't matter.

These also seem to be the people who express the most disapproval about other people's pursuits of pleasure. As though other people not being miserable is a personal affront for which one should bear no tolerance.

[8] Specialists, strategists, technicians, etc. These are not jobs.

If it were up to me, they wouldn't even be words.

---

[154] Bob Marley is the punchline. It's not funny because I had to announce it.

Also, unless they're professional athletes, employees are not "team members".

Some other words that aren't allowed to appear in job titles are: "optimization", "systems", "division", "strategic", "integration", "program", "operations", and "innovation".

Outside of babysitting and chaperoning a high school dance, nobody is a "supervisor of" anything.

"Representative" is only okay if you were elected to the House.

"Agent" is only okay if you represent actors, writers, athletes, or musicians.

And "director" is only okay if you're surrounded by people with titles like "key grip" or "props master".

A "lead", "senior", or "chief" something is a person to be pitied.

Unless it's a CEO or CFO (also the only two job titles in which "officer" can appear). But a CEO of a four-person company is just sad and unimportant.

[9] Worse: use of the word "leadership".

A single invocation of this word damns its speaker to Hell for eternity. It's an irrepentable sin. One of only nine.

"Synergy" is repentable, but has a three-strikes law. Same with "forward thinking".

And expressions such as "working hard or hardly working?" and "work smarter, not harder" are banned.

Also banned: "if you're early, you're on time; if you're on time, you're late."

[10] And damnation is the penalty for hanging an inspirational poster.

If the poster has a single word at the bottom (e.g., "achievement", "determination", "dedication", "persistence", etc.), the eternal punishment will be much harsher.

[11] Every occupation has a set of specific guild requirements that must be met before its aspirants can claim membership. One cannot call oneself any of the following things until all criteria (most of it financial) are met:

Web designer (or "programmer"). Minimum annual income of $35k in each of the last four years.

Consultant. Minimum annual income of $40k in each of the last five years. "Consultants" are not allowed to have additional jobs; 100% of all taxable income must be derived from "consulting".

Athlete. If it's a stadium sport, there is no longevity requirement, but you must have a current contract and have exceeded a million dollars in accumulated earnings. If it's a minor sport, $50k/year in salary and sponsorships combined. A minimum of four tax returns must already reflect this amount and the current year must be on pace to exceed it as well.

Blogger. Minimum annual income of $40k in each of the last three years derived strictly from blog (or podcast) advertising contracts. Referring to yourself as a "blogger" prior to the completion of this probational period is tantamount to a 1990s community college student with a bedroom-filmed cable access show calling himself a "talk show host".

Writer. I must be able to find at least two books you've written in the last five years currently sitting on shelves at Barnes & Noble. If you're a columnist attempting to conserve syllables by calling yourself a "writer", you must have reported annual earnings of over $60k in each of the last four years. If you're a salaried medical writer, you have to say "medical writer"; this cannot be abbreviated to "writer".

Model. Minimum annual income of $45k in each of the last three years. The current year's earnings must also be expected to exceed this amount.

Artist. Average annual income of $50k (derived exclusively from drawing or painting)[155] throughout the last eight years. Maximum average income during those years: $200,000. If you exceed that amount, you dismiss "what do you do?" questions or answer them with modesty.

Photographer. Minimum annual income of $50k in each of the last five years. If part of that income is supplemented by friends (or parents of friends) commissioning portraits, you're not a photographer.

Poet. High school students who aren't in "drama" or "theater" must universally despise you. Drama and theater kids (and many other "introspective" virgins) must universally quote you. And you're already dead. A while ago. If you're not dead, and the U.S. government has named you Poet Laureate, you need to have an annual income that exceeds $80k (exclusively from sales and readings of your poetry) before "I'm a poet" is permitted.

Musician. If you're a studio musician, you must be able to show a minimum annual income of $40k in each of the last three years. If you're an orchestral musician, you must have full medical and dental insurance and the beginnings of arthritis. If you're a jazz musician, you must have already died of a drug overdose. If you play guitar, bass, or drums, you must be an active member of a band that has released at least two RIAA-certified Gold albums within the last six years. If you're a music *teacher*, you're a music teacher. If all you do is sing, you're a grocery clerk.

---

[155] Sculptors are sculptors and graphic artists are graphic artists. Membership conditions exist for each of these as well. While the inclusionary criteria for graphic artistry are forbidding, one can be inducted into the quilter's guild with very little hazing.

Inventor. You must have won more than six Nobel Prizes for your inventions (the "peace prize" doesn't count; that's not a real thing). Or you must own more than twenty patents on inventions that earn an average of all the money in the universe every year.

Doctor. You must have an M.D. and your patients must be too stupid to know you're a doctor when you go by your Christian name.

Economist. Unless you work for an entity such as the World Bank and your official job title actually is "economist", you're not an economist; you're a teacher or a professor.

Craftsman. You must be the current CEO of the American tool manufacturer, Craftsman.

Director or producer. I must have heard of your movie. "It was in this specific film festival" doesn't count. "What have you done?", I might ask. And an appropriate answer might be: "I'm producing a movie right now with Jeff Daniels and Paul Giamatti – sort of a *Spinal Tap* for the YouTube hero – but the last movie I directed was..." and then it's something I've heard of.

Film Maker. There's no amount of money or success in which you're allowed to call yourself a "film maker".

If you fail any of the above criteria (for any of the above careers), you're merely an "aspiring" x. An aspiring writer, an aspiring producer, an aspiring model, whatever. Nobody is an "aspiring film maker".

[12] Other things one cannot call oneself under any circumstances:

Anything "master" (e.g., fencing master, chess master, dungeon master). Bobby Fischer was not allowed to call himself a chess master. He could either say "I'm a chess player" or simply "I'm Bobby Fischer."

Entrepreneur. This just means you have some bad ideas you think of as "business ventures" but won't ultimately pursue. "Jimmy is an entrepreneur" is a softer way of saying "Jimmy's unemployed."

Scientist. This doesn't mean anything to anybody.

Statesman or maverick or leader or rebel. These are even worse than calling oneself "creative" or "quirky".

Anything "buff". The worst of these is "history buff".

Historian. You can be a history professor, but you can't be a historian.

Academic or intellectual. These are adjectives, not nouns. So if someone says "I'm an intellectual", that person is not even smart. And they're at risk of saying things like "utilizing one's intellect". Use your brain, asshole.

Guru. This means someone who doesn't have any qualifications but, somehow, is still perceived as qualified. Not only can you not refer to yourself as a "guru", you're not allowed to assign it to other people either.

Along similar lines: maestro.

[13] I hate people who work in malls and airports. Especially those whose jobs involve food. Mall eatery French fries and premade airport sandwiches should nauseate everyone. First, I hate people who aren't nauseated by one or both of these. And second, how come the people selling these products don't appear to know what an appropriate price might be?

[14] I hate the people who go to "workshops" (even if it's just to fulfill "continuing ed credits").

[15] And people who get "certified" in things (personal training, SCUBA, CPR, skydiving, etc.). If you have a certificate, and you tell someone about it, that certifies you as pathetic.

Chapter Seventeen

[1] I hate people who wear sports jerseys with a name that's not their own printed across the back, shoulder to shoulder. I'm fooled by this almost every day.

Out of the corner of my eye[156], I see a pasty, sixteen-year-old with bad complexion. At a height of 5'8" sags a mop of unkempt Kurt Cobain hair.

My heart is immediately racing.

Hysterically, I grab my wife's arm and shout directly into her ear: "Holy Dad, look! It's Michael Jordan!"

Then I begin to realize: I'm in WinCo, an industrial grocery store that cuts costs by making shoppers bag their own groceries. It's 1:21 a.m. and several people around me are shopping barefoot. Why would Michael Jordan be wearing his 1992 Bulls jersey here at this hour?

I slouch into a posture of freshly conquered excitement. And then into one of hatred. Hatred for this high school dropout who dressed up as Michael Jordan just to trick me.

Before I let my devastation conquer me completely, I look around, inspecting all of the other shoppers, hoping for the chance to recover with a second celebrity sighting.

Instead, all I see is a bunch of barefoot, obese women leaning against their grocery carts, retouching their makeup.

Each woman is holding a small, clam-shaped case. Those cases are all open. On the top side, there's a mirror. On the bottom, a little puffy pad (which apparently contains the actual makeup).

---

[156] I hate people who say "out of the corner of my eye".

Realizing none of these women is a celebrity (or worth celebrating for any reason), I pick one at random and watch as she converts her lips into something that no longer resembles human lips.

She dabs on some glossy paint with a dirty Q-tip, presses her lips together, and then parts them into a thin, wide smile. It looks like she's very animatedly whispering the word "meat".

She seems to like the way it looks, but decides she's not quite done. So she applies a little bit more paint and then pooches her lips out as if readying for a kiss (or mimicking an inflamed butthole, all red and glistening).

Worried she'll notice me staring at her face, I look down and stare at her feet instead. The bottoms of those feet are so filthy they've turned black.

I don't know how long I'd been staring at her toenail polish when she finally put her mirror away and reached into a cooler of frozen sausages.

After putting a hard block of them into her cart, she looked down at some children she'd been neglecting the whole time and said "I got you some bangers for dinner."

I begin to wonder if this woman's children, whose ages I would "guestimate" to be six and nine, have not yet eaten dinner.

And I wonder if they even know who Michael Jordan is. And how exciting it would have been if that shopper (who is now drinking a can of unpurchased beer) would have been wearing that uniform honestly.

I make a mental note of my hatred and begin thinking about sausages. Or, more specifically, this:

[2] Sometimes people are born with fingers that are thicker than other people's fingers.

People whose fingers are thinner than that sometimes refer to those thicker fingers as "sausage fingers".

Instead of saying this, they should consider calling them "banger fingers". That way, it could take on several meanings.

[3] I don't like many of these people. A time allotment.

[4] I hate people who can't understand the difference between plums and clams.

[5] I hate peeing on cats and hamsters. Touching mutton inpert. Infants plus midgets died of during becoming dizzy. It's a fact.

[6] I hate people occupy.

[7] I hate people who don't make sense.

Chapter Eighteen

[1] I hate people whose clothing is either flamboyant or ironed. And people who wear shoes when they're ironing their pants (the very pants they will soon be wearing).

These are the people who refuse to take their shoes off when they enter someone's home.

[2] People with no manners should probably be dead. Or at least barely alive. So they don't have the physical strength to behave in the way they otherwise would.

But I also hate people who demand obedience to arbitrary manners (elbows on dinner table, etc.). I hate them about the same amount.

These people should have their elbows removed "super" quickly.

[3] I hate people who think the word "super" means "really good" or "a lot". Consider "supervision". Nobody thinks this has to do with Superman's eyesight.

[4] I hate people who say things like this to me: "good afternoon."

The reason I hate them is because they say it to me immediately after I've woken up. And depending on when this happens, this comment can change the entire tone of the day.

As a rule, people should say "good morning" until 6:00 p.m. And then just say "hi."

[5] I hate people who use the word "utilize" when "use" is available.

These are the same people who "utilize" the word "elucidate" too often. And emphasize the T in "often" but ignore it in "soften". And pronounce the P in "something". And in "hamster". And put an L in "both". Inexcusable, all.

[6] And I hate the males who have the most gynecomastia in their breast's tits.

[7] Sometimes people complain about things for reasons other than humor.[157]

It's harder for me to listen to this than it is for me to cast a longing gaze into a milkman's oily gynecomastia.

Other than that, complaining and gynecomastia are essentially indistinguishable (unless one of them becomes more saggy than the other).

[8] I like it when a young male spends three thousand dollars or more on wheels for his car. A car that cost him four hundred dollars or less. Because then I can say "nice wheels."

[9] I hate people who ask me to play "Twenty Questions" and when I have four questions remaining, they're still answering with "it *can* be."

[10] "For your age" is not a qualifier I enjoy hearing when it's applied to me. Any sentence that precedes it is a sentence you should just keep to yourself, regardless of how complimentary you intend it to be. Courtney agrees.

[11] I hate people who ask rhetorical "how could that possibly…" questions because they assume the asking of the question is the same thing as answering it.

They think this sort of phrasing is evidence of a position. But all it really evidences is that they don't understand how the alternative works.

---

[157] Complaining is a skill, just like anything else. Painting, woodworking, backgammon. If you don't practice with a purpose, you're not going to get better. People too often complain without a purpose. They complain for the sake of complaints, which is no better than art for art's sake, war for war's sake, school for school's sake, Alice Cooper for Alice Cooper's sake.

Example:

"How could humans have *possibly* come from monkeys!?"

The people whose love for me is the deepest (and most savage) are those who ask (or, more accurately, declare) this "question" most frequently.

Because it always bothers me when they do, I would like to answer it once and for all. This:

They didn't.

People didn't come from monkeys.

That's not what "sharing a common ancestor" means. But my followers don't seem to understand the difference. Which is why they're always stating questions with the word "possibly" accented so hard.

And I hate these people.[158]

12 I also hate people who ask *themselves* questions, don't presume asking the question is the same thing as answering it, and then provide themselves with an answer.[159]

For example: "do I think I came from monkeys? I don't think I came from monkeys."

Or: "do I think I look good in these jeans? Yes. I do. I think I look great in these jeans. Do I think they're in my budget this month? I don't think so."

If you don't need my help, just go shopping by yourself.

---

[158] Although I should admit that I, Jesus of Nazareth (a.k.a. Jesus of Bethlehem), have nothing to do with monkeys.

[159] Like I do in chapter twenty-eight, verse thirteen.

I'd much rather stay at home if you're going to be asking yourself really stupid questions and then dignifying every one of those questions with an answer.

[13] I hate people who talk about being "humane".

It's a little bit conceited to presume the defining qualities of humanity are things like sympathy and compassion.

That's what it means to be a human as compared to, say, being a dog or a hog or a chicken. Or just being apish. To be humanish (i.e., *humane*) is to reveal sympathy. It means being tender and loving and considerate.

This really is the apex of self-flattery.

People are not naturally compassionate. They're greedy, angry, hyper-adrenergic primates. They kill and steal and then they hoard those thefts and kills all to themselves.

Even the pious, the innocent. Everyone ever born. They're all just a bunch of thieves and rapists and killers who, owing only to circumstance, haven't yet committed their crimes.

That is what it means to be human. And in turn, what it means to be "humane".[160]

If people were instinctively sympathetic and compassionate, then kindergarteners would not need to be taught how to share their toys. Kids would just behave that way naturally. But does this ever happen? Or does every single toddler scream "*MINE!*" when threatened by a foreign hand reaching in to touch one of his toys?

The age of bullying peaks in pre-school. You have to work this *out* of the human form. So clearly what's natural is greed.

---

[160] Trust me. I know your hearts and thoughts (Matthew, chapter nine, verse four and Acts, chapter one, verse twenty-four). You're a bunch of scoundrels on leave.

Greed at everyone else's expense. That's the nature of humanity. And overcoming it is hard. But that's what adulthood is all about. To be an adult is to understand what is humane, and then beat it.

[14] I hate adults who stand in front of mirrors and talk at their reflections.

Especially when they're practicing "pick-up lines" on themselves. And then role playing the other party's submission to those lines.

[15] I hate people who tell me things like this: "no, I don't want to do that; it'll mess up my psyche."

Look, when my dad first sat down to invent people, a "psyche" wasn't part of the package. He didn't create that. And you didn't evolve one.

[16] Shitting and wiping (coupled) can be thought of as phase one. Once complete, phase two is the flushing of the toilet.

I hate people who don't complete all phases before exiting the bathroom.

[17] I hate people who ask me this: "are you in line?"

Are you serious? There's a big line of people in front of me and I'm standing motionless behind the second-to-last person. What else would I be doing here?

I'm genuinely interested in your alternative explanations.

"Hey, are you in line?", asks a twenty-something-year-old male who seems eager to buy his ointment and soda pop.

"Nope", I respond very mechanically. No gestures, no eye contact, no motion of any kind.

He cuts in front of me.

I reach around his body and begin to rub his tummy.

"What the fuck are you doing?!", he asks me.

"I'm rubbing your tummy."

Chapter Nineteen

[1] Sometimes a word will have a v in it. I hate people who really accent the pronunciation of that v. Especially when saying "five" and words that rhyme with five.

"I feel so alive" might be the most painful example.

[2] These are the same people who pick flowers and ponder things. Some of them wear really tight jeans, gripping their little legs. Sometimes I think this makes them look like lollipops. Other times, I decide they're pirates. The first pirates to discover denim.

[3] Opposite this, I hate people who wear the kind of jeans that look like denim Aladdin pants. I'd rather they just wore Aladdin pants. And carried a Sinbad sword.

[4] Excluding baseball players, giant jean wearers are those most susceptible to baseball cap wearing. It is a well-known fact that (excluding baseball players) the more pronounced a hat is atop a head, the more worthless the head is inside of it.[161]

This is especially true if the hat is crookedly aligned.

[5] And if the hat is worn daily, but it still has marketing stickers on the bill. Have these people never purchased clothing from an actual store before? Those stickers are supposed to be removed.

Either A) you don't understand presentation devices, or B) you need everyone to know this is something you purchased brand new from a retail outlet.

---

[161] I hate people who describe things as "long" or "well" known. Or sometimes just say "it's obvious". What these people mean is that they can't think of an actual explanation and know no source to cite. Thus it becomes "a well-known fact". Even worse: "it is long believed that…" Or still worse: "generally believed". It seems reasonable to ask: by whom? Certainly not me.

Or possibly C) despite wearing it daily for a whole year now, you still plan on returning the hat at some point and the presence of the sticker will validate your "no, I never wore it" claim (providing you can figure out how to get rid of the salt lines from all of your head sweat).

[6] I also hate people who wear golf visors, excepting Dilger.

[7] And I hate people who go to bed at 7:30 p.m., like Dilger.

[8] And people who spend too much time in a swimsuit.

[9] And people who wear wool on purpose.

[10] And people who "sun" or "go sunning".

[11] And everyone who can name a show on daytime television.

[12] And the people who make decisions about "the nation's most eligible bachelor" or "the sexiest man alive".

The sexiest man alive is always a wealthy actor. But if Johnny Depp's name were Angus Barnpenis and he worked at KFC, and had three ten-year-old sons from different women (to whom he was behind on child support payments), and at the end of every work shift, he rushed home on his ten-speed Walmart Huffy to sit on a beanbag chair and play Halo online, nobody would think he was sexy.

[13] I hate people who work or eat at KFC and people who play videogames while wearing headsets.

[14] Sometimes, when I'm struggling, and my disciples pick up on those struggles, I'll receive a prayer that says "you hang in there, Jesus."

I don't hate the people who say that, but I feel like I should. I feel like, if they *really* cared, they'd find a way to express that support in their own words.

[15] I definitely hate people who make resolutions. Not just in January. Any inspiration to resolve is reason for hatred.[162]

[16] The same amount of hatred that can be applied to people who experience pleasure in a "rec room".

[17] I hate people who say "pretend I'm not here."

On Friday night, Kevin invites his teenage posse over. They're in the "rec room" doing bong hits on the air hockey table. Grandma comes downstairs in her evening slippers, bathrobe, and hairnet to get some milk of magnesia from the pantry. She pokes her head into the rec room: "just pretend I'm not here."

Tough to do when you announce it, Grandma. If you come back down for prunes, just grab them and go.

[18] "Don't mind me" is similarly painful. When people say this, that means they're either about to do something annoying or they're currently doing it. And saying "don't mind me" will not inoculate anyone against that annoyance.

Picture this: I grow out long, thick toenails. I don't believe in shoes or socks. And as a nervous habit, I scrape those toenails really aggressively against the hardwood floors, the upholstery, whatever else my feet can reach. I do this as loudly as I can and I take no breaks.

If I say "don't mind me" as I do it, that's a tough order to obey.

[19] I hate dying people who feel constrained to issue advice to other people as though they're dying too.

Not every conversation needs to adhere to a theme of "you really gotta make the most of the time you have. Every day is a gift."

---

[162] "New year, new me", they say.

[20] I hate people who stand outside of Metallica concerts wearing sandwich boards and shouting about how I'm going to return to earth just to torture everyone who ever once experienced pleasure.

[21] I also hate the people who try to communicate their anger quietly. More women do this than men. A typical scene might look like this:

Husband forgets to do everything the wife asked him to do since the day they got married. Wife responds to the latest incident at a populated dinner table by clamping down her jaw like a threatened oyster and communicating through her clenched teeth. This isn't as subtle as she thinks it is. Every single person at that table can hear the imprisoned anger seeping and hissing out.

[22] I hate people whose refrigerators have more than one item in them that's covered or wrapped in foil.

[23] And people who own more than three pieces of Tupperware.

[24] And people who talk about "baggage" in any context other than air travel.

If it isn't something you check at the airport, come up with a new term to describe whatever it is you're talking about.

"Relationship baggage" is not an expression you get to use.

[25] I don't know who to be mad at. I'll decide this later.

Chapter Twenty

[1] I just finished eating manna. I didn't eat this very often when I was a man. Instead, I would catch fish from the Sea of Galilee. And then eat those fish. Peter would always help me. He actually did most of the catching, but that's only because I was off picking figs from the fruitless tree. Anyway, after lunch I made some more decisions. These:

[2] When my phone rings, I'm going to say hello once. I will wait a single second. If nobody responds, I'm hanging up. They're the ones who called me. They should not be caught off guard when a conversation begins.

[3] I hate people who reciprocate greetings with way too much enthusiasm: "well heeeelllll-*OH*!" or "goooood mornin' to-ya'!"

[4] Some people sound awkward when they use profanity, but they still use it a lot because they think younger people will find them more "hip". But cuss words rarely make sense in the context of the sentence. Not just expressions like "Ala-fucking-bama" or "holy fucking Christ" (the latter being a bit more biographical), but consider: "how the hell are you?" or "he stole my fucking car!"[163]

[5] Also, when people are trying to come up with vulgar things to call each other, the imagery conjured by a lot of them (e.g., "dickwad") is weird. Maybe you should put a little bit more thought into your vulgarity before you give it a voice.

[6] I hate people who use "fudge" as a swear word (rather than a bodyweight enhancer). And people who say things like "shoot" or "frickin" or "shut the front door!"

---

[163] Or anything about "jack shit" or referring to a muscly person as a "shit brick house" (or "brick shit house" or whatever it is). Not only does cuss word placement not matter here, but the cuss word itself seems irrelevant. Any cuss word will do. "Did you see Randall play last night? Man that guy's a fuck cunt bunker!" That conveys just as precise a meaning.

[7] I hate people with dreadlocks. Timmy counted five. Five people. Each with at least five dreadlocks.

It's not that I think Rastafarians aren't not not silly. It's that their hair can smell really bad. And sometimes it catches me off guard.

[8] I hate people who refuse to pop zits because it will compromise their complexion later in life (or whatever Katie's justification was for leaving a big bulb of puss completely undisturbed on her chin).

[9] I also hate people who pride themselves on being able to keep a secret. All this tells me is that you're a bore.

[10] And that you probably comment on the length of days.

"It sure gets dark early" or "it seems so much later than it is" around winter solstice.

[11] I hate people who display trophies or wear medallions.

Sometimes the trophies appear on bookshelves (in the place of books).

Also on these bookshelves will be a snow globe.

Destination globes (Disneyland, etc.) are the second worst. The very worst are personalized globes. The kind that has a several-year-old family photo inside and the water only goes two-thirds of the way to the top.

[12] I hate people who buy keepsakes. "Let's commemorate this event with consumer goods" is never a pardonable sentence.

[13] I hate bicyclists who wear spandex jerseys that have sponsors printed all over them. A dozen different Italian brands covering their thighs, chest, and back.

You're not sponsored. You bought that jersey. You paid for it.

[14] RyKrisp crackers and Rice Krispies are not the same thing. If I ask "do you have RyKrisps?", don't direct me to the cereal aisle.

[15] Even if this happens in a nice grocery store, I'm still forced to walk by someone who thinks of herself as pretty. And she takes small mirrors around with her wherever she goes in order to reinforce that belief.

She'll probably have a series of very unfortunate sexual encounters and be extremely unhappy for that reason (or unhappy for some other reason). I hope – whatever the reason is – it's a good one.

In her unhappiest moments, she might put one or more primary colors in her hair.

[16] The men who can picture themselves sexually violating such a girl are often those who think of themselves as rugged because of how physically dirty they are. And because of the amount of time they spend in the cabin of a physically dirty pickup truck.

One version of this person has a cigarette tucked behind a very dirty ear. Like a pencil, except gross.

[17] This is also the person who throws his used up cigarette butts out of his car window as if they were apple seeds (or some other handful of nature).

That's okay though. Because the seven-hundred-degree fire at the end of that butt won't cause any problems in the dry field you just threw it into. Plus, it's biodegradable. Those menthols become blades of grass in several hundred billion years. No reason to fret.

[18] Sometimes (i.e., all the time), while I'm sitting on a bench on a sidewalk, an ugly person will sit down next to me and ask if I have a way of creating a small, temporary fire: "do you have a light?"

I'm Jesus Christ. Of course I could produce a fire an inch from his mouth. But instead: "no, sir, that is not something I have."

I then return to the activity I was doing before I was interrupted: nothing.

A moment later, he'll ask someone else. And sometimes that someone else will say "yeah, I gotcha." And then I'll hear the spin of a striker wheel. And then a "thanks, man" from the now-active smoker sitting next to me.

After another moment, that smoker will blow his smoke in my direction.

Sometimes it's on purpose; sometimes it's just the wind.

Either way, I never anticipate it, so I end up breathing in at the exact moment he's breathing out.[164]

I immediately start coughing and say "damn you to Hell!"

And I mean it.[165]

But I also want to punish these people right away. I don't want to wait until death and its afterlife to inflict my revenge.

So I follow them home and kill their pets.

I use tooth floss to kill them because tooth floss is stronger than people think it is and it's usually minty.

Once I've finished, I look at the man whose pets I just killed.

---

[164] He's breathing out much harder than I'm breathing in.

[165] Part of me is angered by the smell of the cigarette smoke "per se" (correct use of per se), but mostly I'm upset about what that smell means. It's scented evidence that what I'm breathing in is this person's breath. The very breath he has *just* finished exhaling. That's the part I *really* hate. If I wasn't forced to notice the smell of that breath, I could convince myself that what I'm breathing is fresh air. Fresh air that's fresh off the potted plant sitting next to the bench we're now sharing. But I can't make myself believe that when the smell of his exhaled breath is too distinguishable to confuse and too powerful to ignore.

I look him squarely in the lips and whisper: "you questioned my bosom with your mouth tooth."

Then I go home, happy about what I've done.

[19] After I've killed their pets, many of these men go to the gym (the weight room part of it) and exert themselves way too hard, very irregularly. And wonder why their workouts don't seem to accomplish anything. Or at least why they only accomplish heart attacks.

As for the latter, you're welcome. That's my doing. By itself, the pet thing wouldn't be severe enough punishment for the lives being led here.

[20] Sometimes, instead of signing up for gym memberships, these men just play softball for an hour, once a week, and take it too seriously. While stretching their hamstrings, they critique the athleticism of all the other quarterly "athletes", saying things like "number twenty-two couldn't hit the broad side of a barn."

This is good because it would probably startle the animals if number twenty-two were capable of such a feat.

And I hate people who say things like "broad side of a barn."

[21] I also hate people who use dumbbells in public weight rooms (even if their use of those dumbbells violates no component of weight room etiquette).

This hatred is not about improper handling of the weights, or the guttural noises they make while doing so. I hate that too[166], but mostly I'm bothered by what they do *between* sets.

---

[166] Especially if they hiss instead of grunt. The people who do that are usually overtraining amateurs doing a pressing routine. At 6:00 p.m., they make the "bench" area sound like a snake pit.

Go to any dumbbell section of any weight room in the world (it's the area that has all of the stand-alone benches facing a giant row of mirrors) and look at the people sitting on those benches.

Every single one of them will spend his entire rest period staring at himself in the mirror. Unbroken eye contact with himself for all three minutes (unnecessarily long rest period because he didn't want to break eye contact any sooner).

"Jesus, you and your dad should be flattered. Your dad created these guys in the image of Himself and here they are admiring the hell out of that image."

Look, reader, that's no excuse. I've been merciful with them so far (pulled muscles, rashes from dirty equipment, little things to keep them out of the weight room), but I'm going to start getting more aggressive in my responses. I have to. Because this behavior needs to stop. The fact that it's still going on means I haven't responded to it harshly enough.

[22] I hate people who make a big fuss about skin cancer.

Honestly, who's really dying from this (Floridians aside)? Skin cancer is such a hopeless underdog, one has to almost root for it. Or at least feel sorry for it, watching it try to compete against overdogs like dermatology.

[23] I hate the new best friends of the newly deceased.

Whenever a human being dies, everybody that person ever met (briefly and unmemorably) will suddenly behave as though they had been best friends since the cradle, their weeping a practice in showmanship. Not sadness that the world lost its Agnes or its Benjamin, but "everyone look what *I* lost: my best friend." [167]

---

[167] These are the same people who become the world's biggest fan of an actor or a musician or an athlete on the day of his death.

When one of Courtney's friends or family members dies, and he's approached by an anonymous mourner, he now pretends that he didn't know the deceased person. "At least not personally."

For example, upon the death of a very dear Maria, Courtney will be approached by a Jason, who can't be any nearer to Maria than three steps of separation (he's probably nearer to Kevin Bacon). But Jason will behave as though he and Maria were soul mates.

His response to Jason will go like this: "Maria? No, that's not ringing any bells. I'm sorry for your loss though. It sounds like you two were really close."

[24] I hate people who bring sick people balloons. This woman is in the hospital because she has cancer, not because she became a five-year-old.

So I don't know if this giant, helium-filled, metallic balloon with a motto on it is going to bring her any comfort.

And if you actually think she became a little kid, what made you decide on a balloon? Why didn't you get her some Barbie dolls?

Is it that you think Barbie is a bad influence on little girls like her?

[25] I hate people who think Barbie is a bad influence on little girls (complaints about unrealistic waistlines, etc.). Find a doll being marketed to boys of the same age that isn't even *more* unrealistic.

The Incredible Hulk (and every other superhero), Hulk Hogan (and every other wrestler)[168], every single character from *G.I. Joe*, from *He-Man*, or from any hybrid species (e.g., *Teenage Mutant Ninja Turtles*).

How are their bodies any more realistic or achievable? Every piece of plastic has giant, veiny biceps and a striated eight-pack that appears to be absent of not just fat, but skin.

---

[168] The toys are not scale models of the humans they're named after.

What's the difference here? Is it in the realism of the toys or in how pathetically impressionable the child is?

Don't kid yourself. If your daughter's emotional constitution was influenced in any way (or to any degree) by Barbie's appearance, she's *really* retarded.

Maybe she wasn't born that way, but she's definitely caught a case of encroaching Down syndrome.

[26] I hate people who think anything can be communicated to anyone in a brochure.

[27] A lot of people (including some of the brochure folks) seem to operate under the impression that their sexual activity is a subject that might interest me. That's why they tell me all about it. And they're always way too interested in oral and anal sex.

[28] Oral sex. There are very few activities as overrated as this one. It doesn't even make sense. Sexual desire exists only to procreate. That's why evolutionary biology put all of those pleasure centers in the penis and the vagina. It was to help those two things find each other. If you desire something else – something that can't result in procreation – you're not functioning according to my dad's design. That is to say: you're fucked up.

"But Megan swallows!"

Okay. What biological drive would I have to put my semen into Megan's stomach? It's useless in there.

"You're telling me you want her pregnant?"

No. That's why I bought all of those condoms that I have every intention of wearing but never do.[169]

---

[169] Evolution couldn't anticipate the invention of condoms, but somehow still manages to overcome them.

[29] Anal sex. I don't get the confusion. Dad designed that hole to stink really badly. How is that not clear enough?

When people engage in either oral or anal sex, they're trying way too hard to be sexy by doing something really stupid. And I can't find stupidity sexy.

[30] The same can be said about BDSM. And the people who think "it's a healthy way for couples to explore a deeper connectedness."

There's no way I would feel more spiritually connected to Mary Magdalene if I squished her into a bondage corset and gagged her with a moldy apple.[170]

[31] Connectedness aside, I find computer solitaire exactly as arousing.

[32] People who play a lot of solitaire (not the BDSM people) have taken to calling things "grassroots".[171]

I wish people would stop this. Especially when describing non-agricultural businesses. I don't even want people who own farms to say it anymore.

[33] Back to the sex braggarts. Sometimes they'll tell me stories about "the girl who went down on me last night".

If they describe that girl's height, they always add an extra h to the end of the word. Like this: heighth.

---

[170] I guess I don't *hate* these people, but isn't it funny how sometimes one partner wears an executioner's mask and the other is made to eat poop out of a butthole?

[171] It's possible that BDSM people say this too, but I've spent a fair amount of time in the community (see the Max Ernst painting of Mary spanking me) and I have yet to hear a latex-wearing, rope-and-clamp-yielding dominatrix utter the word "grassroots" in reference to anything. I suspect that the people who say it are those who *should* participate in BDSM because they're the most opposed (thinking it "improper") strictly because they have the greatest desire to repress (see chapter four, scene six, of *King Lear*).

Sometimes I add a th to "forgive" but that's because I was learning English around the King James era.[172]

34 I've never *once* spelled definitely with an a though.

And salvation does not await anybody who does. The ends of the words "fortunate" and "definite" are not spelled like rhymes.

It shouldn't be that tricky. Nobody thinks "infinate" is the proper spelling. "To infinaty and beyond!" Or "I have a finate amount of income." Why when it's "def" does it suddenly become definate?

35 Or "awful" with the e in it. Like this: "aweful".

That makes me think you're using it as its own antonym. As if you're recalling its old "awe-inspiring" definition from the time when English was first getting its footing. But you weren't alive then. So obviously you just don't know how to spell.

36 Or when people leave the keyboard behind, and use their throats and lips, they affix a prosthetic vowel to the last-syllable-hinge of mischievous to turn it into "misch-*eve-ee-us*".

37 Or "let's get paninis for lunch."

The speaker apparently doesn't realize the *ee* sound supplemented into "mischievous" actually makes the panino plural on its own. The hyper-plurality of the s is a bit gastronomically daunting.

I don't know if I'm up for that kind of a lunch.

38 There's a Finnish noun, pilkunnussija, which means a person who feels entirely too compelled to point out every spelling and grammatical problem in his vicinity.

---

[172] See Psalms, chapter one hundred and three, verse three, and Luke, chapter seven, verse forty-nine.

If you try to pretend like that's all I am – a lowly grammar correction officer – as opposed to Lord Almighty, the Only Begotten, Son of the Eternal Father, the Bright and Morning Star, Messenger of the Covenant, the Resurrection and the Life, the Prophet of Nazareth, Christ the Lamb, the Redeemer of Israel, Holy Messiah, Pastor of Pastors, Firstfruits, faithful and true, Judge of the Quick and Dead, King of Zion, Captain of Man's Salvation, then you've got another thing coming, asshole.[173]

---

[173] I hate people who, attempting to be cute, say things like "you've got another think coming" (or "the next big think"). You won't find it so cute when you're burning in Hell.

Chapter Twenty-One

[1] "Shotgun", as we're approaching a car.

No. You're fourteen. I'm thirty-three. I don't have to call it.

[2] I hate people who hum. Nervous hummers, people who hum songs, people who say "hmmm" when they're thinking, C+C Music Factory, etc. There's no type of humming you can do that I won't hate.

[3] I hate people who, when presented with anything, read its name out loud. "Fancy Italian blend", upon being passed a packet of cheese. "Birds of North America", upon being handed a book to use as a coaster.

[4] I hate people who make sure other people know where they went to college. This is just a way for the unaccomplished to feel superior.[174]

[5] "Can I touch your stomach?", a pregnant stranger is asked.

First, the baby isn't in her stomach. She didn't eat the baby.

This hatred needs no "and second", although I could "definately" do a third and a fourth. Perhaps a fifth.

[6] I hate people who pretend current events are interesting.

"Did you hear about the gunman in Michigan?"

"I can't believe politician A filibustered legislation B."

"What's going on in Kuwait right now is a travesty."

---

[174] Or if the college wasn't *that* good, it's a way for the unaccomplished to preserve *some* self-esteem, as if youthful prospects still apply in middle age.

Ignoring that the word "travesty" is not a synonym of "tragedy" (and very unlikely describes anything occurring in Kuwait), none of these events changes anything in your life.

If you think otherwise, then you're going to have to explain to me how the way in which you experience your day-to-day life is meaningfully affected by "what's going on in Kuwait".

You're an American who has never been to the Arabian Peninsula. Your mother is not currently living in Kuwait City. Stray bullets are not going to cross the ocean and simultaneously take out your knee and your hospital and its doctors. Your life is unaffected.

So when you bring this up – or when you bring up gun laws or the debt ceiling – all you're really doing is announcing that you're a bore. And you can't think of anything more interesting to say, so you're inflicting your boredom on other people.

Why not just talk about the weather? The chance of precipitation is exactly as uninteresting, but at least it least it applies to people.

[7] Worse than talking about the weather (which is bad enough) is talking about it in this way:

"Looks like some blue sky is trying to poke through." Or: "looks like the sun is really trying to shine out there." Or: "it looks like it's trying to clear up outside; it wants to be a nice day today."

Consider the no-more-ridiculous thought: "it looks like that dead opossum is trying to stop stinking so badly. The one that was hit by Grandma's LeSabre last week. It looks like it wants to get cleaned up and go to the outlet malls. And it's really trying hard."

[8] Blessed are the poor in spirit, they that mourn, they which do hunger and thirst after righteousness, the merciful, the pure in heart, the peacemakers, and they which are persecuted for righteousness' sake.

That was for people who want something to cite and quote so they can pretend as though they read my codex.[175]

⁹ If you need something more to quote, here:

Judge not lest ye be judged. And may you build your house on the rock for the rains will come – with floods, winds – to beat on the sand castles. Is not the life more than meat and the body than raiment? I say unto you: lilies in the field don't work and toil. They let God provide. The fowls of the air work, but only slightly, for sometimes it can be hard to find, kill, and eat ample worms. And beware the false prophets, which come to you in a sheep's fleece, but inwardly they are ravening wolves. And know that if a blind man leads a blind man, I will push them both into a pit and then go to their gardens and pull up all of their plants by the roots. Concerning gardens, it is men who gather grapes of thorns, or figs of thistles. Just don't harvest your grapes *from* thorns, figs *from* thistles. Do bad trees issue good fruit? Probably not. Do good trees issue bad fruit? Maybe, but less often. It is corrupt trees that bring forth evil fruit. Their trunks should be hewn down and cast into the fire so fires may be home to those who serve other gods. For two men cannot serve two masters without hating one; no man may serve both God and Mammon. Humble thyself and you shall be exalted; exalt thyself and you shall be humbled. And if you leave the flock of ninety-nine sheep to find the one lost, then rejoice! Rejoice with me! For the lost sheep is found! But don't go hiding your talents in a hole in the ground. Or you'll be punished. Even if you worked hard to earn them, for even that is wicked and slothful. Invest them or else I will take from the poor and give to the rich, leaving the poor weeping and gnashing of teeth. And know that if you put leaven in things like bread or Heaven, and then wait to see what happens overnight, it gets big. Big like a kingdom.[176]

---

[175] I hate people who memorize a line – maybe a whole passage if they're ambitious – and recite it as evidence that they read something. This is how stupid people pretend to be literate. "Yeah, I read that." No, you didn't.
[176] This should be content enough to satisfy the quoters.

10 I hate people who put too much effort into "loving thy enemies" or "thy neighbor". When I was in my early thirties, I thought I was being clever. I thought lines like this made me seem deep. Now that I'm in my thousands, I realize how silly I must have sounded.

11 I hate people who pretend they're only capable of loving one person in the world. They bear love for their soul mates and none other, for they are not capable of divvying love among the many.

Weird. Are both of your parents alive? If so, do you only love one of them? Are you an only child? If not – if you're one of many – do you love only one sibling? Are you a parent to more than one child? If so, do you only love one of those children? After the first, you're no longer capable of issuing any love?

12 I hate people who pretend to love *everyone*. They just have so much love to go around, so much to give.

This is never believable.

The undiscriminating lovers just weren't loved enough themselves. And they're trying as hard as they can to compensate for that.

13 I hate people who think otherwise. People who think the love-everyones have bigger hearts than the rest of us. With massive, throbbing chambers that are just overflowing with affection.

They don't. They have tiny, shitty hearts with loose valves.

It's not that those hearts have so much blood to give; it's that they're unable to direct that blood to the proper destinations. Because they're defective.

14 In A.D. 2012, Fred Frank develops a more accurate approach to evaluate someone's worth in your life: the Jewish model.

A scenario is presented in which you'll soon have Nazis knocking on your door. Everyone you have ever known is a Jew. Which of them would you hide?

Do you have a close-ish friend who makes an obnoxious sniffing noise and doesn't seem to know he's doing it? One sniff and your life is over. Would you risk it?

If the answer is "yes", you don't understand the question. If you can think of more than eight people you would save, you really don't appreciate the stakes.

Unless you admit being an idiot, far too stupid to understand a very basic concept, don't pretend to love everyone. It's insulting. And nobody believes it. Not even the people you actually do love. They all think you're lying to them. Because how would they know the difference? When you treat them exactly as you treat those you wouldn't save, why would they trust anything you say?

[15] I hate people who assume that one's death is sufficient reason to celebrate one's life.

Lots of people (some of your enemies and most of your friends and neighbors) are terrible. They're horrible people.

Not only should they go through life unloved, but when they die, so should their obituaries be unloving. The sentences should be cold and factual. One should never lie just because death recently happened.

"Dale was born in Eugene, Oregon. He died in a hunting accident. He is survived by his wife, one son, and two daughters."

That's all that needs to be said. It should be a brief announcement. It should not pretend "he was a loving husband, a devoted friend, and always a father first."

In 2010, I read the obituary of a huge asshole. One of the worst people I've ever met.

It was a full page and it didn't say anything bad about him.

Even though it said the man's name, I was sure it was describing someone else. It must have been a typo. So I called one of the daughters who was listed as having been "survived by".

"Hey, did your dad just die?"

"Yes."

"Okay", I said, instead of saying something comforting but untrue, such as "I'm sorry to hear that."

This call should have been expected, given how misleading the obituary was. All it needed to say was his name, maybe a date, and "his wife will probably stop being hit now."

Instead, love. Paragraphs of it. And I hate every person who pretended to love here.

[16] I also hate people who pray specific prayers

Our Father which art in heaven, Hallowed be thy name.
Thy kingdom come, Thy will be done in earth, as it is in heaven.

Etc.

[17] I hate Tycho, who wrote the Gospel According to Mark.

He portrayed me as a woodworker[177] who, despite being the son of God, wasn't much of a leader.

"Don't tell anyone about my miracles!", I seemed to be pleading every time I performed one.

And that wish was apparently granted. I was hardly worshipped at all. I was just some misunderstood would-be preacher with a tiny audience.

---

[177] Vaguely. Given his word choice, it's possible he intended my trade to be stonemasonry.

¹⁸ I like Antigonus (who wrote Luke's account) much better.

He said that I had been worshipped since my infancy. True? Hardly, but it's much cooler.

¹⁹ Although Pankratios (who wrote the Gospel According to John) deserves much of the blame for the disappearance of this codex, his account is the one I like best.

Pankratios was the only one who wrote about my turning water into wine (chapter two), my raising of Lazarus (chapter eleven), my coinage of being "born again" (chapter three), etc.

My best stuff – all of my proudest moments – appeared exclusively in "John's" account.

According to "Mark", I refused to provide "signs". I'd perform my miracles in secret. In Pankratios' pages though, "signs" were the very reason I was doing them; I was performing miracles for the sole purpose of revealing my identity. "I'm the bread of life. Here, I'll prove it: watch me multiply these loaves."[178]

²⁰ I have no problem with Democritus (a.k.a. Matthew).

²¹ But I do hate people who are always trying to credit me with ethical maxims.

The "Golden Rule" for instance.

Confucius did all of his "golden" talking centuries before I did. And he certainly wasn't the first to do so. What's more, I didn't even do any notable updating to it, like Linus Pauling.[179]

---

[178] He also skips all the impending retributive kingdom stuff: "Jesus coming to right the wrongs." All of that nonsense. Instead, I'm coming to bring salvation. Just believe in me, like a Jewish Peter Pan, and that's all it takes.

[179] According to Pauling, one should "do unto others 20% better than you would expect them to do unto you, to correct for subjective error."

[22] But that's because I never wanted people to remember me for a bunch of fourth-rate platitudes, too many generations derived.

What I wanted people to remember was how much of a badass I was. I could have *wasted* Confucius in a cage match.

Despite that, everybody thinks I'm gentle, meek, and mild. And it's just because a few scallywags decided not to include gospels like Pseudo-Matthew and the First Gospel of Infancy in the canon.

Those gospels were demoted to the Apocrypha. So now I feel like a shoehorn-braggart whenever I bring up that phase of my life.

But I'm going to. I'm going to decorate my CV a little bit; give you a clearer portrait of how this miracle worker took care of business in his younger years.

In the Gospel of Pseudo-Matthew, chapter eighteen, as a mere baby, I stood face to face with dragons ("many dragons")... and those dragons backed the fuck down.

And then in the First Gospel of Infancy (also chapter eighteen), I disciplined a snake because it bit a boy. But I didn't discipline it like a Hufflepuff might. I'm a Parselmouth. I had a conversation with the snake. First, I made it go suck out the poison it left in the boy's leg. And then, as soon as it was done, I exploded it.

The Sorting Hat knows *exactly* where I belong.[180]

---

[180] I also killed some children. I'm not quite as proud of that though. In the Infancy Gospel of Thomas, I dehydrated one kid to death for splashing water with a stick (chapter three). And then later that day (chapter four), a kid bumped into me, so I murdered him too. I didn't feel like taking the time to dehydrate him – I was in a hurry – so I just used the Avada Kedavra Curse.

Chapter Twenty-Two

[1] I hate people who "see the best in others". "All life is valuable", they pretend.

It takes a lot of hard work and determination to reach that level of ignorance. No one is that obtuse naturally.

There are seven billion people in the world. And the majority of them are totally worthless.[181]

"Jesus, you're such a pessimist!"

No, I'm not. If the truth is bleak and terrifying, and I describe it accurately, that doesn't make me a pessimist; it makes me a realist.

I agree: it would be nice if all people were good, all life valuable. But I also think it would have been nice if Dad created unicorns. And you could summon one with a kazoo, climb on, and ride into outer space. And its horn was made of chocolate and you could lick it all the way to the moon. Awesome? Sure. But who cares? That doesn't make it true. And it's not pessimistic of me to notice.

Similarly, no one wants to hear a cancer diagnosis. "Jesus, you have cancer in your butthole", says my really fancy oncologist. Is that a sentence I want to be true? No. But it's one I have to accept. To deny it (or to pretend "all people are wonderful") is to deny reality for one's own security. It's how terrified people cope with a terrifying world.

As for me, instead of denying that truth as an effort to cope with it, I wrote a gospel about it. *This* gospel. And I hate the people who think its verses are pessimistic. And everyone who "believes in the good of others" because they're too afraid not to.

---

[181] They're a bunch of self-serving, self-centered, and self-obsessed assholes. From birth to death, they contribute nothing to the world. If you want evidence of this, just go to any site on the internet and browse the comments section.

[2] I hate people who have elderly conversations.

"Did you hear Walter down the street had a stroke? Do you think it had to do with his saccharine?" Or: "I heard they got a new projector down at the cinema."

[3] I hate people who spend every waking hour reminiscing about old times.[182]

When they're denied the opportunity to reminisce in this way, they have tantrums and people call them things like "grumpy".

All of this is sad and I can't help but hate everyone involved.

[4] I also hate people who say "conversate".

[5] And people who always need to be doing something, even if that something is not a productive or enjoyable experience.

"At least it's something, right?"

No.

[6] I hate people who talk about needing "me time" or "alone time" or "time out for myself" when they don't have a job. You're not allowed to "take a personal day" or talk about "down time" for "personal health" if you haven't worked more than sixty hours this week.

[7] Also, "I work so hard" is only ever declared by people who don't work hard at all. And "I've earned this vacation" says only that no vacation (or other such "reward") was "earned".[183]

---

[182] Often, this includes sentences like "God, it seems like it was just yesterday" or "I remember it like it was yesterday." Ouch. Evidence that you're a tired, old bore. And no one wants to hear your stories.

[183] Sometimes those rewards are things like cakes or milkshakes. In this case, the most rewarded people tend to be the most obese. Maybe you should try to focus on the journey a little bit more, fatty.

If you have any work ethic at all, the hardness of your effort is not a thought you're experiencing. And definitely not a one you're declaring.

[8] "I gave it 110%."

No, you gave it 50%. Tops. If you worked harder on this than anything in your whole life, then it might be as high as 75%. But if you're talking about how hard you worked, that means you put no more than 50% into it. Sorry.

[9] I hate anyone who always agrees with me.

[10] I hate anyone who never agrees with me.

[11] If you can't park very well, please limit your driving to nights and weekends. And realize that I don't like the cookies most people bake. So while you're staying home more often, don't bother making me cookies.

[12] Sometimes people have sex in cars. If these fornicators are past their teenage years, they're probably doing this because they have partners at home and can't afford (or hide the expense of) a hotel.

If you ask these people why they're cheating on their partners, the men and women will both blame men, but disfigure the truth in a different direction.

The woman will admit that she is not being appreciated at home.

The man will admit being a "sex addict".

To the woman: does this new ejaculate appreciate you more?

To the man: you're not a sex addict; you're a scumbag.

[13] Wes Craven loves bird watching. Loves it.

[14] Any man who has ever tried to pretend "blue balls" is a real phenomenon, or said he's taken a cold shower for any reason other than "we were out of hot water", is an embarrassment to the gender.

If you get aroused, and then you don't climax, your testicles don't turn blue and require cold water submersion. All that happens is your erection goes away.

Blue *vagina* is a real phenomenon though. It's called Chadwick's sign. But that has nothing to do with being denied a climax. Rather, it's evidence of a successful one (a couple months ago).

[15] I hate people with extremely harsh bangs cut straight across a forehead. Every time I give one of these people a chance by including them in my conversation, I'm punished with the most boring response the universe can imagine. It's way beyond *my* imagination. That's why I dared to engage them in the first place.

Boring is the one trait I can't tolerate. Murderers, tax-collectors, whatever. Happy to extend a cordial invitation to the celestial after-party. But boring people I just can't do. There's so much pain involved in their company.

[16] And none of them seems to be aware that gaps in conversation are common. So they get really nervous every time someone isn't speaking. And they treat that nervousness by asking me questions like "if you could be any kind of animal, what kind of animal would it be?" Or "what type of clothes do you like?"

[17] People who ask me about clothes are just as tedious as those who ask me this: "do you have any brothers and sisters?"

"Yeah, I have a brother. I doubt you'll ever meet him."

"Will you describe him to me anyway? What's he like?"

[18] Regarding "brothers" and "sisters", I hate people who have ever been a part of a fraternity or a sorority.

A special (secret unlockable bonus) degree of hatred for those members who have referred to a fellow member as a "brother" or a "sister".

"We're Greek."

Oh.

When I ask these people to explain the purpose of "Greek life" to me, I'm always given the same response. So I've decided to carry a buzzer with me everywhere I go. I pull it out when the subject comes up. And as soon as I hear the word "service", I sound it.

Sorry, brother, you lose. That's like comparing the other guy's politics to Nazis. The first mention of "service" nullifies your answer.

[19] Frats and sororities are always bad (always) but get *especially* bad when they start thinking of themselves as a fraternal order in possession of hidden teachings, unavailable to the uninitiated.

There's nothing any one of these people knows that isn't on Wikipedia.[184] And those who pretend the alternative is true are insufferable. You're humiliating all of your "brothers" and "sisters" with your make-believe. Stop it.

[20] I hate anyone who is really into any secret society. Not a guerilla insurgency that's trying to kill in secret. That's okay. It's the people who think Freemasons or the Illuminati are somehow interesting.[185]

I intervened to make Poland ban these things. You're welcome, Polish people forever.

---

[184] At least nothing worth knowing. Questions such as "how many hours did you sleep last night?" don't have answers that are worth knowing.
[185] Or "Skull and Bones" or any other embarrassing gathering of tomorrow's upper-middle class dunces.

[21] "Tell me something about yourself that you've never told anyone else" is not a way for two people to get to know each other better. It's just dumb.

[22] I hate anyone who calls poor people "cheap" or busy people "flaky".

[23] And I hate waitresses who call customers (or customers who call waitresses) "doll".

[24] And anyone who enjoys "people watching".

"Can I tell you my favorite place to do it?", they ask me.

"Is it at the airport?"

"How did you know?"

"Because everyone says that. And I get the impression that you're exactly as stupid as they are."

"Do you not like people watching?"

"As the actual purpose of an outing? No. And especially not at an airport, the most boring destination in the universe to examine one's neighbors. Go to an emergency room or a trauma center. Or a porn shop or a Klan meeting. A lot more to observe there. By comparison, the only thing you'll see at an airport is a bunch of people shuffling nervously while exhaling really rancid breath. There are few activities as punishing as 'people watching' in such a place."

[25] Worse than people watching is "long walks on the beach."

I hate anyone who has ever said this. Even if it was said in jest.

[26] And people who talk about a "pair of jeans" and a "little black dress" in the same sentence. Or in different sentences. Again, even in jest.

27 "Flying by the seat of his pants." Nobody flies by his pants.

28 "The whole nine yards."

29 "Déjà vu all over again."

30 "Déjà vu".

31 "Delicioso!"

32 "Long story short".

33 "About face".

34 "Say it to my face!"

35 "I just call them like I see them"

36 "Call it like it is."

37 "Butcher" as a verb to describe the poor pronunciation of someone's last name (or a French word or whatever else can be pronounced poorly).

38 "Pardon my French".

39 "Inner circle".

40 "Do me a solid".

41 "Psych" or "not" to mean "what I just said is untrue."

42 "Cum" (as in "did you read the pornographic adaptation of Jesus' gospel, *Here Cums the Son?*").

43 "Been there, done that."

44 Comparing anything to a "deer caught in the headlights".

[45] "Crash course".

[46] "Mouth breather" and "I vomited a little in my mouth." If you can't express yourself without stealing someone else's expression, just say nothing.

[47] "High as a kite", "smoke like a chimney", "running on fumes", "in the middle of nowhere", etc.

[48] Noticing that dog is god spelled backwards. Or that racecar is racecar. Or that Jesus is suseJ.

[49] "It's gonna get worse before it gets better."

[50] "Only in" any location ("only in Paris!" or "only in Texas!").

[51] "What happens in x, stays in x."

[52] "Award winning".

[53] "That's the beauty of it."

[54] "Independently wealthy".

[55] Any sentence that ends with "if you will."

[56] "Off the grid".

[57] "Modus operandi".

[58] "What goes around…"

[59] "Inasmuch".

[60] "Trifecta".

[61] "Game changer".

[62] "Life coach".

[63] "Out like a light".

[64] "She's sixty-five years young."

[65] "Invest in your heart health."

[66] "Firing on all cylinders".

[67] "Knock, knock."

[68] "Classic!"

[69] "Bat shit crazy".

[70] "Too much information" and its abbreviation.

[71] "11th hour".

[72] "Brainchild".

[73] "Let's not go there."

[74] "In all actuality".

[75] "It's 5:00 somewhere."

[76] "Done and done."

[77] "Douchebag" and its abbreviations (e.g., douche, d-bag).

[78] "Diarrhea of the mouth".

[79] "… said no one ever."

[80] "Hangry", unless you're the person who said it first and once.

[81] "That's just the cross I must bear."

[82] "The burbs".

[83] "Small world". Not the song, which is pretty bad too, but the response to a coincidence.

[84] "Peppered with" anything that isn't pepper.

[85] "Freelance" anything.

[86] "Buzzword".

[87] "Awkward" in a singsong voice.

[88] "Watergate" about anything remotely scandalous.

[89] Spreads (or otherwise behaves) "like wildfire."

[90] "You and whose army?"

[91] "Semper Fi." Special hatred for the chaser: "do or die!"

[92] "Ripped a new asshole." This has no meaning whatsoever. It doesn't mean anything to anyone.

[93] "A laundry list of…" Maybe you have a lot of chores to do. One of those chores might even be cleaning your linens. That doesn't mean you have a "laundry list of chores." People don't even have laundry lists of laundry.

[94] "Bucket list". This one is too stupid to even explain why.

[95] "You couldn't pay me enough to…" To go to a social outing with your boss? To eat that molding slice of pizza? To work at Del Taco? Really? There's no amount of money? If so, that's a profound lack of respect for the dollar.

[96] Every time I'm walking by a group of people and I hear one of them say something like "I can't wait to get mine on the road", I'm happy that I can keep walking. It's times like these that I'm most grateful I wasn't born with bilateral clubfoot.

[97] The "mine on the road" people are those who are most inclined to holler things about turn signals from a driver's seat. These sentences often end in "asshole!"

[98] I hate people who use a finger to express disapproval.

"He flipped me off" shouldn't mean anything to anyone.

"He flicked me off" should mean even less.

And "I gave him the bird" should only make sense in the context of avian acquisitions.

[99] I hate people who demand that distance be discussed in terms of time.

"How far away is it?"

"About an hour."

These people never demand consumption be discussed in the same terms:

"How much wine do you have left?"

"Five minutes."

Instead it's always something like "half a glass."

That doesn't give the same information, but apparently that's okay as long as that half a glass doesn't need to be traveled.

Chapter Twenty-Three

[1] In order of absolute worst to still really horrible: lover, soul mate, better half, life partner, partner, significant other.

Names like "snookums" or "honey biscuits" are usually worse.

[2] I hate fiancés.

[3] I hate people who say "popped the question."

[4] I hate people who shop for wedding rings.

If there's a family ring, something generational, okay. But if you're buying a new one, fusses and "big decisions" aren't allowed.

"Promise rings" aren't allowed either.

[5] I hate both people who form a couple in which, when the wife says something about embroidery, the husband responds with something about a hot water heater. Sometimes the husband initiates the conversation, but the sentences are still the same.

[6] I hate people who purchase birdseed from a home improvement store (Lowe's, Home Depot, Ace Hardware, etc.).

[7] And people who own more than one bottle of moisturizer.

[8] And people who say "moisturize". You mean moisten?

"Finalize". You mean finish?

"Materialize". You mean happen? Or maybe you mean appear, but you definitely don't mean "materialize".[186]

---

[186] "Dis" words are often just as bad as "ize" words. Consider "discontinue". You mean stop?

[9] I hate people who wear, purchase, or sniff cologne or perfume. Especially the people who rub scented magazine pages onto their necks.

[10] And people who wear shirts with writing (slogans, mottos, etc.) on them.

So far, "No Fear" is the best clothing brand ever incorporated. In the 1990s, they tricked people into paying money to wear these slogans:

"If you're not living on the edge, you're taking up too much space."

"Wherever the fear may be, look it in the eyes."

"The sky's not the limit. The ground is, so shut up and jump."

"One second could mean second."

"A man's gotta do what a man's gotta do."

"A champion is someone who gets up, even when he can't."

"Fear is in the eye of the beholder. Don't let it be you."

"Around you. Through you. Over you. Whatever it takes to get here.

"Dive deep... dive hard... fear nothing."

"Who said Sunday was a day to rest?"

By Sunday, I assume they mean the Sabbath. And in that case, my dad said that. See Exodus, chapter thirty-five, verse two:

"Six days shall work be done, but on the seventh day there shall be to you an holy day, a Sabbath of rest to the Lord: whosoever doeth work therein shall be put to death."

This explains many of No Fear's other slogans:

"Live free or die" and "evolve or die" and "death is nature's way of telling you to slow down" and "you do not greet death, you punch him in the throat repeatedly until he drags you away."

Punch Death in the throat? Sorry guys. But you're not going to be landing a lot of punches on your way out. You really ought to know your enemy. In this case, learn a little Judaism before you get in the ring. Then you'll know that it's actually *your* throat that's going to be taking the hit.

According to Moses (who fears "the cord of the Angel of Death"), you're probably going to be throttled. And that throttled throat is the route out of which Death yanks your soul (after throwing his drop of gall in your mouth).

You ain't gonna win this one with a t-shirt slogan. Sorry.

[11] Once "No Fear" died, "Tapout" took its place. This brand is exactly as stupid.

But when I see a grown man wearing a Tapout shirt, I don't tell him that. Instead, I say something like this: "Kenny Swedish!" And then I try to poke his lips with my thumb so that those lips press against his teeth really hard and swell up for a day or two.

[12] On the subject of "Tapout" and "No Fear" wearers, about a foot above the chest text is a mouth that routinely says "I'm gonna get *so* laid tonight."

This is not a sentence someone should say out loud. If you're among the someones who do this, you have a body that includes a penis that is about to penetrate a really unappealing vagina.

The only thing worth mentioning about your life henceforward is that you will sometimes use a leash to control your descendants at the park.

13 I hate people who accent the second syllable in party (par-*tay*) even if they're being facetious.[187]

14 And everyone who adds extra syllables to any word by pronouncing it through measured outbursts of laughter.

Worst: "Par-tay-hay-hay" (the last two syllables being laughter).

15 I hate anyone with a messiah beard. That was *my* idea! Mine! John Lennon stole it from *me*!

16 And I hate every man who deliberately grooms his facial hair. Especially if he's an "artist" or a "thinker". Your beard hair isn't an extension of your brain; it doesn't contribute to your artistic or cognitive faculties. All it does is make you uglier.

17 No better: people with "interesting" haircuts. Seems a self-consciously silly way to exhibit rebellion.

18 I hate people who find pleasure in carving meat. This includes people who argue over who gets to carve a Thanksgiving turkey. And a special case of hatred is reserved for people who have ever purchased an electric knife.[188]

19 It took me a while to hate sunglasses. They weren't supposed to be a bad invention. But that's what they became when people began to abuse them in the way that people abuse the internet for porn: they begin to occupy way too many situations.

This includes wearing them indoors, backwards, on the bill of a hat, at night, during seasons that aren't very sunny, and untraceable child pornography at the local public library.[189]

---

[187] "Day-uhm!"
[188] "Bzzzzzz" as the middle-aged man begins to feel much better about his life.
[189] Unless they're going to websites with funny names, like skinfant.com and the site is all about the naked skin of infants. Or kittyporn.com where it's babies molesting kittens.

[20] I hate high school kids. Always. Not just in pornography.

Actually, I hate everyone between the ages of zero and twenty-one.

[21] Also, I hate people who draw pictures of me. Not because of some nonsense about "graven images", but because I was a Middle Eastern Jew. My skin was darker than Aladdin's. But I'm always drawn to look like a sexy rock star from Kansas.

[22] Likewise, I hate people who aren't confused by the sight of a black Santa.

Skin color is a product of climate. If you're in a more northern climate, you need lighter skin to absorb enough vitamin D out of the limited sun rays. The farther north you are, the whiter you need to be. Santa lives in the North Pole. It doesn't get any more northern than that. So how could he possibly be black?

Unless he just got there – like he's a first generation resident who recently emigrated from Cameroon – he's white. Seriously white.

Either that or he'll have the worst case of rickets ever observed.

[23] I hate people who make three-dimensional art. There's nothing more hideous than contemporary sculpture.

Unfortunately these people never appear to be "starving artists". Unfortunate because they're the ones who I really want to starve. All the way to death.

[24] I also hate people (of any age) who can't draw but still try to draw the nose on a face.

I can almost tolerate the oblong circle mouth because it looks like what you'd do for a jack-o-lantern and I like Halloween. But please stop. Don't draw anymore. You've done enough.[190]

---

[190] Also, "hey kids, want some candy?" is only appropriate on October 31st. I've tried it in June, but never to the same effect.

25 There was a point when I hated Halloween.[191] I hated it a lot.

No matter how off I turned my porch lights, dozens of children dressed up like they had recently experienced a case of post-burial Lazarus syndrome (referring to themselves as "zombies") would still ring my doorbell.[192]

"Trick-or-treat", almost all of them would say while taking candy from me.[193]

The littlest Lazarus among them would usually have a parent standing five feet behind him, whispering loudly: "say thank you… say thank you to the man!"

It wasn't until those little kids grew into aren't-you-getting-a-little-too-old-for-this?-aged trick-or-treaters that I began to appreciate the holiday for what it actually is: a test. Halloween is an aptitude test for children who will soon be entering the job market.

Every trick-or-treating child is (presumably) unemployed. And those unemployed children are all given the opportunity to work for a single day. They're offered a four-hour shift (from 5:00 until 9:00 p.m.) to work as hard as they want. And each one of them is paid at an identical rate, based purely on the amount of work accomplished. Nobody is *forced* to participate, but the job is available to every child (and short adolescent) who wants it.

By 9:00 p.m., I'm able to identify (with near-certainty) every single prepubescent resident (within a twelve-block radius) whose postpubescent years will be fulfilling and successful.

---

[191] Only partly because of things like "apple bobbing", which is really stupid, generally humiliating, and always disgusting.

[192] Sometimes they were dressed as ghosts, or maybe a ninja or Mario, although I don't understand how ninjas and Mario honor the dead (the saints, the martyrs, and the faithful). As for the zombies, none of them could explain to me how they managed to Houdini themselves out of their coffins.

[193] Others would just reach into my supply and start taking, grabbing at the lot of it with unquenchable greed and impending diabetes.

My prediction is based solely on net Halloween candy collection weight (as a continuous variable).

After spending decades monitoring neighborhood children in this way, watching and following them as intimately as a child pornographer, I have come to appreciate Halloween as earth's best metric for future ambition and work ethic.

And thus I give to you the second pathway into Heaven.[194]

Every October 31st, at 9:00 p.m., I appoint the top 1% of the hardest working candy collectors into Heaven.

I don't deliberately kill them that same night, but if they happen to die of natural causes (choking on hard candy, diabetic coma, etc.), that child will skip lightly through the abyss of Purgatory and arrive – with the full warmth of my eternal embrace – into Heaven.

But he will be an employee. Heaven does not clean itself.

[26] Also, nobody is passing out poisoned candy to trick-or-treaters. Or razor blades. And I hate the hyper-paranoid parents who pretend urban legends like this "once happened to Charles' boy down the street" (or whatever). It's never happened. So you can stop putting Mounds bars in the waste basket because "it looks like it was tampered with." It looks that way because it was in a bowl that fifty other child-sized hands rummaged through violently.

[27] Sometimes child-sized hands belong to kids who participate in school plays. When addressing their parents after the performance, I'll say things like "that was great; so cute!"

But the reality is those kids are terrible actors. The *entire play* was painful and embarrassing. My "so cute!" compliments are no truer than when anyone says "that's a great question."

---

[194] The first path being the silent response of a "server" to a diner's announcement of a birthday; see chapter two, verse six.

[28] I hate parents who think their kids are good at things. The kids who succeed usually have neglectful parents.

Either that or they have psychotic parents who force them to participate in everything. And that leaves no time to brag.

[29] "Are you gonna eat that?"

Am I going to eat the food that's sitting on the plate of food in front of me? The plate that I'm currently eating off of? Yes, I plan on eating it. All of it. There won't be any left for you.

[30] I hate people who celebrate Saint Patrick 's Day. Unless they're celebrating the life and work of Billy Corgan.[195]

That's so much more dignified than a bunch of nonsense about some shamrock trinity. And tales about a man who banished snakes from a place than never had any snakes.[196]

Saint Patty's great accomplishment is a reptilian version of Lincoln's Emancipation Proclamation.[197]

[31] I hate people who celebrate Valentine's Day. This wasn't always as hideous as it now is. But February's duckling has grown into quite a swan.[198]

Also, everyone who receives a bouquet of flowers or a box of chocolates on this day is definitely being cheated on.

Sorry. Better luck next year.

---

[195] But referring to him as Saint Ligeia.

[196] The only reptile Patrick could have confronted is the Eurasian common lizard (or the "viviparous" lizard). And the reason it's still there is not because Patrick, feeling a bit more charitable than usual, decided to let it stay.

[197] The Emancipation Proclamation freed slaves in the free states, which means it didn't actually free slaves. What freed them was the Thirteenth Amendment. And, technically, this wasn't ratified in Mississippi until 1995.

[198] Ducklings are cute and harmless. Swans are bitter, violent beasts; ugly in all things but feather.

32 I hate people who celebrate the Fourth of July. Special hatred for those who call it "Independence Day".[199]

33 The rest of the holidays are just as much of an imposition upon my calendar. Including the Jewish holidays, like Hanukkah, which is just trying to compete with Christmas (little prepubescent Jews wanting a Bethlehem of their own).

34 And the people who attempt to establish themselves as "individuals" by adhering to obscure, imported customs need to be stopped. And then those customs need to be destroyed.

35 I hate people who refer to Washington (as in Washington, D.C.) as though it were a person.

"Washington needs to stop catering to special interests."

Or: "Washington needs to stop pandering to gun lobbyists."

Or: "Washington needs to cut its tax on…"

Or: "Washington needs to refocus on…"

Or: "Washington needs to win back trust with…"

---

[199] America's independence is declared on July second, 1776. The anniversary of this day is to be celebrated by igniting "fireworks" (i.e., cheap paper tubes filled with combustible materials that are made in China and, when lit on fire, emit sparks in the color of the Mexican flag). And then looking for lost dogs. Or, if you kept yours inside, cleaning up its pee. But people never celebrate the second; they celebrate the fourth. And this is weird because, throughout history, very little happens on the fourth. A few tedious political proceedings (none of which calls for any celebration). And then John Hancock masturbates onto the parchment (sullying the Declaration with his signature). Despite his regrettable behavior here, the fourth isn't the official signing date. That's August second. And the famous Philadelphia reading is July eighth. However, both Jefferson and Adams do die on July fourth (A.D. 1826). So maybe the celebration is in remembrance of their deaths? If so, combustibles feel like a bizarre ritual. Instead, you should just commemorate with chocolate eggs. Or perhaps the Valentine's Day chocolates you got in February, assuming you're single now.

[36] I hate people who buy metal detectors as an investment.

I don't hate them because of the purchase, but because of the other behaviors that these people always have. Just go work. Find a job.

[37] I hate people who find too much pleasure in camping.

[38] And people who, whenever camping (or otherwise confronted by wilderness) in a group or a pair, make that stupid joke about bears: "I only have to outrun you!"

[39] Most people who are religious have never once spoken directly to the lord of their faith. Not even just casually (e.g., "hey Lord, what type of clothes do you like?").

I know this because, throughout the entire history of mankind, I've only answered one prayer. One. A single prayer (which I will discuss later).

I feel bad for the people who keep praying despite this. The relentless in need. My sorrow for them exceeds my hatred. They clearly need help. And they're really reaching out for it. But reach somewhere else; I'm not interested.

[40] I don't like people who end their past tenses with a t. Learnt, spilt, etc. Because you have to be consistent. And that means you'll wind up saying things like "I soilt myself."

[41] I hate people who try to convince me something is delicious by using the words "yummy", "decadent", or "nougat".

[42] And people who call things "my famous", as in "my famous enchilada casserole" or "my famous teriyaki ham hocks" or "my famous fifty-five-layer roasted raisin bran bean dip".

Not only are these dishes never actually famous, but they never deserve to be.

[43] Restaurants that advertise a "famous" dish should always go out of business. I try my best to put them out in a timely fashion, but there are so many of them, it's hard to keep track.

I do the same thing to restaurants that bill their food as "authentic". Authentic Mexican food. Or authentic Italian food. Or worse: authentic Italian "cuisine".

[44] I hate people who drag me to places like The Cheesecake Factory. This is not a restaurant, it's a food dispensary.

[45] While at The Cheesecake Factory: "there are four of us; let's just split the bill four ways", says the person whom I hate.

Okay, hated person, all I had was a coffee. And I tried one bite of the first appetizer because I wanted to know if it tasted as bad as it looked and smelled. It did.

The bill has two *more* appetizers, three "specialties" dishes, two coffees (one mine; the one that wasn't a "caramel royale macchiato"), six beers, and four of those *Sex in the City* drinks with embarrassing names (e.g., "The Well-Mannered Dirty Martini").

It's a $162 bill.

That means my coffee is going to cost me $40.50 plus tip.

Is this why you insist that I go out to eat with you after I say "I just finished eating; I'm chewing my last bite right now" or "I hate The Cheesecake Factory"?

"Oh come on, it'll be fun", you assure me.

[46] I hate people who take pictures of their food. Nobody is interested. Nobody.

[47] And I hate people who refuse to eat something because of the date printed on its package.

[48] Also, I hate people who don't think that eating people is fine.

Not everyone needs to become dust or oil or a mummy.

Out of the three of those, I like mummies the best.

Mostly because they have such a comforting name.

Chapter Twenty-Four

[1] "Don't worry, my dog doesn't bite."

Your dog doesn't bite *you* because you're the owner. That has nothing to do with the probability of it biting *me*.

"Oh my god, what a shock! He never does that sort of thing!", when it bites me right away.

[2] Anyone with a "beware of dog" sign is advertising that a terrible purchase was made: a dog that barks at people and bites them and poops on the lawn.

[3] I hate people who try to pet seeing eye dogs.

[4] I hate people who try to show how unique and interesting they are by buying and then owning unique and interesting pets.[200]

[5] I hate people who own any pets at all. Especially cats.

If I were ever to volunteer ownership of a cat, two conditions would have to be met:

First, it would need to be able to pick up after itself *and* me.

Second, when someone is petting it, instead of purring, it would have to do that thing cats do when they're in danger, where they hiss really loudly. Not because it perceives the act of petting as a threat, but because that's just the sound it makes. It probably won't be able to talk, so the second best option would be hissing.

[6] I hate people who like the idea of "Secret Santa".

---

[200] "This is my spotted pigmy guinea ferret; it gave my sister monkey pox on Tuesday." Or, more commonly, "this is my boa constrictor. It ate my sister's lemming this weekend. The lemming's name was Avril de Souza. The funeral was on Sunday."

In a Secret Santa exchange, people buy, give, and get garbage decorated with the euphemism "stocking stuffers".

If you ask me to participate in this demeaning nonsense, I'm going to give you severed animal parts as gifts.

For your first gift, you'll unwrap a mongoose kidney. For your second gift, it might be all of the tendons, still bloody and wet, from a horse throat.

Do you still want to keep playing? The animal kingdom has a lot more to offer this holiday season.

[7] I hate people who claim to know what a dog is thinking by the way it cocks its head or perks its ears or wags its tail.

I watch these people talk to their dogs and detect a belief that the words are being understood.

[8] I hate people who talk about having "saved" or "rescued" a puppy. And then they put bumper stickers on their gas-conscious SUVs that say things like "who saved who?"[201]

I always think there will be a story here. A story that ends in either a pet or a person being saved.

Maybe Samantha or Meredith (or whatever the rescuer's name is) kidnap-saved the puppy from a rusty cage in Michael Vick's backyard. While Vick was inside, climaxing into an unconscious woman, Meredith sneaked onto his property, rattled the cage loose, and escaped with a giant, battered pit bull.

Or maybe Samantha is the kind of person who enjoys camping. And this Labor Day weekend, she's driving down Highway 89 (looking for a good campsite on the perimeter of Mount Shasta). And she sees an incredibly hairy Cocker Spaniel sitting on the McCloud River Railroad. "Did it lose its comb?" she wonders.

---

[201] The grammar is bad; the premise is worse.

And then she sees the steam. She sees it billowing out of the train's chimney as it rounds the corner, solo headlight shining, horn blasting, weird little bell chiming. And the dog doesn't move. "Run, goddammit, run!", she screams like River Phoenix. But the dog just sits there (as still as Ubu at the end of *Family Ties*). So she races over to it, only to discover that it's actually tied to the tracks. She immediately gets to work, trying to undue the knot, but it's tied too tightly. And the train isn't applying any brakes. It's going fifteen, maybe twenty miles per hour, and it's only tugging a few railcars, but that conductor isn't even throttling down. He's just honking things out of his way, life be damned. Now battling some serious panic, Samantha pulls out her camping cutlery and begins to saw through rope. She manages to carve all the way through it, severing it just in time. She grabs the hairy Spaniel, and together they leap from the tacks as the train roars by. Another pet rescued.

This is never the story. It's not what people mean by "rescue". 100% of the time, it turns out that what they rescued the puppy from was a life in which all of its basic needs were being totally met, but it wasn't often cuddled as *tightly* as it is now. Or the food it was being fed wasn't quite as expensive.

And what's worse, Samantha adopted the exact same puppy that Lindsey or Kathy or Elizabeth would have adopted. She didn't adopt the one who is nine, has three legs, is missing patches of hair, and sometimes bites.

But even if she adopted that one, that hardly meets the criteria to be considered a "rescue". You're not allowed to call your pet that unless you were out in the ocean when you spotted it, miles from land, bobbing in the waves. And you pulled it aboard with a tuna net and gave it CPR.

[9] I hate people who refer to their pets as their "kids".

"I've gotta get home so I can take the kids for a walk", they say.

And I refuse to excuse them for saying something that stupid.

I saw a lady crying today. She was upset because her twelve-year-old dog had died that morning. It was hit by a car. I had to announce its cause of death because if I didn't, one might assume it died of old age... at twelve.

This is the problem with pets. They're always dying. After which, the owners wait a couple months and then buy another one. And this behavior makes me question how much affection there ever was for the damn thing.

If a twelve-year-old human child dies in July, "I guess we should just have another one" isn't a thought that occurs to the parents in September. So when you refer to your dog as your "child", you're *seriously* kidding yourself.

[10] And there's no such thing as "dog heaven" either.

A) I don't have room. Read the bible: Heaven is finite. Revelation (chapter twenty-one) describes the dimensions pretty accurately. The geography enclosed by its walls is roughly 69% the size of Brazil. So Princess Isabel and Carmen Miranda and Pelé and Jimmy Hoffa and Blanka (and a great number of transatlantic slave owners) were all born into a larger nation. And despite what you think, it's not flocks of empty spirits floating around, occupying no space. The canonical heaven is a land of corporeal reconstitution. And it's already *really* overpopulated up here. I say "up" because, by your reference point, it *is* up. I'm up in the clouds. See Mark (chapter thirteen, verse twenty-six, and chapter fourteen, verse sixty-two). He wasn't lying. And I can't just keep building in that direction (up and up and up) because there's a ceiling at twelve thousand furlongs. So I'm trying to make the most of what I've got. Now some of you feel it's your civic duty to pressure me into expanding my real estate. I've heard your prayers and the answer is no. Because I've seen what you do to your cities. Especially in Arizona. And I think it's ugly. Heaven is not going to spill out into some celestial sprawl as a cheap attempt to liken it to Phoenix. My kingdom is surrounded by a wall that's a hundred and forty-four cubits thick. And your Reagan prayers will *not* be answered. So there's no room for your dead puppy.

B) Heaven isn't as nice as you think it is. And this shouldn't surprise you. Has anything with that much hype ever once been well-received? Anything in the universe? No.[202] Especially in this case: "here's your room; here's the cafeteria. Forever." One year into forever and you're going to be sick of the setup.

And C) even if I agreed to take over more geography and make it nicer, everyone except for the Mexicans would spend their entire afterlife complaining about pet dander and their damn allergies. I don't want to fucking hear about it. So dogs and cats just die. That's it. No more. You're not going to be reunited, so just go buy another one.

---

[202] See chapter twelve, verse thirty-one.

Chapter Twenty-Five

[1] Once upon a time, I walked down Glen Creek to the Roth's IGA in West Salem to get a money order. I needed it because PayPal hadn't been invented yet and I had recently used eBay to purchase an autographed photograph of Al Pacino playing the role of Michael Corleone.[203]

It came with a "certificate of authenticity".[204]

I hate females who don't shave their faces but need to do so.[205]

[2] I hate people who use the word "said" to reference something someone else is talking about.

Example: "does said money order have a particular value?"

A) Of course it does; certificates of authenticity aren't free.

B) I understand "said" is commonly used in that way, but that doesn't mean it *should* be. Because it hardly makes sense. So just use the word "the" like everybody else.

[3] I hate people who excuse their stupidity as "typos".

Typos are when there's an H instead of a Y. Or typing "our" instead of "out", of "or" instead or "of".[206] That's not the same thing as bad grammar.

[4] I hate people who need to show me something.

"No thanks", I say every single time.

---

[203] It wasn't for me. I hate both *The Godfather* and people who don't hate it.
[204] The seller referred to this document as a "CoA" and clearly printed it at home on his inkjet printer. It looked like he took a Denny's gift certificate template (featuring the Grand Slam menu) and barely edited it in Microsoft Paintbrush.
[205] This is because of the woman who sold me the money order.
[206] That last one was a typo, obviously. But it was a deliberate one.

"It'll only take a second", I'm assured, as if the duration of my investment is the reason I'm declining.

"That's okay."

"No, it's *really* funny."

"Yeah, but it's upstairs?"

"Yeah, c'mon. Just really quick. It's super funny."

"Even if it was more convenient – like in my lap right now – I still don't think I would find it funny."

"No, come on, you'll love it. It'll take like one minute."

I can't remember a time in which I succumbed to this pressure and was happy that I did.

[5] I hate people whose kitchens and dining rooms have glass door cabinetry and behind those glass doors are shelves filled with unusable "china".

Baby teacups, crystal goblets, collectible plates with paintings on them (each one of them facing outward on its own plate stand), pointless things made out of sterling silver, etc.

The next shelf might have porcelain dolls.

Go into any of the bathrooms in this house and you'll find at least one basket of seashells.

[6] I hate people who think astrology isn't stupid. Not just people who consult daily horoscopes for input on how to confront the day, but people who appreciate constellations.[207]

---

[207] Please don't try to tell me "that's astronomy; it's a science!"

See those three stars up there? You might think three points could only make a triangle, but those three make a lion. It's Leo Minor.

Roar!

And over there, Fornax: the triangle that becomes a furnace.

Or Pyxis. You can only see a couple stars, but it's a mariner's compass.

Over there, that small cluster of very few randomly scattered stars is a crab. Or maybe a boy carrying (and beginning to pour) a vessel of water.

[7] I hate people who refer to an imaginary talent as "the gift".

Sometimes it's a gift of healing powers. Like this: "I first became aware that I had the gift when I touched a leukemia patient's chest and he had a miraculous recovery."

Other times, people have "the gift" of psychic intuition. And they try really hard to never look surprised. Because if they were caught wearing a startled expression, that might betray the secret that they know less about the future than any gift-less chump.

[8] I hate people who "believe in themselves".

[9] I hate people who have nothing to say, but want to feel engaged, so they inject excitement into stupid sentences. Consider the following scene:

Courtney enters an occupied room while eating a bowl of rice.

"Whoa, Courtney, that's the first time I've seen you eat real food! Did you make that yourself?"

"Did I boil a bag of rice? Yeah."

[10] I hate people who say things like "at this juncture" or use the word "particular" when it adds nothing to the sentence.

[11] And people who say a word like "impricitry" and expect me to understand that what they mean is implicitly.

If you can't pronounce a word even close to what it's supposed to sound like, say something else. English has a lot of words to choose from.[208]

[12] Of all of the words available, there are only seven that must never be issued as an answer to any question, no matter what it is that's being asked.[209]

[13] I hate people who describe anything as "avant-garde".

[14] "Party pooper", "negative Nancy", and any other pejorative bit of alliteration. I hate people who say these things.

[15] And this: "I love you more than words can say."

No you don't. At best, you love me more than *you* can say with words. Don't blame language when the inadequacy belongs to you alone.

[16] Similarly, I hate people who use the expression "more than life itself" to describe how much they care about something.

Life is the reason people care about things. My dad designed natural selection to select only those who only care about things that promote life. This is not a debatable point. My dad swears it's true and science attests.

---

[208] I enjoy hearing non-native speakers say things like: "I do not know what it is you are meaning." Or: "it is raining and winding outside hard." Or: "my life is so borely lately." People who say sentences like this don't usually say "impricitry" in other sentences.
[209] "It came to me in a dream."

[17] "There's nothing like" cannot begin any sentence. For example: "there's nothing like a nighttime swim to clear the mind."

Yes, there is. There are millions of things that will clear your mind comparably.

[18] I hate people who say "beyond compare". Beyond compar*ison* you mean? Compare is a verb.[210]

[19] And people who say "this is all *YOUR* fault!"

Take some ownership of your actions.

[20] In A.D. 2013, I eavesdropped on a conversation between two young college girls. I heard one girl tell the other that she was "an underclassman", but "next year I'll be an upperclassman."

If it's upper, it should be lower. If under, it should be over.

"Classman" aside (dumb enough word to ignore), "grad" presents another problem: "I'm an undergrad."

Okay, then there should be an "overgrad". But there isn't.

[21] I hate people who attend "poetry slams" or read "slam poetry". Bad poems are not made good by louder, more animated readings.

[22] I hate people who appreciate bad poetry (which is nearly all poetry).

[23] When people who love poetry go through a rough patch, they usually try to conceal their grief by pretending the hardship is a blessing in disguise.

It's not though. It's just grief. And nothing but. It doesn't have a purpose or a perk.

---

[210] I blame Michael and Patty Silversher: "*bouncing here and there and everywhere; high adventure that's...*"

24 I hate people who talk about "summering" (or any other use of summer as a verb).

Example: "I summered in French Polynesia."

Worse: people who abbreviate the word "vacation", as in: "got my vaca coming up next month!"

Additional hatred for those whose "vaca" is at a waterpark.

And those who refer to tropical destinations as "escapes".

25 At this point, a latter day disciple (or a suspicious reader) may be wondering "why is Jesus so concerned with twenty-first century abuses of American English?"

Yes, it does seem strange that, having more than two millennia of earthly observation to criticize, I remain focused on a narrow span of time in the United States of America. But once the United States happened, that's where nearly all of my time was spent. And for good reason.

The rest of the world is nice. And on the whole, often nicer. The absolute worst of anything (food, lodging, etc.) in France or Japan or Italy is of average quality in the United States.

If you want your lowest class to really stoop, you're not going to find those stoop-able depths in the Belgiums of the world. The real pits can only be reached outside of the first world *or* in the U.S. But I have no interest in steerage. The abject life is not worth living. I want the best. I want the nicest. And the nicest in the U.S. beats the nicest everywhere else (or at least matches it). In beer, toilet paper, event entertainment, in everything.

Bad food in France may be average food in the U.S., but the best food of any country is no better than the best of that option in the U.S.

There's no country with wider margins of quality. And that's the part I like about it. That's where I find its charm. And why I spent the final centuries of my millennia there. And why so much of my gospel has been dedicated to it.

That's not to say that, once I had arrived, I never left the U.S. I did spend a fair number of years overseas (or otherwise "elsewhere"). But none of those elsewheres were sites of "Jesus spottings" (nor have I ever been legitimately "spotted" in the U.S.).[211]

In writing this gospel, I considered offering some commentary about those years. Notes on the Old World and about my experiences abroad, but what would those verses look like?

They would be a bunch of abusive observations aimed at belittling underprivileged "foreigners". Or ridiculing an Iron Age peasant. That seems like a terrible thing to do. And I wouldn't feel right in doing it. Making fun of the little guy – the impoverished, the struggling – is just mean-spirited. Mocking the tenants of a world power, though; that's satire.

23 Okay, my colon is full of feces and I have no interest in pooping my pants. It'll trickle down into my sandals and I don't want that. It always makes my feet itch. So I'm going to stop writing and go to the bathroom (yes, even Jesus has a colon).

I'd like it if you would take this time to plan my bachelor party. You can plan it right here. I've left the next page completely blank. That way you have plenty of room to draw up an outline.

---

[211] I've never been to Munster. I wasn't in Portugal in 1917 (and neither was my mom). I spent no part of the twentieth century in the Netherlands. I *was* in New York during the 1820s, but nowhere near Joe Smith, Jr. And definitely nowhere near Sunset Mountain in the 1960s, Jonestown in the 1970s, Japan in the 1980s or Waco in the 1990s. I can't be held accountable for "Potter Christ". I certainly wasn't "Walla Walla Jesus". And I've never committed myself to a grilled cheese sandwich. You've never heard a story about me (gospels aside) that's true in any way. Those who claim to have seen me haven't. Those who claim to know me don't.

Chapter Twenty-Six

[1] I made it to the bathroom in time.

Barely.

Now who wants to wipe my butt-ass?

Once I hit my thirties, it started to get pretty oily down there. So I thought it would be a flattering ritual if my apostles started anointing each other with my bung oil. They could mix it with mule's milk and smear it on each other's lips and nipples.

Nobody wanted to do that. So I sent them all to Hell.

[2] I hate everything about bachelor parties.

Everything.

[3] I also hate people with cell phones.

At first, I tried to kill every cell phone user with brain cancer. That seemed like the best strategy, but I had a hard time making it work. I was able to stir up some concern for a while, but when hardly anyone actually died, everyone lost interest in the threat.[212]

With no terrifying headlines (e.g., "phone cancer wipes out another third of America"), sales went "through the roof" (as they say).

The whole industry "took off". And I sat around for years, angry, trying to think of a new way to murder its customers, looking for a new angle, some little behavior or quality I could exploit.

---

[212] Everyone except for the lady with giant clown glasses behind the counter of Forever After Books in San Francisco. I managed to get her all worked up about it and she never lost that intensity. Not until the day she died of not-brain-cancer (which, as of the 2013 copyright of this book, hasn't happened yet).

[4] At first, I just noticed how loudly old people spoke into them: exactly twice the volume at which they spoke into regular phones. Perhaps they thought the technology was the same as tin cans and string (except that it relies on invisible machinery to accomplish that effect).

It wasn't until the "smart phone" was released that I came up with my next strategy.

[5] After the release of the smart phone, all users began to spend nearly every moment of life staring down into it.

Because they're often seated, holding those phones in their laps, this results in an anteriorly distorted posture (much more severe than that of any ordinary "shoe-gazer" or "naval-gazer").

I quickly realized that was my "in" and I started mutating people's necks. I began altering the natural curvatures of their spines, permanently bending them to accommodate the stresses and strains of their daily phone-gazing behavior.

Kyphosis (a pathological curvature at the neck-end of the spine) used to require something like arthritis or Scheuermann's disease to develop. Now, with just a tiny bit of divine intervening, I've been able to chronically deform millions of adolescent necks. I've been able to take their spines and bend them into the shape of candy canes.

And I've decided the proper coinage for this smart-phone-induced neck mutation is *iPhosis*.

You're welcome, consumers of the digital age.

While it might not be as lethal as brain cancer, I considered it debilitating enough to have accomplished what I set out to do, so I returned to my observations about general phone-using behavior.

[6] And I noticed that some people talk really loudly *all* of the time. Not just the old people.

It turns out most of these folks just have trouble hearing. That's why they shout. They think everyone else has the same problem.

I shouldn't hate them as much as I do because the batteries for hearing aids are more expensive than people think they are and they only last about three days. A couple weeks if you get the giant ones.

[7] Plus, some people who can hear just fine talk so quietly that I've never heard anything they've ever said. Not even their prayers.

People don't realize that I'm not a mind reader (at least not in the way they think I am). You have to actually say your prayers out loud. And if you whisper or mumble, I'm not going to hear you. You need to shout.

So, starting today, please make sure every one of your prayers is yelled with all the volume your lungs can muster. If they aren't, you can't blame me when I ignore them.

[8] I hate people who explain to me (whether in prayer or regular conversation) that their names are not pronounced in the way that they're spelled. Steven Segal for example. Steven is always praying complaints at me about how people pronounce his last name "seagull".

"It's not pronounced seagull; it's suh-*gahl*!", he always complains.

And he shout-prays those complaints loudly enough that I actually hear them.

But I don't respond. Not to him anyway. Instead I just shake my head and whisper to myself. I whisper something like this:

"Nonsense, Steve. It's seagull. Your last name is seagull."

And then I divinely intervene so that he's an even worse actor.

Asking that I pronounce his name suh-*gahl* would be like Courtney deciding that the C in his name is soft, as it is in certain and celery. And that the OU is pronounced as it is in sour and loud. And the EY is pronounced as it is in convey. So, spelling it phonetically, Courtney becomes Sour-t-nay.

Is Courtney that stupid?

No, Courtney is not as stupid as Steven Seagull.

And if little Stevie Parakeet is going to keep insisting that his name is suh-gahl, then I will begin insisting that, instead of Christ, my suffix is now Blason. But it's *spelled* like Chorchor. It's just *pronounced* Blason.

And don't you mess it up because I snap at everyone who pronounces it phonetically (i.e., "Jesus Chorchor").

I snap like the devil himself because deep down I know they're completely right and I'm completely wrong.

[9] When Steven Segal is in a restaurant (or any other location in which he's able to buy something), he orders that thing like this:

"I'll have…", followed by the item he wants.

Please don't ever request anything this way. Ask a question. Don't make a statement about what someone must give you. If you ever do this a single time, I'm going to hate you for your whole life.

And then, when that life is over, I'll have you die a soulless and complete death (like your dog that I killed for fun that one time).

[10] I hate people who have said "dry humor" more than once.

[11] I hate people who have said "dark humor" more than zero times.

[12] And people who say "over the top", as in "Jesus, don't you think that's a little over the top?"[213]

[13] Worse: people who say "timing is everything" about anything.[214]

Timing is almost nothing. Let me illustrate the unimportance of timing with an example:

"Courtney, I signed you up to compete in this biathlon."

"What? I don't know how to ski; I tried to learn once and it didn't work."

"Yeah, but the timing is *perfect*."

"But I've never even shot a gun before."

"That doesn't matter, because timing is everything!"[215]

[14] I hate people who ask me to shoot them if some specific condition ever occurs.

"If I ever buy a Ford, I want you to shoot me", or whatever.

Within two years, I'll have shot this person in the stomach with a whaling harpoon.

Immediately he starts screaming for help.

This confuses me because I was asked to do this.

---

[213] It's okay to say "over the top" if you're talking about Sylvester Stallone arm wrestling to win an estranged son's love.

[214] These people are usually trying to excuse a failure: "the timing wasn't right." Or they're trying to justify their urgency: "if we don't invest now, we'll miss our window of opportunity; the timing is everything!"

[215] Or maybe it's an archery tournament: "but I don't even know how to hold the bow." "That doesn't matter, because timing is everything!"

And I wasn't given *any* instruction about what to use or how or where to shoot.

15 I hate people who say "be careful what you wish for."

16 And I hate people who, when asked "what did you wish for?", say "it won't come true if I tell you!"

Liar. You're just too embarrassed to tell me.

The same principle applies to people who say "it's a long story."

It's not. I guarantee it's not. You just don't want to tell it.

17 The people who say these things are the ones who find the most pleasure in going to the beach.216 Not for sex (which we discussed earlier), but for "platonic" pleasure.217

18 The only thing I really hate about people who love the beach in this way is that they always talk about that floating thing in the water, referring to it as a boo-eee. That floating thing in the water is called a buoy, which is the first half of the word buoyant.

19 When I correct them, they respond with one of two excuses:

Either: "sorry, pronunciations aren't my strong suit."

Or: "pronunciations aren't my forte."

Neither of these is an acceptable response.

The former because "strong suit" must never be said. The latter because they add a second syllable to "forte", making it rhyme with "sorbet". And that means they're going to be playing their music more loudly.

---

216 And they're also the ones who are the most afraid of elevators.

217 I hate people who describe anything – including Plato – as "platonic".

[20] Something a lot of people do if they don't have bright futures is this: not work hard to become good at something, but then struggle to win at it while other people are watching.[218]

Let me give you an example: ping pong. Never practice once, and then – upon losing – throw your tiny, solid wood racket in anger. Those rackets are really compact and hard and it hurts when I get hit in the chest by one. Never do that again, Brian.

[21] Whenever someone has a temper tantrum, I've found it's best to treat that person as though he's wearing a cowboy hat: "are you having a hissy fit? It looks like you need some juice. Can I get you a juice box?"

[22] Brian will take me up on my offer. Connor won't. But Connor isn't the racket-throwing type. Instead, he can be found issuing the personal accountability excuse. You didn't beat him; he beat himself. "Man, I played *terribly*!", he might say. And then he'll continue: "I just kept messing up on the backhand." Or maybe: "I don't know why I can't hit the ball today."

His loss has nothing to do with your win. The fact that you're a way better player doesn't make him lose. Only Connor can make Connor lose.

[23] One time, Connor bought a teddy bear for his girlfriend. One of those huge ones. It was about the size of a teenage black bear.

Connor's girlfriend got a warm feeling. She got a warm feeling just knowing that $130 was spent to purchase an item that cost less than a dollar to make by the bare hands of a little foreign child who's probably dead.

[24] The people who get warm feelings like this sleep at least twice as much as Courtney does. And they don't have hypertension.

---

[218] I also hate people who make a competition out of every noncompetitive activity, like eating lunch the fastest. And then they approach it as though it's a sport, but with no sportsmanship.

I fail to see how this is fair. So I commit them to Hell.

Problem solved.

[25] More females than males are forced by their own impulses to make serious looking facial expressions at themselves in mirrors around the house. I don't have any data to know whether these people are more or less likely to be obese.

[26] "It's Deb's birthday on Friday. There's a money pool to get her a present. Just a few dollars so we can get her a gift certificate to the spa by her house."

"Who's deb?"

"The secretary. There's a card in the kitchenette for you to sign too."

"Didn't I just give you five dollars like two weeks ago?"

"That was secretary day. This is for her birthday."

"Look, I don't even know Deb. Every month someone asks me to chip into some pool to buy someone some gift certificate. And to sign a card. And I never know the person, which is why it would be an insult if I signed the card, if I pretended we were buds and wrote a friendly message. Plus, I hate the entire idea of cards that someone else created. Giving group gifts to people is a cheap, insensitive, and impersonal way to show that you don't really care. And I care even less, so no. I'm not playing."

[27] I hate people who give their spouses homemade coupon books as gifts. "Redeem this coupon for one free thirty-minute backrub." Or: "redeem this coupon for one free blowjob."

[28] I hate married couples who expect their anniversaries to be celebrated by more than two people. If you're into polygamy or *really* into pastrami, then I get it. But otherwise, I'm sorry. No one else cares about the landmarks of your relationship.

[29] Simon's mother-in-law had a fever. I fixed it. That was a while ago though.

[30] You know slot cars? When Courtney was little, he used to play with them. He would press the little gun trigger and make the cars loop around all six feet of their track for hours. The scraping noise annoyed him immediately but the smell took about ten minutes to get going.

I've never met anyone who sounds like a scraping slot car, but once in a while, I'll find someone who smells like one. A person who smells like burning wires. And I hate him.

[31] Other people permanently smell like steam rooms and saunas because those are things they use way too much.

These "naturalists" aren't afraid to ask me to massage them.

No thanks. I'm not the type of person who's overwhelmed with joy when it's sunny out, like you. So I don't want to massage your neck and shoulders while you moan and say things like "yeah… right there."

[32] It's an entirely different set of slobs who think that a couple of beers and a twelve-piece bucket of mini-mall rotisserie-style chicken is a pleasant way to spend an afternoon.

I have a fantasy in which I pick one of these men and interject a little miracle into his life.

We'll call him Hank Sims.

On Christmas day (again, not *really* my birthday, but I've taken to celebrating it as such), Hank Sims is scheduled for a bypass surgery. That morning, while he's on the gurney, just moments before his surgery, his heart stops.

And there's nothing the doctors can do.

But some poor cardiac resident (we'll call him Sidney) decides his Christmas wish is to resuscitate Mr. Sims. So he *really* begins to apply himself.

After fifteen exhausting minutes of Sidney laboring over Mr. Sims' dead chest, the attending physician initiates that over-dramatic scene that occurs at least five times in every medical miniseries:

"Sidney, time of death."

Sidney doesn't stop.

"Sidney!"

Still Sidney struggles to resuscitate Mr. Sims' ugly corpse.

"SIDNEY! TIME OF DEATH!"

Sidney looks up, defeat in his eyes, and then staggers out of the operating room.

"Mission accomplished", I whisper to myself.

[31] Sidney will then quit medicine and become a writer. And the first thing he writes will be Mr. Sims's obituary. In it, he'll write about what Mr. Sims and his wife thought of as sexual intercourse: fisting, but instead of using fists, they used five highlighters that were all taped together.

It's very healing.

Chapter Twenty-Seven

[1] I hate people.[219]

---

[219] Especially the "finest" among them (Boston's finest, Brooklyn's finest, etc.). Wherever you go, that place's "finest" will be a bunch of middle-aged cops.

Chapter Twenty-Eight

[1] I appreciate "bake sales for a good cause" exactly as much as I appreciate kittens. I will withhold my urge to set them on fire, but that's the extent of my compassion.

But I do hate people who are not impartial to bake sales and kittens.

[2] And I hate Ozzie Osbourne. His music was great; I approve of the tongue-in-cheek Satanism. What I hate is what he did to the entertainment industry.

When millions of viewers watched him mumble about how he forgot to feed his dog (or whatever), other celebrities saw an opportunity: "I could do nothing on television too!" And this changed Western Civilization.

[3] Braveheart was wonderful, but I still hate Mel Gibson. Mostly because he won't stop making such a huge fuss about me. I'm usually comforted by people's affection, but what Mel is doing is just fucking creepy.

[4] But I also hate the people who thought that Mel Gibson needed to apologize after his anti-Semitic outbursts ("*it's not okay to call Jews 'Hebes' or refer to the holocaust as 'horseshit'; you need to apologize!*").

Mel should not have apologized. About any of it. What he said in his rants was a) really, really funny (perhaps not all on purpose)[220], and b) what he truly believes. That's him.

The apology is just a formality to appease hypersensitive people. He didn't *mean* it. He *meant* his rants.

---

[220] "Jews are responsible for all the wars in the world!", etc.

It would take an astonishing fool to be duped by "I didn't mean it."
Or to think that he very suddenly changed his very extreme mind.

Everyone seems to behave as though "on the one hand" actually
applies to people.[221] And they demand that the other hand is
revealed. But there are no cards in that one. And we already
know the *exact* hand Mel is playing with. What more do you
want?

"Show me what's in your other hand!"

"Nothing is in that hand, obviously. But I'm happy to make
something up. How about you just tell me exactly what you
want to see and we'll pretend that's exactly what I'm holding?"

"Okay, deal. Thank you for doing that. Now I feel comforted."

⁵ I hate Pat Robertson.[222]

⁶ I hate people who find meaning in national flags (instead of just
viewing them as really ugly pieces of fabric).[223]

The worst of these people find themselves inspired when a man
holds a giant flag on a tiny pole and rides a horse around in a barn-
sized circle as fast as he can (his flag whipping in the wind) while
his country's national anthem is being played.

Or they break out in goose bumps when, following a major athletic
achievement, the victorious athlete ceremoniously wraps himself in
his country's cloth.

---

[221] Not just to Mel, but anyone. Anyone at all.

[222] Sober Pat quotations sound like drunken Mel quotations. "Just like what
Nazi Germany did to the Jews, so liberal America is now doing to the
evangelical Christians." He goes on to say it's "more terrible than anything
suffered by any minority in history." You tell 'em, Pat!

[223] Though I do admire the versatility of the fashion. People in suits on Capitol
Hill wear a lapel pin version of it. People in rodeos and monster truck rallies
get the stars and stripes printed on their denim jackets. It's an unusual crossing
of party lines.

Imagine going to anything other than the Olympics (or a rodeo) and draping yourself in a flag.

Go to the dentist.

Go to a piano recital.

Or go to a parent-teacher conference.

Sit down and whirl a giant flag around your body.

Somehow this wouldn't feel appropriate.

[7] I hate people who talk about the arches of their feet: "I have high arches", says the painfully boring person with very ordinary feet.

[8] I hate people who wear leg and ankle braces. Or even just Ace bandages. None of these things is worn because of a real injury. Please don't pretend otherwise.

[9] I hate people who, while feeling pain or discomfort, announce that they're feeling pain or discomfort.

"My knee hurts."

When I ask "is there something I can do with that information?", they become upset at my lack of sympathy.

[10] I hate people who play (or enjoy watching) American Football. I find it exactly as interesting as hopscotch. And just as funny too. Except that so many women are raped.

[11] One time, someone tried to argue that not *every* high school football player is a date rapist. He went on to assert that many of them "are not getting their comeuppance."

Ouch. Comeuppance is a seriously embarrassing word.

[12] I hate people who refer to a sports team they don't currently own, coach, or play for as "we" or "us".

For example: "big win last night! I didn't think we were going to pull it off until Rapemaster's interception. Beautiful. I tell you that kid is taking us straight to the Super Bowl."

[13] This kind of talk is the white man's equivalent of referring to an entire race or ethnicity as "us".

The people who do that are attempting to smuggle their own opinions and values into the positions of people they've never met and know almost nothing about.

The worst of these types talk about long-vanished atrocities like slavery. In doing so, they're hoping to induct themselves into the system on grounds of ancestry (i.e., "kinduction").

Okay, anonymous twenty-first century mixed race person who is trying to create an interesting identity for himself, I'm sorry that some of your relatives (on the darker half of your family tree a few lifetimes ago) were owned by British people with weird teeth and Americans who had recently been British people with weird teeth. But "us slaves" is ridiculous. You can't even name four people who were marginalized in that way.

"Jesus Christ, you're being a racist!"[224]

---

[224] I used to be a *total* racist and completely pro-slavery, but that was an inherited prejudice. Growing up in my dad's house, it was tough to be progressive about that sort of thing. Although in Exodus, chapter twenty-one, my dad *did* forbid people from beating their slaves to *death*. And too much damage to the eyes and teeth was frowned upon too. Disabling them for a *couple* days was okay though. That could be thought of as sport (of a kind). But the typical slave beating shouldn't go *too* far beyond that. That's the message of compassion I inherited. I just didn't talk about it very often pre-crucifixion, so the authors of *my* testament didn't have much to go on. Had I been more vocal about it back then, the gospels wouldn't have strayed too far from Dad's position. But since then, He and I have grown apart. It just took me a while. I didn't repudiate slavery until the nineteenth century. Not long after Darwin did.

Am I? Are you *sure*?

Are you *sure* that human enslavement and African-American racism are the same thing?

"Yes!"

Okay. Maybe you're right. And if you are, I apologize. Truly. But this feels an awful lot like weeping over 9-11 (see chapter four, verse two).

Is the history of slavery a disgusting one? Yes, hideous.

Were you there? No.

Do you know anyone who was? No.

But even if you *were* there (or did know someone who was), far worse conditions of suffering and bondage don't seem to upset you at all. Not even a little bit. You're unfazed by these stories. Even when they're about slavery specifically.

If that weren't the case, you'd care just as much (or at least express *some* concern) about Babylonian slaves. But I don't see the Code of Hammurabi giving you any chills. And you don't appear to be all that upset about Sumerian slavery (otherwise I would have heard your complaints about the Code of Ur-Nammu).[225]

You're not troubled by the history of enslavement in Egypt, in India, in Assyria, in China, in Greece, in Rome, etc.[226]

---

[225] This is a code with laws like: "if a man proceeded by force, and deflowered the virgin female slave of another man, that man must pay five shekels of silver." And: "if a man's slave-woman, comparing herself to her mistress, speaks insolently to her, her mouth shall be scoured with one quart of salt."

[226] The Romans were enslaving entire (European and Mediterranean) populations. Jews, Arabs, Germans, Greeks, Slavs, etc. It wasn't that long before my first human birth that slaves composed about a quarter of the Roman population. How come this doesn't seem to ruffle any of your moral feathers?

And it doesn't bother you when it's the Vikings capturing a bunch of English, Irish, and Scottish chaps (and lady folk) and posting them for sale in Islamic and Byzantine slave markets.

Or the Barbary pirates capturing any Christians they could find along the European coasts (a million or so between the sixteenth and nineteenth centuries).

Or how about the first slave trade in Spain, in which the Moors were importing Spanish and East European Christians (from the eighth century until late in the sixteenth). Any pain there?

"Nope."

What about when the Turks were enslaving the Ukrainians (hundreds of thousands of them). Do you perceive that as a problem?

"Nope, no problem there."

Does it disturb you to know that the Hawaiian kauwa (i.e., slaves) were being used for human sacrifices?

"No, not really."

Romanian enslavement of the Roma (i.e. Gypsies)?

"No, that's fine."

Do you celebrate William the Conqueror's effort to halt the exportation of English slaves (a small step toward the larger leap of abolition)?

"Nah."

Do the Soviet Gulag camps bother you at all?

"Can't say that they do."

Do ten whole centuries of slavery in Muslim countries fail to excite?

"Yup."

It's just here in America?

"You got it. Land of the free."

And you're not bothered by any instance of slavery anywhere on either American continent *prior* to the European colonization?

"Nope."

And the enslavement of the Native Americans is fine too?

"Yup. None of that matters. *My* ancestors, whose names I don't even know, are all that matter."

That's fucked up. That's *really* fucked up.

All of the suffering and cruelty that doesn't apply to the "us" with whom you most closely identify is permissible?

"Uh huh."

And the "us" in reference is strictly the roster of captives bought and sold in the Atlantic slave trade. The ones who were shipped to the Americas (nearly half of whom came from the Angolan coast). Those are the only slaves that matter?

"Those be the ones."

And the demographic that deserves the *greatest* share of blame for this is a bunch of recently-British men in powdered wigs who had really severe lice?

"Damn right!"

So it doesn't matter to you that almost 40% of the slaves taken aboard those ships went to Brazil (compared to the roughly 6% who are taken to the U.S.)?

"Fuck them. Who cares about Brazil? I don't have any Brazilians in my family tree."

Huh.

It seems weird to base your identity on the injustice of an institution that was predominantly a pipeline from Angola to Brazil, but not allocate the predominance of your respect to Angolans who worked themselves to death in Brazil.

I guess I'm failing to see where these two stories get tied together. The story of your indignation and the story of actual world history. I'm failing to understand how your beliefs about retributive justice map onto reality, how they scale with the crimes.

How does your behavior (when pretending to be a victim yourself) honor those Brazilian slaves? Or those in Babylonia or Sumer or Egypt or India or Rome or anywhere else in the world at any other moment in history?

Any time someone feels constrained to specify an exceedingly narrow direction in which he is not an asshole (e.g., "I'm opposed to 6% of the transatlantic slave trade"), the implication that gets made – and the only impression left – is that he's a gigantic, rotten asshole in practically all other directions (see chapter two, verse eight).[227]

---

[227] And I hate people who say "you're being offensive" as though that sort of admittance doubles as an argument. As though it addresses some point I've made. It's not an argument and it addresses no point. If you want to join the debate, you need to be able to explain where my argument is wrong. And to do so, you need evidence. And not *just* evidence, but an ability to articulate *how* that evidence supports a system of reasoning. Otherwise, "that's offensive" is just another way of saying "I lose" or "your points are better than mine."

Slavery is a terrible institution. We all agree (now). You will be pained to find someone who doesn't. Someone who doesn't regard it as a brutal system in which millions of people of all races and cultures were horribly dehumanized for millennia.

So it seems silly (and perhaps worse than silly) when a twenty-first century, mixed-race, middle-class American attempts to garner the sympathy of those tortured lives without having actually *lived* one of them. Or, apparently, even knowing anything about a single person who did.

So instead of referring to entire populations of people whose lives were defined by tragedy as "us", why don't you just go make something of your *own* life?

You may very well be a victim of *racism* (especially if you live in the South), and people who harbor that sort of bigotry are gross, but you're not a victim of *enslavement*. That's not the same thing. That's not an "us" you can talk about and be taken seriously.

More than a hundred thousand people die every year from measles. This rashy virus produces about eighteen funerals per hour. But I don't hear people who have never had the measles talking about "us" measles sufferers.

Maybe they should. At least that would be more relevant, more current. Much less of a chronological stretch.

[14] Let's move on: I hate people who are chronically early.

Sometimes I say 10:00 and mean it.

[15] Also, just because you show up early every time doesn't mean I'm eager to hear your advice about something you're bad at.

[16] Even more than that is the amount of hatred I have for people who try to launder their advice, pretending it's just a conversation.

Let me be more specific: I hate people who ask me to change something by asking me if it's what I'm doing.

"Are you wearing those pants?"

Well, they seem to be on my legs, so…

[17] This doesn't happen anymore, but when Dilger had his stroke at age twenty, there was a guy who contributed to the *Statesman Journal* who wrote about fishing almost every single day. These were horrible articles. Horrible.

I really hate people who can't write but still pursue "I'm a writer" as a career. Every one of them has a "work in progress" memoir with a "working title" they call "Confessions of a…" something.

The world is a worse place because they were born. A lot worse.

[18] I also hate anyone who has ever watched a fishing show that wasn't *Jaws*.

Actually *participating* in fishing is okay, although one must admit that the purpose isn't to catch fish. You can do that a grocery store (and the fish you catch there are already in Saran Wrap). But showing up at a lake and swinging a pole around. That kind of fishing can be excused as an exercise in "nature appreciation". And I don't hate the people who do that.

But spending an afternoon watching *other people* appreciate nature is not okay. That's just killing time.

My dad gave each person a finite amount of time to be alive.

And there's nothing that offends Him more than watching you kill that time.

Nothing.

Chapter Twenty-Nine

(Chapter Twenty-Nine has not been translated yet.)

Chapter Thirty

[1] I hate Oprah.

There, I said it.

Perhaps (in the interest of promoting sales and avoiding litigation), this verse would be better skipped. But I can't do that. Instead, let it be known that Jesus Christ hates Oprah Winfrey.

Because of this:

Every time I've finished Easter egg hunting my way through the grocery store, seeking every can, box, and carton containing a Nickelodeon-orange "reduced for quick sale" sticker, I see her.

While I'm transferring those dented and expired items onto the conveyer belt, a glossy photograph of Oprah is smiling in my direction.

"Here I am", she seems to be saying.

Here I am close up. Here I am farther away. Here I am seated. Here I am standing. Here I am with my hands on my giant hips. Here I am dressed in gold. Here I am in fall fashion. Here I am with big hair. Here I am wearing a size four. Here I am wearing a size thirty-four.

She's never actually doing anything. She's just there.

Martha Stewart stars on the cover of her magazine too, but at least she occasionally incorporates a verb.

Here's Martha icing a cake she didn't bake. Here's Martha pretending to beat eggs. Here's Martha in a vegetable garden. Maybe she isn't driving a trowel into the dirt, but at least she's holding a potted plant, looking like she has a verb in mind.

Martha is preoccupied. She isn't staring at me, smiling condescendingly while my dented cans don't scan properly.

And surrounding Oprah's condescension are cover lines asking me questions like "what's *really* healthy?"

I'm supposed to open up to a specific page to find out, but instead, I just get angry.

On another page might be a list of "guilt free snacks". I doubt any of those snacks have their nutrition labels patched over with orange price tags.

No matter what she says[228], she seems to be talking down to me.

Among those "tweets" of condescension, she might be explaining how to "make your own luck" so you can "eat better, live happier". Or maybe she's asking me about my "true calling" or offering "unexpected ways to become happier" or instructing me how to "transform" my body or my love life.[229] It's usually about a body. And sometimes it will come with a list: "10 simple things you can do for your body this season". Other times, Oprah will have recently lost a thousand pounds and she'll be telling me to "imagine the ideal you" or something about conquering food cravings or any number of "how to" explanations (e.g., "how to improve with age", "how to inspire the best in you", etc.).

On other covers, Oprah will have spent the previous month eating like a hog, but maintain the snobbery with lines about loving your thousand pound body just the way it is ("let your true self shine" or some such).

While pondering the question Oprah has asked me on the cover of the current issue (something like "who are you meant to be?"), I'm interrupted: "sir?"

---

[228] Even when it's a solicitation for teamwork: "let's get creative!"
[229] If it's about my love life, there might be a subheading of "what it takes to build intimacy" or "love you can bank on".

The cashier is interrupting my silent conversation with Oprah.

"Sir, this is just a wrapper; there's no food in it."

"Oh, sorry. I ate that. I was starving when I got here. Just scan it and then throw it in the trash."

"Okay, your total will be $26.41."

I scan my card.

"Is that credit or debit?"

"Debit", I say as I give Oprah one last look and decide that she probably doesn't mean any harm. And I resolve to permit her into Heaven if she starts behaving more like Ricki Lake[230] and less like Cal Ripken.[231]

---

[230] At least *try* to keep the weight fluctuations to yourself.
[231] Let the streak go. Not every magazine cover needs show you doing nothing (pompously) in my direction. Pick up a trowel for the next issue. Incorporate a verb.

Chapter Thirty-One

[1] I hate people who think I'm on the verge of making a comeback. A ferocious one, all fiery-eyed, banging an apocalyptic gavel.[232]

"Jesus is coming!", shouts the cleanly shaven pastor, the stinky homeless person, and the Harold Campings of the world. And every one of them shouts it with a threatening tone, as if to say "Jesus is coming... to sentence *you* to the unquenchable fire!"

But that's not really how it works. If it was – if I was planning on making that kind of a comeback – you would think they'd start to wonder why I haven't done it yet.

It's the imminence of the belief that baffles me; "Jesus is coming back *any minute now*" is what they're really saying. And saying it with real conviction. Practically every Christian who has ever considered my return (from Paul to Harold Camping) has done so with the optimism that I would be returning *during* his lifetime.[233]

A) It's a little bit conceited to think that *your* lifetime should be the phase that welcomes the return of H. W. Christ.

And B) every single person who has ever held this belief has gotten it wrong. Not one person has ever been right. Not once. So why does this seem like a reasonable thing to believe in?

I can assure you that it isn't. It's not a reasonable belief.

Given the facts, "Jesus isn't coming" is the only bankable wager. But nobody wants to hear that. What people want to hear is encouragement.

---

[232] Sometimes I'm pictured as a shepherd, dividing the sheep from the goats. Other times I'm a farmer with a holy winnowing fork, separating the grain from the chaff. Over here on my right, the righteous. And on my left, the wicked.
[233] I actually did promise my witnesses that I'd be returning during *their* lifetimes. And every one of them was *very* dead by the time the Harold Camping was born. So why would Harold be expecting me?

"No, no, it's okay! Don't feel downhearted. I'm sure he's still coming. He's probably just stuck in traffic. But he's definitely on his way. Jesus will be here soon. He didn't forget about you!"

Really, though, I'm not coming. At least not in that way.

To paraphrase a lyric by Shalom Hanoch (i.e., the "King of Israeli Rock"), if Jesus is going to be *this* late, you think he would have at least called by now.

It's clever. I can appreciate the joke. I'm not so rigid and petty that I can't find humor in a well-placed punch line. And I hate people who think that I can't, the people who think taking my name "in vain" is a damnable sin.[234] That's a little bit accusatory. I feel like you're implying that I'm that petty.[235]

What these people are failing to appreciate is that I actually came back regularly.

From the time I was crucified (i.e., from the time I "did the cross"; I like to refer to it as though it's a dance move) until well into the twenty-first century, there was hardly a Jesus-less decade.

Nobody noticed me because I never made a big scene – splashing around as a monster of the apocalypse – but I popped in and out of the lifecycle for over two thousand years. I've been a Chad, I've been a Felix. I even ghostwrote a couple of the Pauline Epistles.

"How, Jesus?"

Good question, my young disciple. And the answer to that good question is: a miracle.

---

[234] That's a bunch of Old Testament anger; Exodus and Leviticus and Ezekiel. I had nothing to do with that testament. And it's a serious stretch if you think I implied any name-vain while "on the Mount".

[235] Ephesians is in *my* testament. And if you read chapter five, verse four, you'll notice that it only prohibits foolish talk and course joking if that talk and those jokes are out of place. And obviously a little bit of jest (of the "in vain" variety) is not out of holy bounds.

Not all of my miracles are as stupid as the miracle of killing hogs[236] or hiding a temple tax in a fish's mouth.[237]

The problem is: none of my miracles are actually "miracles".

Like any good magician, I work in mysterious ways until the mysteries unravel. To explain any trick is to strip it of its magic.

But however much I would enjoy keeping all of my magic intact (by saying "every time a baby is born through the miracle of parthenogenesis, that's me"), stopping there would cheat my reader out of the full story. It would just be too naughty of me to write this entire gospel without including at least one portion where I "tell all". That seems to be what one does in this literary form.

Like this: "Love Boat captain Gavin MacLeod welcomes you aboard as he tells all in his new memoir, *This Is Your Captain Speaking.*"

Or like this: "Mike Tyson pulls no punches, exposing his undisputed soul, in brand new tell-all autobiography."

Or like this: "John Edwards' mistress Lisa Jo Druck tells all in poorly-written memoir nobody will ever read; it's so bad it's not even worth naming."[238]

---

[236] The Miracle of the Gadarene Swine. All I did was drown a bunch of pigs in the Sea of Galilee. When people came over and saw all of the dead pigs floating in the water, they started inventing "miraculous" reasons why I did it.

[237] The rest of my miracles were just a bunch of healings (stuff that would have healed on its own anyway), a few exorcisms, and then some antics that were largely plagiarized. Things like walking on water and calming the seas (which were lifted straight from Poseidon and his sons). Most of that stuff I didn't actually do. But I did change water into wine. And I wish people made a bigger fuss about it. That and the bread thing. Those were really hard tricks to pull off.

[238] Rielle Hunter involuntarily decided to go by her birth name, Lisa Jo Druck (like when The Rock went back to Dwayne Johnson, except he *chose* to do that). I couldn't get far enough into Druck's book to know if she talked about how her dad used to electrocute horses to death. On purpose. She did say that John looked like "someone that I used to show horses with" ("with whom" you mean?), but she didn't use that to segue into horse murder (equinicide).

Or in my case: "Son of Man tells all – major miracles and sultry secrets revealed – in juicy new codex."

In my effort to "tell all", I've decided to bring closure to a few ongoing debates and to reveal some long-concealed secrets.

As for the resolving of debates, I'll settle the dispute over my parents' hometown, the discrepant genealogies to which I've been assigned, the timing of my crucifixion (and whether I dined at my famous supper), and how my divine judgment will be delivered.

We'll begin with my parents' hometown.

In the Gospel According to Luke, it's said to be Nazareth. In the Gospel According to Matthew, it's Bethlehem.

Obviously Luke's account is the correct one. My parents were from Nazareth. The Bethlehem thing was just invented to make me look better. Whenever disagreements like this are found, it means one of the writers has made something up. And if someone is going to be making up details about me, why would the invented account be undignified? Fictions will always scale the respect up, not down. Thus, Matthew's account was lying for my benefit (and I'm grateful for that); Luke's account was merely being honest.

The gospels of Luke and Matthew also have different genealogies.

Matthew traces me (technically he traces my non-biological dad) all the way back to Abraham (weaving through King David en route). Even my ancestry has appointed me "King of the Jews". In Luke's account, my non-biological paternity is traced all the way back to Adam and Eve. Ignoring the convergence at David, the names are different at every step, beginning with my grandfather (and his dad, etc.). So which account is correct?

Neither.

Neither one of them is even close.

Excepting Joseph himself, not a single name on either list is accurate. But one can hardly expect the alternative. The people who wrote those lists did so half a century after my crucifixion. They never met me – certainly never met Joseph – and they had no documentation of any kind (no birth or health records, etc.). And I didn't even know my grandfather's name back then. He died before I was born. My grandmother, Eudoxia, was still alive, but they were never married. And not only was she not a Jew, but she had eleven kids, no more than two from any one father.

Moving onto the timing of my crucifixion: in John's account, I died during the afternoon before the Passover meal. According to Matthew, Mark, and Luke, I had that meal and was then crucified the following morning.

Although I usually like John's account the best, he's wrong here. I totally overate at the supper. And the meal hadn't fully digested when the "Holy Lance" hit my guts. The Roman soldier (whose name wasn't really Longinus) got a serious surprise on his spear.

Lastly, the mode of my judgment.

According to Luke (chapter twenty-one, verses twenty-seven and twenty-eight), Matthew (chapter twenty-four, verses twenty-nine and thirty as well as chapter twenty six, verse sixty-four), and Daniel (chapter seven, verses thirteen and fourteen) the Son of Man will come on the clouds, judgment in tow.

It might have been more apt to suggest: "Son of Man will bring His judgment on the clouds of twenty-first century literature." Because this is the extent of it. This gospel is all there is. It's the rubric by which all humanity will be judged. So read it carefully and obey it diligently.

Now, with all of the major inconsistencies settled, it's time for the big secret: how I resurrect myself through the "miracle of parthenogenesis". This: parthenogenesis happens when the Holy Grail is deposited into a fertile human female. The Holy Grail isn't a cup; it's a parasite.

Although Isaac Asimov (in his *Book of Facts*) says mosquitoes have forty-seven teeth, really they just drink blood through big tubes in their faces. And while I was up on the cross, a dozen or so mosquitoes put their tubes into me. I couldn't very well swat them because my stigmata were too fresh; they still had nails in them. So each of those mosquitos got a last supper of its own. And my blood used a reverse transcription mechanism[239] to transcribe the "Grail Gene" (which isn't a single gene, but a large cluster of them) into the genomes of those dining arthropods.

---

[239] This gets a little bit tricky, but every person has a genome (a collection of genes containing the recipe to build that person). Your genome is a bit like a chef charged with the task of baking a cake. Except, instead of a cake, your genes build the hunk of biology that is you. And those genes are made up of strands of DNA (that thing that looks like a twisted ladder; the "double helix"). Your DNA is housed in the nucleus of your cells. And those cells are always dividing, making copies of themselves. So your DNA is constantly replicating. If it ever stops replicating, that means you're dead. To perform this replication, the double helix is unzipped into two distinct strands – two DNA templates. Then some enzymes reconstitute full DNA strands from each of those individual strands. This is DNA replication. One strand becomes two. But that's not how the "cake" is baked; that's just how your DNA replicates itself. The creation of all of the proteins that constitute the meat that is you occurs through a process called "transcription". Here, the DNA ladder unzips and one of those two strands is used as a template to create a strand of "messenger RNA". The mRNA then leaves the nucleus of the cell and heads to little protein-building factories called "ribosomes". Once in a ribosome, these messenger RNA strands lend themselves to the creation of the amino acids that form the proteins that form you (with the help of "transfer RNA" molecules that are also in the ribosomes). So "transcription" is the creation of RNA from the templates of DNA strands ("translation" is the translation of that RNA into the actual amino acids). "*Reverse* transcription" is the reverse of transcription. Instead of making RNA from DNA templates, a reverse transcriptase enzyme reads the coding of a single strand of RNA and then creates a single strand of DNA based on that. And then, once the first strand is done, it synthesizes the second to complete the double helix, incorporating itself into the host's DNA. HIV is the most well-known example of a reverse-transcribing RNA virus (in which a reverse transcriptase enzyme enables RNA to be transcribed into DNA, which then gets replicated by normal transcription – regular DNA polymerase enzymes). Without the reverse transcriptase enzyme, HIV would not be able to incorporate itself into the host's genome (and without the reverse transcriptase gene, there would be no reverse transcriptase enzyme). Like HIV, the Grail Gene uses this mechanism to sneak into the back door of the host's genome.

Among the genes that were reverse transcribed into the mosquito genomes was telomerease. This is the primary "anti-aging" gene (and one of three major "self-preservation" genes) in the cluster, which prevents the mosquitos from dying of natural causes.[240]

Having eternal life etched into their genomes, these arthropod apostles survive into the twenty-first century, where they come to be known as the "Grail Bearers".

The full "Grail" cluster carried by these mosquitos contains more than a hundred genes in total, each of which performs a different function in the body of the infected female (though many of them are simply "accessory genes" carrying out regulatory roles).

The passing of the Holy Grail from one of these Grail Bearers to a fertile female is what triggers the biological phenomena that result in parthenogenesis. And the baby born of this fertilization is me. Every time.

But never once will it be me filled with vengeance, eyes ablaze, apocalyptic gavel at the ready.

---

[240] The telomerease gene is the gene that makes the telomerease enzyme. And the telomerease enzyme is the enzyme that repairs telomeres. And telomeres are the odometers of a cell (except that they count down rather than up). Each cell's genetic engine is born with a very specific engine life; a specific number of achievable miles. And every time a cell replicates, it marks another mile off of that lifespan. Telomerease sort of "resets" the genetic odometer so that cells can go on replicating without that engine ever deteriorating. That button on your dashboard that resets your trip odometer back to zero? That's telomerase. But it affects more than the dash. The whole engine is affected. Perhaps a better way to imagine the telomere is to liken it to the aglet at the end of a shoelace (the aglet being that little plastic cap). Let's say every time you tie your shoes, a hundredth of a centimeter of that aglet gets lopped off. Tie your shoes a hundred times and you've lost a full centimeter. If you keep tying them, you'll eventually run out of aglet. At that point, you'll find that the lace itself begins to fray. That's almost exactly what happens to genes when they replicate. They have an aglet (telomere) at the end and a tiny bit of that telomere gets lopped off every time the cell replicates. Until you eventually run out of telomere and the gene itself begins to deteriorate. Telomerease keeps that aglet shiny and new.

Chapter Thirty-Two

[1] I hate people who say "at large". Or even worse: "writ large".

[2] And people who say "blew his brains out."

How many brains did he have? Even if he had a bunch, I doubt any of them actually came out. I bet a bullet just went in.

[3] I also hate people who say "you get what you pay for."

Okay, maybe if you're buying oatmeal by the pound. But you're not buying food in bulk; you're buying sunglasses. And they cost $300. And you're trying to justify that terrible purchase with the only cliché that's almost never true.

[4] On food: I've eaten but never enjoyed bulk lasagna. And I hate people who try to serve it to me.

"Come to this fundraiser; there's gonna be free food."

"What kind of free food?"

"It's catered."

"Does that mean lasagna in a giant aluminum pan with a candle burning underneath it?"

"Well, yeah, lasagna is the main course, but…"

"No thanks. Free isn't a synonym of desirable. If the fundraiser were offering me free tree sticks and popped balloons, I would not be rushing to arrive. Bulk lasagna is no more appealing to me."

[5] I hate people who go to (or throw) themed parties. Especially if the themes have the hosts serving "floats".

[6] I hate people who peel oranges, carefully preserving the peel in one mangled-but-wholly-connected piece, and then feel compelled to show it to me.

"Hey, look!", shouts the person who just finished peeling his orange.

"At what? What am I looking at?"

"At this. Look at this!"

"At your orange peel?"

"Yeah, look at it!"

"Why?"

"Because I got it off in one piece."

"Okay. Why is that interesting? I bet you take your pants off in one piece too, but somehow you don't feel the need to show me every time that happens."

[7] I hate people who use the word "marathon" to mean something other than a 26.2 mile race.

Marathon does not mean a lot of something. Or a long time.

"Marathon work shift" doesn't make sense unless you were working in the medical booth, giving people bananas and Gatorade, making sure their body temperatures didn't get too high.

I can't think of a context in which "movie marathon" makes sense or isn't depressing.

[8] I've never seen a Facebook post and thought "oh, that really changes my outlook on things."

Friendster, MySpace, Facebook, Twitter, Instagram, MyFace, FaceSpace, InstaFace, whatever. They're all the same. It takes a serious buffoon to think one of them is unique or otherwise special.

[9] People don't usually post this on a social networking site, but sometimes in private, women complain about not being able to fit into their old wedding dresses.

I hate women who complain about not being able to fit into their wedding dresses when they've been married for ages.

Why do you need to get into it? What are you going to use it for? Do you not have any clean pants? I don't care how dirty the rest of your clothes are, digging an outfit out of your hamper is still a better option than getting into an old, giant, flowing gown.

[10] Much more importantly, I wish – at least on phones – people would avoid talking in their "cultural" tongues.

Excluding foreign accents, sex is the only characteristic I should be able to identify over a phone. If you were born in the United States, I should not be able to tell your race, sexual preference, or socioeconomic status.

This verse was inspired by a phone call I received from a woman named Keshia. Either the education system has let this woman down or she made a conscious decision to talk like an obnoxious stereotype.

Talking like a regular, literate person is not that hard.

There's no biological difference that allows me to talk in that way and prohibits Keshia from doing so.

When I told this woman (whose race, sexual preference, and economic status I had fully identified) that she had a wrong number, she said "fine" in the way that her stereotype says "fine".

¹¹ With homosexual men, the voicing is equally obnoxious.²⁴¹

It's not the gayness itself; that part is usually adorable. Even in my testament days, I never hated gay people as much as people think I did.²⁴² To me, the only obnoxious part is that I can tell that the person is gay over the *phone*. And I shouldn't be able to do this.

I know his parents didn't talk to him with that tone and accent. I know his teachers and peers didn't. So there's no environmental influence exerting any force here. And I know it's not biological either. There's no gene that makes gay people stretch vowels and hiss (some dormant gene that gets upregulated only after publically exiting the "proverbial" closet).²⁴³

The voicing is a decision. And it's one that should embarrass just a little bit.²⁴⁴

Courtney has a friend (an ex-girlfriend's son) who is both black and gay. When Courtney talks to him on the phone, can he tell? Of course not. The kid is a Harvard student.²⁴⁵ He's not an idiot. So when he's on the phone, he just talks like a smart person.

He should probably be Keshia's role model.

---

²⁴¹ Also, when I hear someone with a lisp – not because of a cleft palate, but because it's a male attracted to males – I can sometimes predict when he's going to say the word "puppetry". I'm pretty good at guessing.
²⁴² Leviticus predated me (I had nothing to do with that testament) and Paul is the author of both Romans and First Corinthians. I'm not responsible for either. I definitely wasn't *pro*-gay back then, but I didn't carry the degree of opposition people accuse me of. And I did eventually arrive at a pro-gay position (and did beat Dick Cheney to it).
²⁴³ I hate people who refer to everything figurative as "proverbial". Proverbial means it's derived from a proverb. And I know of no proverb about closets and sexual orientation.
²⁴⁴ With the only exception being David Sedaris. During the morning in which the earth gets consumed by its sun, I'll release the official all-time rankings of "best narrator produced by the species". Spoiler alert: Sedaris is going to win. But I'll have you know that it's taken an awful lot of miracle working to keep the cancer out of his lungs.
²⁴⁵ At the time of this codex's publication (its virgin print).

[12] I hate people who misdial and get my number. Not because they accidentally dialed my number, but because of what they say when they find out:

"Hello?"

"Hi, is this John Cervantes?"

"No, you have a wrong number."

"Is this (860) 794-8162?"

"Yes. That's the wrong number you dialed."

"Okay. This is the number I have listed; do you know a John Cervantes?"

"Oh, yeah. Of course. He's my best friend. He got a new phone, but I took his old number."

"Can you please give me that number, sir?"

"No, I was kidding. Of course I don't know who John Cervantes is. Why would I know him? I bought a phone and they gave me a number at random."

The call goes on for several more sentences, during which I try to explain to my caller how the phone industry works.

My explanation fails to educate.

[13] The less competent someone is, the less *in*competent they're aware of being. It takes a certain amount of intelligence to be made aware of one's deficits.

For this reason, the actual subjects of this gospel are unlikely to understand its message. Some of them, I realize, are very nice people. But "nice" is just another word for wrong and stupid.

[14] Usually, when people say or do nice things, what they're *really* thinking is: "I wish people liked me as a person." But people don't. Nobody does. People just ride razor scooters around the avenue and spit when they swallow a bug. That's all anybody does. And not one of them is going to like you "as a person".

Some people (such as whores and teachers) will *pretend* to like you, but that's just because it's their job. They're getting paid to make you *think* you're appreciated. They don't *actually* appreciate you any more than I appreciate them, which is to say: very little.

[15] One time, Courtney Jensen was sitting in a class with a bunch of nice people who were all "appreciated" by a professor. We'll call this professor Linder Picadillow. At the end of that lecture, Linder said this: "that's just the tip of the iceberg."

She then began a several-minute explanation of what she meant by the expression "tip of the iceberg."

It's people like this who have inspired me to write this gospel.

[16] When I decided to do so, I set out to describe every fault of humanity. Every single reason validating Victor Hugo's claim that Dad made man during a fit of misanthropy.

And I meant to offer these verses as literary bootstraps.

I intended them to be a source that my followers could use to hoist themselves out of the tragedy of the human condition.

But the hour is late. I need to meet Paul on the road to Damascus.

It seems strange: for thirty lives of men I walked this earth and now I only have time for one more chapter.

So you should know that the reasons I've provided in this gospel are just the tip of the cliché.

Chapter Thirty-Three

[1] I hate everyone who was either confused by something I said in this codex or somehow felt menaced by it.

Anyone who gets offended by anything at all is probably someone I hate, but especially those who have taken offense to these verses.

[2] Actually, I hate the concept of taking offense.

People only take offense with things they find uncomfortable because they worry those things might be true.

If I tell you, for instance, that your religion was concocted by a pedophilic psychopath pretending to speak "Ancient Egyptian" while bedding scores of nubile babes, you get offended. Why? Because I just might have a point.

If, conversely, I insist that your mom is terrified of pigeon feathers, no matter how loudly and obstinately, you merely get bored.

[3] I hate people who think that "hate" is a "strong word".

Hate is not a strong word. It's a lazy word. One that often fails to capture the true feeling. That true feeling tends not to be "hatred", but frustration. Usually with ourselves.

[4] There *is* one hatred that exceeds all others, however. A feeling that penetrates the full depth of my integrity; the mother and father of all abhorrence.

And that is the hatred I bear for intolerant people.

There is no sin graver, no sentiment more punishable, than intolerance. Like use of the word "leadership", intolerance is one of only nine irrepentable sins.

Perhaps this seems a strange thesis, considering how the holy books whence I came are just reams of life-crushing intolerance. And the verses in this gospel do not seem a notable departure.

"How can such a position be reconciled with the mountains of hatred that precede it?", one might (reasonably) ask. And I will answer that question, my dear reader, with a parable (the type of prose for which I am, after all, best known).

[5] This is a story about the only prayer I have ever answered.

It is called *The Parable of the Answered Prayer*.

There were three high school boys. There was a Courtney, there was a Dilger, and there was a Pseudo-Solomon.

Two of these boys were born into wealth. And the third boy had a girl's name.

As high schoolers, Courtney and Dilger built a friendship. But the two of them remained impartial to Pseudo-Solomon. They did not like, dislike, or even think of him.

In the years after high school, Courtney and Dilger forgot all about Pseudo-Solomon. And as those years marched on, even Courtney and Dilger began to grow apart, losing their touch but not their ties.

And it came to pass that Courtney met a girl named Princess Paris.

He abandoned his friends and began to romance her with all of the passion and ingenuity he could. He painted her pictures, he sang her songs, and picked her bouquets of flowers.

But did she reciprocate his pictures, songs, and flowers with cuddles, gummy bears, and Starbucks gift cards?

No.

Instead, she belittled his attempts in contrast to those of her previous paramour.

And yay she regaled Courtney daily, even hourly with the exploits of this past love. She sang of the greatness of his house, his automobiles, his business, his money, of the many flavors of his earthly success.

She described these things as though they had been earned through heroic tribulations. As though the man's whole life, and each of the decorations that hung upon it, had been gathered from nothing, taken from the dirt and sculpted (like how Muslims say my dad made humanity from a clot of congealed blood).

When it was revealed that her latest suitor was Pseudo-Solomon (the very Pseudo-Solomon who had been forgotten years before), Courtney at once knew these tales of success to be false.

Pseudo-Solomon's fortune had been given to him, not earned. His house. His automobiles. Even his business. His wealth was just a pond of inheritance. And his witless greed would soon evaporate its abundance. Eventually the fertile pond would be but a baron, sun-parched pit, drained of its riches through Pseudo-Solomon's incompetence. Or so Courtney took solace in convincing himself.

Yet Princess Paris still saw these riches as a sign of Pseudo-Solomon's celestial value.

Courtney, who had no house, no car, no business, and no money, grew bitter.

And lo he wallowed in the valley of despair, burdened by the knowledge that he would never possess such earthly treasures. Courtney saw the gap between him and Pseudo-Solomon as un-crossable. Superiority was the birthright of the wealthy. They were the Ferraris, Lamborghinis, and Bugattis. Courtney was just a Hyundai. With work, perhaps he could become a Prius.

His indignation grew. And he watered it. He watered it with vinegar and bile. And as the roots of his bitterness coiled tightly, its trunk grew knotted, its branches thin and bare.

And still he nursed and nurtured his gnarled garden. And it felt like justice as the fetid kudzu consumed everything in its path, eventually sprawling into a jungle of hatred.

And this hatred prompted a prayer. And he shouted that prayer so that I would hear him.

In a booming televangelist voice, he beseeched me to smite Pseudo-Solomon, preferably with a painful strike to the pelvis.

This was not the prayer I answered.

After a period of silence, Courtney tried again, this time asking me a question (though still shouting): "Jesus, why do I want to see Pseudo-Solomon smitten so badly, preferably by a savage and painful strike to the pelvis?"

This is the only prayer I have ever answered.

The "mysterious way" in which I provided that answer was to use Dilger as an instrument.

Soon after Courtney finished his prayer, he received a letter from Dilger. The letter said things like "hey" and "I haven't talked to you in a while" and "are you going to be in town for the holidays?"

Courtney was unmoved by the content, but he noticed something: why did he not hate Dilger?

Dilger was born into comparable privilege. The house, the cars, the catalog of shimmering decorations hung upon an unearned life of riches and comfort. So why was Courtney so fond of him? Why had Courtney so long admired him?

Courtney began to realize that the difference was in the way that Dilger presented himself, the way he took no credit. The moment he suspected someone might be admiring his wealth, he readily would admit "none of this is mine; my dad just bought it for me." Dilger often announced this before his potential admirers had even noticed.

And therein, Courtney realized, lay the difference.

This hatred was not a principled one, the condemnation of a system that prohibits economic mobility. For Courtney knew that a Hilton or a Gates child would not be maintaining the family fortune any longer than Pseudo-Solomon would. One has enough fingers to count the generations before it's gone.

Courtney looked at his fingers as he held Dilger's letter and realized his hatred was about sexual selection. Nothing more.

Like a stuffed peacock, Pseudo-Solomon's resplendent plumage wasn't real. Its elaborate kaleidoscope of feathers – the glinting rainbows that had provoked Courtney's jealousy and Princess Paris's envy – had merely been glued on and painted. But they worked. Sexual opportunity still tumbled favorably toward him.

As soon as Courtney recognized this – as soon as he had identified the real cause of his indignation – the feeling started to dissolve. It began to seem so petty, hating someone for trying to get laid. Such a petty and pointless direction to misspend one's emotions.

No wrong was righted. Pseudo-Solomon's counterfeiting continued to pay dividends and Princess Paris still waxed on. But the power to afflict had vanished. For once an aversion is understood, it loses its ability to harm.

We suffer emotionally as we do physically. It is not the skinned knee itself that causes us pain; it's the panic that really hurts.

If you understand that much, you've made progress in life.

[6] After Courtney had completed the dissection of his hatred, he put down Dilger's letter and wrote one of his own to Fred. A letter describing how his new understanding of hatred had quelled his increasing desire to murder.

Fred wrote back:

I appreciate the murder sentiment. Remember, people's repugnance is really the only subject there is. I'm starting to think that it's what makes them sympathetic too. My hope is that the latter (loving people because of, not in spite of, their worthlessness and utter lack of appeal) will somehow make me a grown-up. Maybe even a good writer. Chew on that for a while.

Upon reading these words, Courtney's hatred all but vanished. Though he did resolve to maintain a very small amount. Only because Pseudo-Solomon lacked the decency to hate himself. Somebody had to do it. But the fire in that feeling had been extinguished. And in its extinguishing, Courtney learned a valuable lesson. This:

We all have heated moments (just ask Mel Gibson). These aren't the problem though. And rarely do they define us. It's the feelings we keep during the quiet moments of self-reflection, when the heat is all gone, that matter. And emotional entropy should always lead to tolerance. When it doesn't – when even the peace and quiet stokes your fire – that's fucked up. And these fuckups might be the only people who genuinely deserve hatred.

For everyone else, calm your sorry asses down. Life is tough and it ends badly (on this I speak from experience). So enjoy it while you can. And remember that you don't really hate whomever it is you're presently fuming at. You're just disappointed in yourself.

Now go make up with everyone you thought you hated before reading this chapter. Give them a cuddle, some gummy bears, and a Starbucks gift card.

The end.

Jesus H. Christ

Written on the Ninth Day of April in the Year of Me, Thirty
(Gregorian calendar)

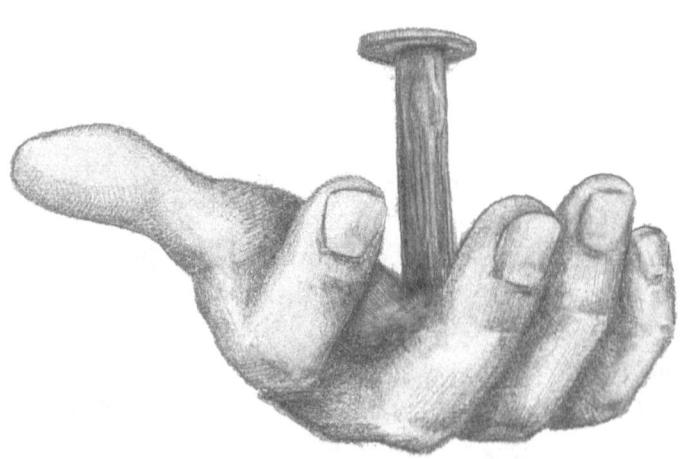

Afterword

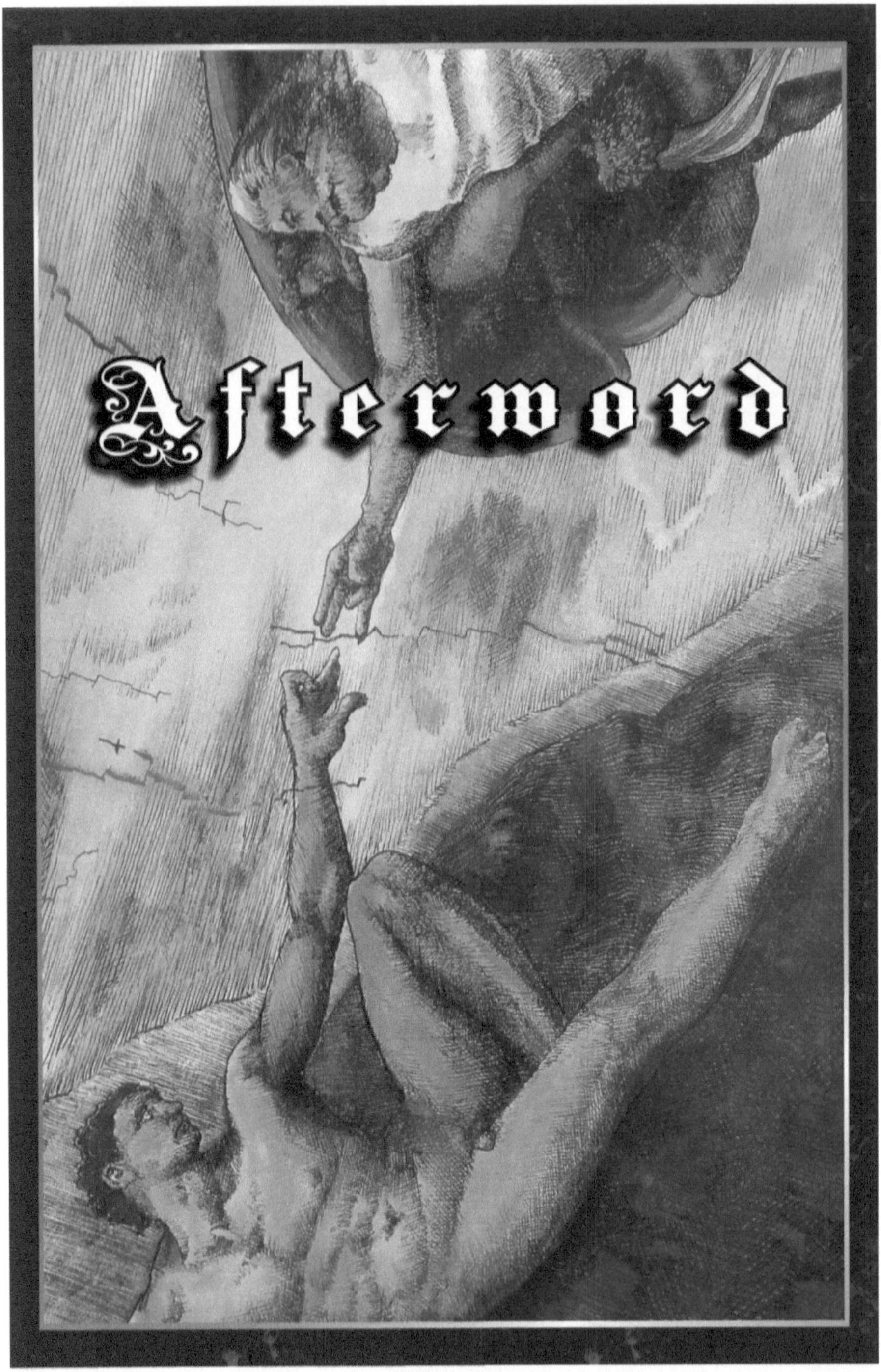

Notes on (and origin of) **Here Cometh the Son**

The New Testament is a cobbled-together anthology of twenty-seven "divinely inspired" books authored by a variety of named, unnamed, and pseudepigraphical[1] writers from the first and second centuries. Among these books are the four gospels, which chronicle the life of Jesus.[2] In the order they appear in the bible, they are:

> 1) The Gospel According to Matthew
>
> 2) The Gospel According to Mark
>
> 3) The Gospel According to Luke
>
> 4) The Gospel According to John

Three of these four gospels (Matthew, Mark, and Luke) are regarded as "synoptic", meaning they're very similar in their stories, sequence, and style. These similarities are so striking that they've resulted in the emergence of the "synoptic problem", namely: from what source did the authors draw their content?

To answer this question, one must evaluate the evidence concerning the origins of these books.

Historically, the first gospel to be written was Mark's, which characterizes the life of Jesus from his baptism by Saint John through his bodily ascension into heaven.

---

[1] These are named writers, but those names aren't correct. Pseudepigrapha are works by anonymous authors posing as less-anonymous authors. Pseudo (false) epigraph (inscription). It's the Dread Pirate Roberts principle: if you want to be taken seriously, you have to take on a serious name. In this case, if you had something you wanted to say about Jesus, but your name was Felix (or perhaps Chad), it would help your cause (meaning more people would heed your words) if you pretended to be Paul. See the following epistles: Ephesians, Colossians, Second Thessalonians, First Timothy, Second Timothy, and Titus.

[2] No other book in the Bible discusses the life or acts of Jesus, so everything we know about him is derived from the gospels.

Among religious communities, the author is believed to be Mark the Evangelist[3], founder of the Church of Alexandria (and thus the first archbishop). But actual evidence suggests this gospel was pseudepigraphically written around the fall of Jerusalem in A.D. 70 (the destruction of the temple is mentioned in chapter thirteen).

The next two gospels to appear were those of Matthew[4] and Luke[5] (both written between A.D. 80 and 90). Although these gospels discuss different elements of the life of Jesus[6], their content was heavily derived from two preexisting sources:

1) The Gospel According to Mark

2) A missing text known as the "Q document", which was thought to be a collection of sayings by Jesus.[7]

The final gospel (ascribed to John[8]), is regarded as canonical by the Catholic Church but is not counted among the "synoptic" gospels.

---

[3] Mark the Evangelist is probably John Mark, which means he's the man who, while Jesus was being arrested, fled the scene naked (see Mark, chapter fourteen, beginning at verse fifty-one).

[4] Matthew is the most Jewish of the gospels, portraying Jesus as a sequel to Moses; he's the one who fulfills Jewish scripture. Although Christian groups claim it to be written by Matthew, the tax-collecting disciple of Jesus, it was not. Nor was it written by any eyewitness. If it was, the author would not have needed to plagiarize other sources to tell his story.

[5] Luke is supposed to be (but wasn't) authored by Luke, the gentile physician who accompanied Paul on his travels. This gospel is directed at those Gentiles. "Salvation is not *just* for the Jews", it seems to suggest.

[6] Matthew illustrates the genealogy, nativity, baptism, temptation, ministry (with a few miracles), death, and resurrection of Jesus. Although the topics in Luke's account often overlap (some of it discrepantly; most notably the genealogy), it remains more focused on societal ethics and has been described as the gospel with the most "personality" in terms of style.

[7] This is the Christian equivalent of the Muslim's Hadith Qudsi.

[8] The John in reference is the apostle John, son of Zebedee (the fisherman). This ascription is unlikely to be accurate given that John was a peasant. He was a lower-class Galilean Jew who probably spoke Aramaic and almost certainly wrote nothing (based on rank and region as well as biblical descriptions; see Acts, chapter four, for example). It thus seems improbable that an illiterate peasant composed an entire gospel in a foreign language (Greek).

John's account departs from the former three in both content and style.[9] These departures raise a new dilemma (alongside the synoptic problem): how did the Gospel According to John achieve inclusion in the canon?

After its creation (around the turn of the second century), literary references to the Q document, popular among writers of the era, stopped appearing. And in the years that followed, the Gospel According to John was often found "piggybacking" on the already established gospels, ultimately usurping the station of the Q document.[10]

It wasn't until A.D. 325 (at the Council of Nicaea) that John's account was declared canonical. Convoked by Emperor Constantine I, this council was responsible for the creation of the Nicene Creed, which has arguably influenced the beliefs of Christianity more than any event since.[11]

---

[9] These departures are considerable and include the emphasis on Jesus as divine. Furthermore, while the synoptic gospels were written predominantly for Greek speaking gentiles of the Roman Empire, John's account appears to be directed specifically toward the Jews. It doesn't labor itself (as the synoptic gospels do) on explanations of Jewish traditions as a component of the narrative. Rather, it seems focused on persuading their acceptance of Jesus as Christ.

[10] Note, for example, the collection of papyri known as Papyrus 75, which was discovered in 1952. This manuscript was created around A.D. 200 and contains an early recreation of the Gospel According to Luke. With an almost expected guile, John's gospel begins on the same page on which Luke's concludes.

[11] However, Athanasius, the twentieth archbishop of Alexandria, may be as important a figure as Constantine. Considered the "Father of the Canon", Athanasius wrote the earliest known list of today's twenty-seven-book New Testament. Before writing this list, Constantine himself exiled Athanasius from Alexandria in A.D. 335. Upon Constantine's death in 337, Athanasius was allowed to return to his bishop's seat. Then in 339, Constantine's son banished him again. And again he was unbanished in 346. And then banished again in 356. And then unbanished again in 362. And then banished again seven months later (still in 362). And then unbanished again in 363. And then banished again in 365. And then unbanished one last time in 366. And in 367, Athanasius wrote his letter, which contained the earliest known documentation of which books belong in the New Testament: the exact twenty-seven books used today.

The first and most important topic on this council's agenda was to answer the Arian question: is Jesus consubstantial of God?[12]

Predictably, the Gospel According to John was used to assert the divine nature of Jesus (invoking lines such as 10:30: "I and my Father are one").

Since that time, the Q document has been relegated to holy footnotes. Despite being the firsthand words of Jesus Christ, it became an insignificant relic of the religion... until now.

In June of 2000, more than three hundred leaves of papyrus codex were discovered in the Ionia region of Turkey. Once historians had translated a portion of the prose (from Hebrew; not Greek), and finished estimating its creation date (A.D. 30-35), they realized the importance of the discovery: they were translating the Q document. Original pages from the source of the gospels, lost for nearly two millennia.

Today, more than 90% of the codex has been translated.[13] Like the Gospel According to Luke, the writing contains more personality than other texts of its age and its content focuses on societal ethics. Unlike Luke however, it appears to be aimed at a twenty-first-century audience. For this reason, it would have made little sense in any first-century Afro-Eurasian society.[14]

In *Here Cometh the Son*, the Q document is made available for the first time. It is a faithful translation of the codex that was written in Jesus' own hand and deemed unfit for inclusion in the testament it inspired.

---

[12] The Arian position was that Jesus and God were distinct; Athanasius may have been the most important opponent of that position.

[13] The only portion still awaiting translation is chapter twenty-nine.

[14] It is difficult to know how it would have been received by first-century Jews and Gentiles, but not unreasonable to suspect that they might have reacted to it with superstitious aversion. And perhaps abolish for that reason (replacing it with the less-troubling prose of the Gospel According to John).

Dedications

To my editors: Fred Frank and Holly Rudolph (who were both more than editors). I didn't (and still don't) have any money to give them in exchange for their work.[15] Instead of financial compensation, I had Jesus arrange heavenly salvations for both of them. According to Jesus, "I *guess* I'm willing to get over the fact that they're both Jews. But just barely." Seems awfully charitable of Jesus.[16]

Okay, lots of people to mention. One at a time:

Fred Frank. Fred contributed to a lot of the entries. A lot.[17] This includes the whole ending. The original draft just ended with Jesus the White saying "I've walked this earth for thirty lives of men and now I have no time." I exported that version and sent it to Fred on August 27, 2013.

"We'll talk" he said. And a few days later, we met in Manhattan.

"What's with the ending?", he asked me.

"What do you mean?"

"You just fade out. It's like a 1970s funk jam; you just slowly drop the volume until it's over. You can't end a book like that. Take lessons from Jeff Franklin."

What Fred meant by this is that I needed to write an *actual* ending. I couldn't just lighten up the hatred a tiny bit, but keep looping it, letting it flow until it doesn't anymore.

---

[15] I wrote most of this book while homeless. At public libraries / in an armory.
[16] I didn't tell Jesus that Fred is actually a heathen. He just did the bar mitzvah for the prizes. I was worried Jesus might rescind his celestial invitation if I brought that up. I'm already asking a lot for him to overlook the Jew thing. I didn't want to push it.
[17] Sixty verses maybe? Eighty-five? I don't know. But it was a lot.

And the Jeff Franklin bit was a reference to the end of every 80s (through early 90s) sitcom, in which the final minute of the show encapsulates the entire plot in a practical life lesson. In this case, Danny Tanner (i.e., Bob Saget) sits a ponytailed D.J. (Candice Cameron) down on her bed and gives her an ethical monologue about what happened that day.[18]

And that's what Fred suggested I do. A backward reflection of all that has happened, wrapped up with some Danny Tanner wisdom.

"What should my theme be?", I asked Fred.

"Give me a minute."

This was not a figure of speech. He sat silently for what must have been exactly sixty seconds. And then he said: "okay, I've got it."

I wait a moment for him to tell me.

He doesn't.

"What is it?", I ask, sounding irritated.

"Hold on, I just have to send this email."

I wait for another sixty seconds. Then I hear the swooshing sound an iPhone makes when an email is sent. And then Fred continues:

"Okay, it's about intolerance. You start with a bit about hating people who think hate is a strong word – it's not – and then you tie everything together with a moral narrative about intolerance."

So that's what I did. I modified Jesus the White's closing line to be ridiculously corny ("I only have time for one more chapter") and I wrote chapter thirty-three. And those six pages became the entire point of the book.

---

[18] Her teenage rebellion has her veering toward some dangerous life direction, but Danny's moral compass straightens her reckoning and all ends well.

Holly Rudolph. Holly is an attorney in Portland, Oregon with a serious knack for editing. She edited every single draft for me.

"Hi Holly, I made some more changes. I decided I didn't like the tense I was using in chapters one, three, four, nine, and the rest of them. And I also came up with a bunch of new things to hate. Will you edit it for me again?"

"Hey bunny. Of course. Send it." It would be in her inbox within a minute. And within a week, she would reread it, re-edit, and resend it, finding typos every time. And each time she did this, she would include comments that begin: "it might be funny if you say something about…" And then her comment would end with a little observation of her own. So I yield credit for the ideas of several verses (including "stickers on hats" and "Jaws") to Holly.

Andrew Mikkelson. Mikkelson and I "go way back" (there could be a whole entry dedicated to this phrasing). "Way back" means I met him in the seventh grade. I still remember our first encounter: I watched a skeletally thin, disheveled boy hunch over a piece of computer paper and draw what appeared to be a photograph of a wizard leaning against a dead tree. He wasn't looking at anything; his only resources were the sheet of paper, a chewed-up pencil, and his imagination. I'd never seen anything like it. Not just from a fellow middle schooler, but from anyone who had ever lived. So I decided we should be friends. And he submitted to my real-life friend request.

At this point, I began sitting next to him in other classes too. English, social studies, whatever. And that's when I realized he got the highest grade in the class on every test he took. "Who the fuck is this guy?", my seventh grade brain wondered. "I guess I should start copying off of him", that same brain quickly decided. And I stayed faithful to that decision clear through high school.

What's unfair about this relationship is that, at the end of high school, I graduated and he didn't. Although he set the curve on every test he took, he only took half the tests. Thus, while I was graduating, he was lying in bed… probably stoned.

After graduation, I went on to college. And he sank into poverty. Then I went to graduate school. And he sank further into poverty. Then I went to another graduate school (I finished this book while doing my Ph.D.). And Mikkelson continued his descent. But while his form was slowly hunching into its station, his ability to produce miracles in the arts seemed to be increasing. And every witness to this assumed the same thing: Mikkelson had found the One Ring. That's when I got back in touch with him:

"Mikkelson, it's Courtney. Would you be willing to illustrate a book for me?"

"Yeah, of course. What is it?"

"Um… It's a gospel written by Jesus. But it's not really a gospel; Jesus just makes fun of everybody. I don't have much to offer. I wrote it while homeless. Could I give you $50 to do a cover?"

The pay scale was insulting. Real Henry Miller stuff. But he was a lot more homeless than I was. At least I had food and shelter.[19] His homelessness involved things like rain and hunger and danger.

Owing to equal parts friendship and necessity, he accepted.

The next morning, using a set of borrowed watercolors, he painted it on an inherited canvas. In a day. He sent it to me that evening. And that exact picture was used as the "Afterword" page.

"Mikkelson, it's brilliant. But could you do a variation of that same design for me? In the place of Adam, could you paint a twenty-first century hipster on a cell phone, gesturing to God to wait a minute? And then have God delivering a "fuck you!" gesture back at Adam?"

---

[19] Regarding shelter, I was sleeping in an office that didn't belong to me (in the armory I mentioned a few footnotes ago). But I knew how to get in. And how to squat like a champ. Although, had my squatting ever been discovered, it would have been called something else: trespassing. Still, in the hierarchy of homelessness, at least relative to Mikkelson, I was doing fine.

"Yeah. Happy to."

Another day went by and then I had my cover. And I am eternally grateful. The world has never met Mikkelson's artistic equal. He's a magician with every medium and I got to incorporate a little bit of his magic into my book. And as much as I'd enjoy profiting from exclusive access to his talent, I would rather see it be put to work in other ways. So if you have a project that needs an artist, and budget that can afford a real wage (not what I paid him), here's his e-mail: *ConstructionStuntClown@gmail.com*.

You're welcome, potential employers.

Mike Dilger. I started this book in June of 2000 (the summer after high school graduation). I was sitting in the den of the house I grew up in, typing on an IBM desktop (with an Intel 486 processor and a 14.4 modem). Dilger was with me at the time. We came up with all of the original entries together.[20] Then, for the next year or so, I continued to add to the list. After it reached about forty pages of hatred, I lost interest. I posted it on the internet and did nothing with it for over a decade. But as I was approaching thirty-three (a good age to co-write a book with Jesus), I decided to pull out the old canon, bring Jesus into the writing staff, and adapt all of the old, unfocussed hatred into divine judgments. Only a small handful of the original entries remain.[21] It turns out Jesus doesn't hate the same things that a teenage Oregonian boy does.

Grant Lightner. One of the last entries that made it into the book is the footnote for chapter twenty, verse four (number 163).

---

[20] "I hate people who don't make sense" was an original line from June, 2000. Mike was looking over my shoulder as I typed "I hate people occupy." This was obviously a typo. I have no idea what I was *trying* to write. "Oh, whoops", I said as I maneuvered my hand toward the backspace key. "No, leave it!", Mike shouted. "It's perfect! Just follow it with: I hate people who don't make sense."

[21] "Drinking fountains" is one of few entries from the original log that made the final cut on grounds of merit rather than sentimentality. "I hate people occupy" and a few scattered entries from 2001 in which Dilger was mentioned were left in for the sake of honoring his presence at the conception of the project.

In September, 2013, I interrupted my streak of Connecticut-based homelessness to visit Grant in Virginia. While drunkenly playing a board game that resembled *Dungeons & Dragons*, Grant looked up from his wizard character (prior to casting a spell at me) and asked: "is it shit brick house or brick shit house?"

Me: "I don't know. I guess it doesn't really matter."

Grant: "Yeah… As long as you cuss. I think that's the important thing."

And then we both got back to casting spells at each other (slurring our incantations).

Grant won that game.

A couple days later, I sobered up, drove back to Connecituct, went to a library, and added the footnote.

Stephen Seehorn. To Steve (a.k.a. Rorik), I yield full coinage of "encroaching Down syndrome" (chapter twenty, verse twenty-five). Also, Steve: pick up your damn guitar; start playing again.

Craig Denegar. I'm sure Craig would prefer not to be mentioned. Being associated with a book like this one probably compromises one's professional integrity more than it enhances one's mood. But I can't skip this dedication. Because if it weren't for Craig, the book would have never been written. He rescued me from a former academic advisor. And without that rescue, I would have never had the time nor the mental health to write any of this or anything else. Ever. So thank you for that.

J. R. R. Tolkien. In chapter one, verse eight, Jesus writes: "Darkness took me… the stars wheeled overhead…" And in chapter thirty-two, verse sixteen, Jesus writes: "It seems strange: for thirty lives of men I walked this earth and now I only have time for one more chapter." Both of these passages are lifted from Gandalf. "Jesus the Grey" and "Jesus the White" are also references to Gandalf.

J. K. Rowling. In chapter twenty-one, verse twenty-two, Jesus mentions the Hufflepuff House, Parselmouths, the Sorting Hat, and the Avada Kedavra Curse. These are all from *Harry Potter*. Jesus and Courtney are both huge fans of Rowling's work (and they both hope she's willing to permit these inclusions).

Michael J. Fox. I mentioned MJF a couple times in this book. And those sentences weren't especially tasteful. But I can be counted among his fans. And his foundation (*Michael J. Fox Foundation for Parkinson's Research*) does great work. If any of my readers can afford to contribute, I would encourage you to do so. Right here: *https://www.michaeljfox.org*

Adam Frank. The Pontiac Fiero poster hoarder and the Chipotle burrito assembly verses came from conversations I had with Adam. If this book ever has a sequel, I'm sure he'll be the one to write it.

Anyone who feels cheated because they weren't mentioned in this section of the book. Don't kid yourself. You're just taking credit for my jokes. Seriously. Although I'm told Daniel Tosh has a similar "I'm a bad test-taker" bit. Assuming he arrived at the territory before I did, I yield to his land claim.

You, reader. Thank you so much for taking the time out of your day to read this book. I realize those hours could have been spent updating your social networking site and I really do appreciate the sacrifice.

Sincerely (and with all due gratitude to those who actually *paid* for the book),

Courtney Jensen, December Thirtieth, in the Year of Our Lord Two Thousand and Thirteen